7/13/00

To [illegible]

Best [illegible]

[illegible]

# Chickens Come Home To Roost

David Moreland

Library of Congress Catalog Card Number: 99-932347
ISBN: 0-9671769-0-5

DEDICATED TO:

Sherry, who endured so much happiness, sadness and love for me. And, also, all of my friends who wrote me letters and stood by me.

"Chickens Come Home To Roost" is a work of fiction. All characters in it are entirely fictional. Any resemblance in names, physical characteristics, or behavior to any individuals living or dead is accidental or the result of coincidence.

PSALM 37 - Holy Bible

"The Lord is laughing at those who plot against the godly, for he knows their judgment day is coming. Evil men take aim to slay the poor; they are ready to butcher those who do right. But their swords will be plunged into their own hearts and all their weapons will be broken."

# PROLOGUE

The suburbs sprawled in Atlanta in the early 1960's. The old farms of the Confederacy were taken apart like a picture puzzle by land developers. Tract houses with straight streets and tall virgin pines covered the red soil. Wheat straw sprinkled the newly sown lawns of Shepard Circle like an early snow. Trips to Green Brothers Nursery on Saturdays had families buying azaleas and dogwoods by the truckload. Seldom did one see a woman at the nursery on Saturdays. It was the social order of the day for the family man to buy the plants and have his colored man plant them. Daddy would take my brother, Mike, and me to select our man for Saturday, like picking a dog out at a pet store.

At the old Farmer's Market in Atlanta, the colored men would bunch together waiting for a white man in a big car to pick them up for a Saturday wage. Mike and I would study his oily face and yellow teeth as our Saturday pick would sit next to us on the back seat. The colored were so different from us; they always looked poor and hungry.

Mike and I just didn't understand. All we knew was that everything had its place, like all kitty cats were girls and all puppy dogs were boys, and all colored folks were maids or yard help. I always wondered why people thought like this. Little did we know until late in life, with the advent of equal rights, that the colored folks were human beings and, contrary to Mike's and my popular belief, colored folks bleed red blood like us, not black.

On Shepard Circle, a turquoise Sears and Roebuck van parked at 1860, and a dozen boxes filled the backyard that May morning. My mother who was a short small woman with a beehive hairdo waved her arms, and in and out of the glass sliding door off the painted concrete patio she directed my birthday party as if she was a director of a Hollywood set.

My mother was a combination of the sexiest Southern Belle I have ever known, and the meanest hellcat that ever lived. Her soft lotioned hands could caress your face like a kiss from a angel, but after a mixture of some high powered pills and a few whiskey drinks her tongue would cut you like a razor. There were a many a night my brother Mike and I went to bed with Miss Jo's cussing tirades. We covered our heads with our pillows as the master bedroom door would open and like a coo-coo bird Miss Jo would pop out every obscenity known to mankind, then slam the door shut with the force of a hurricane. It was not uncommon for frozen steaks and lamps to be hurled at my Daddy across the room.

Miss Jo never physically abused us except an occasional switching of our legs, which we probably deserved. Miss Jo was a woman of courage, fortitude and might, and by God if you ever crossed her she became your mortal enemy for life. Everytime I looked into her large blue eyes I hated her, admired her, and loved her so much.

She was in her early 30's and always wore black, sharply pointed sunglasses. The sunglasses look like the fins on a Cadillac. The may humidity began to rise and the red and black sundress stuck to my mother's body like fly paper. My mother was known as Miss Jo. Miss Jo, with her large bust took her wet tissue and wiped the sweat from her brow to her cleavage.

"Carrie, where are you?," echoed Miss Jo from the kitchen. Again, Miss Jo yells, "Sugar, come help me with this punch bowl. I want to use this ruby glass one."

"Miss Jo, I'm a comin'"," Carrie yells from the back of the house. Carrie, a large black woman wearing a white uniform, sweetly professes, "Princess, dis heat gone be the death of me yet. Laud, Mr. Jesus can't have me now. Miss Jo, git don off'n dat stool. I will git it."

"Carrie, how could I run this house do without you?"

"You shore would have a tore dress for me to sew, Princess, and stretched out arms for me to heal."

"I hope all those damn screaming kids appreciate this birthday party. I have worked as hard as a morter nigger today." Miss Jo lights up a cigarette and tries to put order in her mind of the day's events.

"Master Frankie gon to have the best birthday ever, ifen he don't hide under the bed like he did last time."

Miss Jo burst out laughing. “Frankie got embarrassed and turned red as a beet when Patricia Stone kissed him.”

“Miss Jo, you have two fine looking boys.” Carrie puts her hands on her hips.

In a sophisticated pose, Miss Jo removes her sunglasses and takes a drag on her cigarette and looks out the window.

“Of my two boys, Frankie’s going to be the one to break a woman’s heart. Probably lots of women’s hearts. I predict he will be the handsomest of my boys. Mikey’s the cutest, and I bet he marries a Spanish woman. Carrie, I hope I live to see my boys marry, but I don’t think I will. You know, when I was born, the doctor said I wouldn’t live all that long.”

“The Drs. told that S.O.B. of a husband of mine Frank Sr. he wouldn’t live long either. Well, I guess the damn doctors just guessed wrong. Frank Sr. should of been dead by now. A traveling salesman that’s what I married. A G. damn traveling salesman, and all he lives for is to impress some damn Yankee up north.

“Now, Ms. Jo, Mr. Frank Sr. loves them boys and you too. He would do anything in the wold for any of yoos.” “Now , supposing Mr. Frank Sr. was a liquor drinking man and a devil.” Carrie hugs Miss Jo in a big bear hug.

“You’s got a good home Miss Jo, now, now,” Carrie straightens her posture.

“Go on, Miss Jo...and Mikey marry a Spanish woman. Why, Princess, Mikey would have ta go to Mexico, cause they ain’t no Spanish in Atlanta.”

Cranking out the Miami roll-out window, Miss Jo yells out to the Sears men in the backyard. “Put the swing set over there.”

“We goin’ to let the children go swimmin’ today, Miss Jo?” Carrie asks.

“I’ll be damned, Carrie, put the hose in the pool and fill it up. I knew I had forgotten something.”

“It leaked last time, Miss Jo, and all that water ran down where that Yankee woman lives.”

“Well, I am not going back to McRoys for the 10th time today! We will just make do.”

The shiny red and white poles of the swing set took shape and they looked like large candy canes in the green grass.

"Princess, did you invite the McCurdeys?"

Reluctantly, "Yes," said Miss Jo. "I just can't stand Yankees. They seem so sharp talking, so brash. That damn Gladys McCurdey leaves that flood light on all night. When I was growing up in Atlanta, you never had Yankees living down the street, or God forbid, next door to you."

"I know, Miss Jo," said Carrie. "Atlanta is a changin', Miss Jo. Even in colored town, some of my neighbors are from places like New York or Chicago." Carrie hums "Swing Low Sweet Chariot" as she irons a tablecloth.

"Things shore be a changen, Princess. With all dis here Civil Rights, don't know what to make of it all. Can't colored folk just be happy with what theys got? I been a maid all my life, and so was my mama. I love you, Miss Jo, and your husband man and them boys like they be my own."

"Good God Almighty, Carrie, it is almost 2:00 o'clock. Those damn kids will be here in a moment." Miss Jo goes to the back bedroom where Frankie is looking out the window. Miss Jo sits on his bed and places her hand on his cheek. "Sugar, you need to get up now. All of your friends will be here soon. What are you thinking about?"

"Granddaddy Popos' farm. I'll be glad when school is out. I don't like school."

"Frankie, you will be 10 years old today, and every year gets harder, but you get smarter about things."

"I wish I lived at Popos' all the time."

"I know you love Popo, but you have to be around kids your own age. Now come on Sugar. I hear the doorbell."

All the children and their mothers were like a parade in the front door, "Oh Jo, so good to see you. Where did you get that new furniture? I saw a Riches truck out front the other day."

It was a mixture of boys and girls Frankie's age. All of their party clothes seemed to match. Festive shirts and shorts with black and white tennis shoes. Like cattle, miss Jo herded the kids and their mothers to a safer area — the patio. Carrie stood guard over Miss Jo's pride and joy, her living room and dining room. About 25 kids descended on the back yard like a swarm of locusts. The new swing set was covered in no time with kids, and Frankie laughed with kids he knew and didn't know.

About two hours away in a small hamlet, a black boy Frankie's age and his mother work in an old mom and pop grocery store. A thin black woman neatly dressed in a cotton dress struggles with a 50-lb flour sack to place on a pile.

Mary Harrision had lived all of her life in Eatonton, Georgia. A segregated town where black folks always knew their place, and if a black person ever wanted to buck the system in Eatonton they could be assured a free ride in Mr. Jones funeral hearse.

Mary gave the U.S.A. army her husband Aubrey Sr., and all she got in return was a flag draped coffin. Her only son Aubrey was her pride and joy, and when she looked into his eyes she would tell him "with Civil Rights a coming the world will be a better place to live." Mary loved the Lord and Knew that forgiveness of White folks was the only way to live. When she walked with Aubrey to the colored church white folks that would shun them on the street during the week would file into their white columned church and worship the Lord in their own way.

"Mama, let me help you." said her son.

"Thanks, Aubrey."

"Mr. Parks, all done back here."

"Thanks Mary. I am going to run to the bank. Hold the fort down til I get back," said, the storekeeper Hugh Parker.

"Okay, Mr. Parks. Now Aubrey, I am going to sweep the front of the store, and you stay back here and tear these boxes down."

"Okay, Mama." Aubrey could see his Mama sweeping the old linoleum floor as he tore into the boxes.

The front door jingled as two white men came in. They both looked like they weighed 200 lbs each. Their skins were oily from hair gelatin. They both stumbled and their words were slurred and loud.

"Oh, Mr. Billy, Mr. J.C., how are you today? Mr. Park's gone to the bank. He will be back in a minute." Mary fidgeted around these two powerful men, so she chose her words carefully. The two men just stared at Mary.

"Can I get any groceries for you?"

"You're Tom's girl, aren't you?" said J.C.

"Yes, sir."

"Course, you never know with niggers who their real daddy is, do you Billy?" as J.C. poked his brother in the ribs. Both men reeked of tobacco and whiskey. Mary backed up close to the counter.

"Mr. Parks will be here in a minute."

J.C. strides up to the front door and turns the latch. Billy starts his way around the counter. "J.C. and I been on a hunting trip."

"That's nice, Mr. Billy." Mary shook.

"Yeh, it was nice, but being all alone in the woods for days with just whiskey and a gun makes a real man want more. Know what I mean, Mary?"

"I don't know," said Mary. Mary searched for words. "Let me get you a Coke-a-Cola Mr. Billy."

" Don't want a Coke-a-Cola." Mary knew Mr. Parks kept a 38 revolver under the counter, but her preachers voice kept saying, "Thou shall not kill, Thou shall not kill!" Mary felt faint like she was going to pass out, then Billy's two large hands drew Mary close to his chest.

Mary could smell the under arm sweat of Billy LaSurre and with her small hands she tried with all of her might to pull away. "I don't want to die, I don't want to die!! Please. Please. Tears ran down Mary's face.

"You aren't going to die, less I say you're going to die. I am going to put this big white rod in you."

"NO, NO!" Mary struggled to pull away she felt she was drowning in Quick sand. "Help me!, Help me!"

Billy slapped her so hard Mary thought her eyes had popped from the socket. Her mouth dripped blood on the front of her cotton dress.

"You hadn't had a real man since that nigger husband of yours came back in a army box." Mary kicked Billy as hard as she could in the leg, then Billy socked Mary hard in the stomach. Mary was as limp as a dish rag. Billy kissed Mary and felt her small breasts. J.C. looked on as his brother ripped off Mary's dress.

"Nigger pussy is the best, Billy," said J.C. Billy LaSurre slapped Mary across the face and raped her. "Leave some for me."

From back of the store ran little Aubrey. With knife in hand he screamed, "Leave my mama alone." J.C. comes up behind Aubrey and takes the knife away with little struggle.

"Little nigger trying to save his mama from the big bad white man."

"Leave me alone," struggled Aubrey. J.C. picked up Aubrey and slapped him in the face.

"You're that little nigger that wanted Coke-a-Cola bottles. I don't think we need any more little smart ass niggers like you around."

Mary came to and struggles with Billy, screaming, "No, No, don't hurt my boy." J.C. slapped Aubrey so hard his mouth started bleeding. He picked Aubrey up and slammed him down on the meat block. Aubrey came to and felt his overalls coming off, and his bottom felt cold against the wooden slab. J.C. started slapping Aubrey on the stomach with the flat edge of a meat cleaver.

"Mighty skinny hog for a little nigger boy. Maybe I'll cut your head off like a chicken. Ever seen a chicken run after he's had his head cut off?"

Aubrey's eyes had almost rolled back in his head, and everytime he tried to squirm off the meat block J.C. would slam his head back almost knocking Aubrey unconscious. Aubrey felt everything was spinning like a top from his mother's screams to J.C.'s voice. It was as if everything was in slow motion.

"Ever seem a white man castrate a hog little nigger?" Aubrey didn't respond, he just wondered if it was going to hurt to die.

"'You know what we do with a hogs scrotum when we cut them off...give them to the dogs." J.C. roared laughing like a beast from hell. J.C. pulled a knife from the knife block and said, "You won't make any more little black bastards." With one swipe, J.C. held Aubrey's testicles in one hand. Aubrey screamed and tears flooded down his face.

Aubrey felt his blood running between his legs, and he was cold.

"Hello, Doc Wingate. This here is J.C. Got a little problem down at Hugh Park's Store. Seems a little nigger boy just about cut his little pecker clean off. Yes, he's bleeding like a hog. Okay. See you shortly."

Twenty-five kids yell, "Happy Birthday" as Frankie blows out the candles on his cake and makes a wish.

# PART ONE

It's December in Tucson, Arizona. All of the seasons seem the same in this lifeless desert of a place. Everything here is so hard and barren, and void of the true green color I once knew.

People move here from their northern Midwest climates to warm themselves, but their personalities remain frozen: those northern attitudes. They irritate me with their nasal voices and sharp, brash tongues. These are the people I grew up despising, now I live among them.

Tan mud brick houses dot the moonscape of rocks and sand of Tucson. Tall lifeless sticks with no leaves are called cactus, and their sharp thorns prick at my heart each morning. Mountains surround this town like barbed wire and look down at the barren waterways called rivers. No matter what houses cost in this town, they all remind me of a hovel in Atlanta. A makeshift lean-to for refugees; maybe that's what these poor Indians, Mexicans, and Northerners are, refugees in their own country. That's what I am: a refugee from Georgia.

*Journal Entry Dec. 7*

I am thinking about Eatonton, Georgia, this December morning. All the magnificent old oaks that stretch their limbs out and shade the streets would be barren now. I feel a crisp breeze blowing the leaves across the sidewalks as the writing of chalk across a blackboard. The old antebellum homes with their white clapboard siding and towering columns reflect a purer, simpler time. I miss Georgia, I miss the red clay of generations of my people.

In a section of Tucson called Armory Park are some of the oldest homes.

"Frank, where are you?" an echoing voice booms through the rambling old Victorian house. "Frank, come on, we've got to get these kids ready for school." Up the stairs in the bathroom, Frank and his stepson, a small boy named Willy, stood in front of a mirror. Frank, in his late thirties, is a tall slender man with brown hair and compassionate brown eyes. Frank has a smile on his face. Willy, the stepson, is five years old and has a dust mop of blonde hair on top of his head, like his mother.

"Now, Willy, B'rer Rabbit he done laid this here toothbrush in the middle of the big road, and B'rer Fox sauntered forth and he say 'B'rer Rabbit, iffen you don't pick up that toothbrush, I's gwine to kore you shore."

Willy burst out laughing.

Giggling, he asked Mr. Frank, "What did B'rer Rabbit do?"

About that time, hands reached in through the door and grabs Mr. Frank and Willy by the ears.

"All right, you two."

Willy said, "Oh no, B'rer Fox done got us for sure."

"Frank Moss, I swear Willy is going to end up talking like a black slave," said Leacy, the mother. Leacy is small in stature with long blonde hair, and her big blue eyes glow.

"B'rer Fox, let us go fore we both get kored. Come on, let's go down these here stairs," laughed Frank.

In the kitchen, there was a bustle of activity. All six children are readying themselves for school.

"Mom, I'm going to have Sarah come over. Is that all right?"

"Mom, Willy just spilled milk all over my report."

"Mom, Dad called last night."

Frank looked up from the paper strewn breakfast table and surveyed the room. "Boy, I tell you this house is a highway. I can't figure out if it is 285 in Atlanta or I-10 north on Christmas Eve." Mr. Frank looked up again and six children were huddled around him staring into his brown eyes. "What did I do?"

"Mr. Frank, did you say that you are going to Phoenix?'

"Well, you see..."

Six voices interrupt, "Oh Mom, can we go? There is nothing in this town, but the malls in Phoenix..."

"Frank, just look what you started," responds Leacy.

"But I was talking about I-10, the freeway."

"Oh please, Mom, Mr. Frank is so much fun. Can't we go?" All at once all the girl children placed a big kiss on Mr. Frank's forehead and Willy hugged Mr. Frank's neck.

"Leacy, is it all right?"

"As long as everyone's homework is done."

"Yeah!" as a sonic boom blasted throughout the kitchen.

"School bus!" screamed all the children.

"That poor screen door," Frank scratches his head.

"Here it comes, bye, Mom, bye Mr. Frank, bye, here it comes." Bam! Bam! Bam! Bam! Bam! Bam! As the sound of the diesel engine of the school bus pulled away, the big old house became quiet. Frank got up from the table and went over to the counter where Leacy was chopping an orange. He came up behind her and gave her a big bear hug. He ran both of his large hands up and down her back and gently caressed her buttocks. With one finger, he slowly rubbed her crevice.

"Frank, don't you start anything that you can't finish," said Leacy.

"Oh, I always finish," smiled Frank. "I love you so much, Leacy, and I love all of those six wonderful children."

"Frank, they love you, too."

"Sometimes it is hard for me to believe that so much love and happiness has come my way. I can't believe sometimes that those are Henry's children. They look so much like me," responds Frank.

Leacy stopped chopping the orange and looked straight into Frank's eyes. Leacy hugged Frank and kissed him on the mouth. "I am so glad to have you, Frank." Leacy put her arm around Frank's waist and said, "Frank, we have got to talk."

"Now, Leacy, I am sorry that I forgot the oil change on the van. You see, Willy..."

"Frank, it is not that," said Leacy.

"Have I done something?" asked Frank. You know my E.S.P. on bad things. I haven't sensed anything bad."

"No, Frank. I want you to sit down."

"Well, the last time that you wanted to talk like this, you told me that you were involved with someone else, and I thought that I had lost you." Frank saw in Leacy's eyes a problem.

"Frank, did you read the Atlanta paper a few days ago?"

"No, what's wrong?"

Leacy reached for Frank's hand and said there was an article that said, "Doris Anthony killed herself." Frank sat motionless, then turned and stared out the window. Leacy clutched his hand tighter. She laid her head on Frank's arm.

"Are you all right, Frank?"

With a sigh and a deep breath, he said, "Yes, I am all right." He still faced the window. "You know I had a Sunday school teacher once say that chickens come home to roost."

"What do you mean, Frank?"

As Frank turned, his eyes teared. "All your sins eventually come home. I killed Doris, Leacy, as if I had pulled the trigger myself. I did it through the written word, the novel that I wrote telling everyone what they did to me. Doris had no where to hide. She was a body with the skin pulled back." He turned to Leacy and continued, "I am going to the funeral."

"Frank, I don't want you to go to that town." Leacy states firmly, "I don't want all those memories brought back."

"Leacy, I don't want to go to the service, just the graveside. You know tomorrow will be the anniversary, December 8, 1994."

"I know, Frank, that's why I don't want you to go."

"Leacy, when we got together, I told you I would never keep a secret from you. If I went to Doris' funeral and didn't tell you, then I would have lied to you. I love you more than anything."

"Frank, take Aubrey Harrison with you."

Aubrey was a black man about Frank's age. He spent about ten years in the Army. Aubrey saw more of the world than most white men in Putnam County. The bigots were so jealous of him he never could get work. Frank alone had the guts to hire him. He was to work along beside Frank in his sandwich shop. Aubrey was tall and slender, a quiet, soft-spoken man. He is divorced and has a son named James. When I first came to Arizona, Aubrey moved out here a few weeks later. He is my friend from Georgia.

"Okay, I'll carry Aubrey with me."

"Oh Frank, promise me just the graveside, and come home to Tucson."

"I promise you," said Frank.

**ii**

A couple of days later, Frank laid out a double-breasted suit on the bed and two round trip tickets to Atlanta, reaching in the chest of drawers for a silk scarf. In the bottom of the drawer is a letter and a black diary.

*August 28th, 1994*

*Frank enclosed is the material I received from you in the mail last week. With further reflection and upon counsel, I will not be preparing the lease for your use. I believe the idea that you mentioned Friday about going to another lawyer is a good one.*

*I have had over 24 hours to think about your "visits" to my office this past Friday morning. I allowed myself this time so that everything I say to you will be well thought out and not say it in the white hot anger I felt shortly after you left. I am writing and not confronting you in person because I do not want to enter into a shouting match with you, and I want to have my say without interruption. You have a way of commandeering a conversation.*

*Please listen to what I am saying. Believe it and remember it. I do not want a relationship with you. As to what you thought you saw that night you barged into my home unannounced, that was merely my college friend asleep in my bed. The only relationship I envisioned was of a business acquaintance and eventually a friend, which I no longer want. The possibility of that died when you came to my office last Friday.*

*When I first met you last winter, I looked upon you as a potential friend. At that time, as I told you at our first lunch, I was involved with someone and not looking...*

Frank finished reading the letter. Leacy came up from behind Frank and placed her head on his back, hugging him. "Are you all right?"

"Yes, sugarface, I'm fine." Frank reached his long arms around her back and hugged her. "A lot of memories."

"Please promise me you will just go to the graveside service. I don't want you to go to that town."

"I promised you a couple of days ago, Leacy. I would never do anything to jeopardize you or the children. Aubrey is going with me, remember?" Carefully Frank put the letter and diary in his coat pocket. "All set. How do I look?"

"Like a handsome Southern gentleman."

"My compliments to the lady," said Frank. He walked down the stairs. "Where are all the kids?"

"Some are playing; some are reading. It's Sunday afternoon; all six are doing something."

Frank paused on the stairs with his large hands on the railing. "I sure love them."

"I know, Frank, and they love you." At the front door, Leacy hugged Frank and gave him a big kiss. She put her hands on either side of his face and said,

"You come back to me."

"Love you," responded Frank. He walked down the hall and stepped off the front porch. Pausing, he looks back. "What a beautiful place."

Frank got into his black pick-up and pulled out of the driveway. Sounds of crackling gravel echo through the cool air. Still, gray, over-cast skies shroud the scene. A couple of streets over, Frank pulled in Front of a modest frame house that sat close to the road. A small black boy was playing with a red kick ball in the front yard. The boy is James, Aubrey's son. James recognized Frank's truck. Immediately dropping his kick ball, he ran over to Frank's window.

"Mr. Frank, will you come play with me?"

"Not today, James. I've got my Sunday clothes on."

"Those preachers sure do talk long these days, Mr. Frank. Did they give y'all a break?" Frank laughs.

"No, James. Your daddy and I are going to a funeral."

"Somebody die, Mr. Frank?"

"Yes, they did, James," as Frank hesitates, "in Eatonton, Georgia."

"B'rer Rabbit didn't die, did he, Mr. Frank?"

"No, he's still alive, tricken' ole B'rer Fox. Did I ever tell you, James, of how B'rer Rabbit tricked B'rer Bear out of his fishes?" James' face lights up.

"Tell me, Mr. Frank."

A large black hand grabbed James and a voice said, "He ate them all up."

"Oh daddy, you always tricken' me."

Aubrey laughed with a deep hearty rumble.

"Frank, you look a little shaken," said Aubrey. "I didn't mean..."

Frank's mind flashes back to a cop grabbing him and putting tight silver handcuffs on.

"Ready to go?" asked Frank.

"Yeah. Now, James, be good and mind Miss Effie."

"Okay, Daddy." Aubrey hugged his son and got in the truck.

"Don't you look like a million today, Mr. Aubrey."

"Well, thanks, Frank. I don't know what you are going to do when double-breasted suits go out of style. That's all you buy," chuckled Aubrey.

"Yeah and how about that tie you got on?" Frank laughed and flipped Aubrey's tie up. "Aubrey we have a couple of hours before our plane leaves lets go get a cup of coffee and talk."

**iii**

In a loud coffee shop, Frank said aloud, "Eatonton, Land of Karma and Destiny. Aubrey maybe ole B'rer Fox got mighty tired of the two of us mudding up the stream and stealing the peas out of the garden. Sometimes I think my life is a chapter right out of a Greek tragedy. When did the curtain go up on my life."

Aubrey knew he was instore for along Frank Moss story but Frank had tremendous pain. The pain of returning to Eatonton and all those memories. Aubrey knew is friend dealt with pain by talking and he would indulge him this time.

"It was 1975, the year I graduated from Briarwood High School, home of the fighting buccaneers. God, I was on top of the world then. Became Student Government President my senior year. Fought old principal McCain tooth and nail on the rights of students. That's my philosophy of life as I call it. The rights of others. Ever since elementary school, when I could finally decide what was right and wrong, I felt for people. Never could understand how another child would trip a kid in the hall and throw his books on the floor — just because they were fat or ugly or retarded. Why treat another human being so cruelly for no apparent reason. I made a vow those elementary years that never would I belittle or be hateful to another human being because of whatever handicap they might have.

"I say Mom berate Daddy so many times at parties. I vowed, if I ever got married, never to do that to my spouse.

"Graduation night was also my birthday. Wow, to be 18 on Graduation night! Too bad I didn't drink. We all sang a song based on Robert Frost's poem 'Two roads diverged in a yellow wood, and I took the one less travelled and that had made all the difference.' I said the Graduation prayer that night in front of hundreds of people. What a rush!

"My choice for college was U.G.A. It was a tough school to get into.

Those damned S.A.T. scores. I had a 'B' average in high school, and I could write for hours on what I knew. Fill in the circles I felt was just a cop-out for real knowledge. Somehow, by miracle, I was accepted at U.G.A. That's where I met Lynn Murray; U.G.A. campus in 1975 with some 25,000 students. I came from a school of 750. Everyone knew my name. Here in the vast sea of people, I was nothing.

"Seems like most of my life events happen in the fall. Hell, Aubrey, I guess I will die in the fall. It was fall quarter when classes started. My freshman year I met a guy named Stan Fisher. Stan was a tall, slinky guy. He looked like a string bean. My sophomore year Stan and I decided to get an apartment, be roommates. I couldn't wait. After being cooped up in a dorm room with a window that opened up three inches, and no air conditioner, I was definitely ready for a change.

"One night, after Stan and I moved in, we were talking about finding a girlfriend. Stan spoke up and said, 'I know this one girl from home. I want you to meet her.' Being the horny creature I was, I jumped at the idea. So we drove over to the girl's apartment. There I first met Lynn. She was tall and slender with shoulder-length blond hair. The best thing Lynn had to offer was this great ass. She had these jeans on that were so tight, it drove me crazy. Her face was not all that great - acne and braces - but she had the sweetest smile and a great personality. I loved to hear her voice. She was a Southerner, Aubrey. I haven't dated any Yankee woman that I know of. Stan and I and Lynn's roommate chatted about nonsense for a good while and Stan and I left.

"The next weekend, Stan went home. Before he left he said, 'Frank if you get lonely, here's Lynn's phone number on the back of the telephone book.' I got laughs for years about how I first met my wife; on the back of a telephone book. That night I called Lynn. We talked nonsense on the phone and I said, 'Lynn, why don't we get together tonight? I want to show you my antiques.

Antiques not only made a living for me, but got women, too. Stan let me put antiques in our apartment. It was great. A Victorian sofa with a picture of a Jeff Davis with the Confederate flag on each side of the wall. We even had a fake fireplace mantle. The trick worked every time. Come see my antiques.

"My sales pitch worked on Lynn. I picked her up at 8:00 pm. We had the best time. We went to eat at this pizza place and talked and laughed till late.

I said, 'Lynn, why don't we go to my apartment and look at antiques?'

Lynn responded, 'Now Frank, I don't want you to think I am easy or something.'

'Come on Lynn, it will be fun,' I said.

'Let's go,' Lynn replied.

We got to my apartment, and I gave Lynn the grand tour. Coming back to the living room, we both sat on the Victorian sofa. Bad thing about that sofa was you had to sit up straight. What can I say, sometimes in antiques things look good, but are not comfortable. Lynn and I sat on the sofa, and we were playing cat and mouse games on 'let's go to bed.' Finally, we're kissing and we kissed for hours it seemed. I loved being with her. I never had a real girlfriend until Lynn."

"That Fall was great. Lynn and I did everything together. Now college was a different thing. I was on the verge of flunking out. It was so damned hard. High school had been a breeze, a 'B' average. I really hated college. I couldn't wait for classes to end, so I could go riding in my pickup, see whom I could meet and what antiques I could find. As that school year came to a close, I was really wondering what I was going to do. That summer Lynn and I talked off and on. On her birthday I sent her a dozen yellow roses; her favorites. Sent yellow roses every year for 17 years. Lynn used to say she really didn't know if I cared for her that much, but the roses were always a sign of 'I Love You and I Care.' It seemed we made love all summer. In the car, on a mountain top, in a river...

"We used to lie in bed for hours after making love, and hold each other and talk about our parents.

'Frank, my father you know is an engineer so everything in his life has to be precise. When things didn't go his way he would yell and shout or just sulk. I remember one time my mother got so mad at him she threw all of his clothes in the shower, and turned the water on. My mother was 16 when they married and my Dad was still in college. Both of my parents were poor Alabama folks, unlike your parents Frank."

"Mine were quite different Lynn. My mother or Miss Jo as she is known came from a rich family. Her daddy was a builder. My Daddy came from the country and was poor. How in the world the two of them ever got together, God only knows. Mom said they went on a double date with another couple and mom being the flamboyant Southern Belle chose my Dad over the other man she was with. My mother sure is a hell raiser. One Christmas Eve Daddy and my brother Mike and I were in the guestroom putting together a metal service station and Daddy had pushed a heavy cedar chest against the door to keep my mother from busting in. Mom was drunk as hell and cussing like a sailor. Pounding on the hollow core door, she cussed and cussed. Finally she went to bed and passed out." Lynn and I really had great communication.

"We were back at U.G.A. I was faced with flunking out. I never told Dad what was going on. I pretended a lot. Everything was perfect. That first quarter I did flunk out. Damn it. I hated those professors. No one would work with me, but I guess I never really sought help. I pretended to Lynn that everything was fine at school. I was dying inside. I would pace the floor of the apartment and look out the window and wonder why and what to do. I was so bored. I would drive for miles. Burnt up more gasoline than a route salesman. Searching, looking. What am I supposed to do? The only sanctuary I had was Lynn. She was everything then, but I never could tell her everything, always making sure my facade looked good.

"One day while driving, I decided I would leave U.G.A. and go into real estate. Amid crying for Lynn and sadness in leaving college a failure, with a great sense of defeat on my part, I left.

"I would go up and see Lynn every weekend, just like clockwork. We became closer. I never really loved Lynn to the core of my soul. Something seemed to be holding me back."

"When she graduated from U.G.A., and all along she kept saying let's get married, and I would say, but I have nothing to offer you, no house. I am trying to make it on a commission, I am only a real estate salesman. Lynn was persistent. She loved me so much, but I just didn't want to get married. I just never had the nerve to break off our relationship. I couldn't hurt her. So one day, we were at the Flint River, near the town where all of my ancestors were born and married and died. Sitting in my car, I presented Lynn with my Grandmother's engagement ring. Tears rolled down her face. I told her, sitting there in the car, as a fine mist of rain softly landed on the windshield, as if angels were crying for our happiness or sadness...I said, Lynn, let me tell you all about why I had to leave U.G.A. I felt I had no secrets that afternoon from Lynn. The only one, the main one, I didn't want to marry her."

"We got married on Confederate Memorial Day, April 26, 1980. I chose that day because I felt I could always remember it and not get into trouble. Like forgetting a present. Ah, Aubrey, that first year of marriage was something else. We were so poor. I had bought an old Victorian house, when I was still at U.G.A., one of my damned finds. Lynn thought I had lost my mind. What a great house, Victorian Queen Anne cottage. What a prize! I moved the house to a town 70 miles from it's site. Now you see why Lynn and I were so poor; that house was a money pit. God, Lynn and I were so young. Both of us never had been on our own before. We didn't have the slightest clue about money."

"After about a year in our home, the bank demanded the note because we missed several payments. One day, the bank sent foreclosure papers to the house. We had till the end of the month to pack up and get out. All of that work. I paced the wood plank floors of that house and looked at each room, each pane of glass. The sheet rock I had put up. The sweat, the dirt, the emotional stress of how to finish the place. Each nail, every piece of wood I touched. Finally, I sat down on the living room sofa and cried. Why God? Why do you want to take this from me? Where will we go? What will people think? We had a week to move, or they would put all our belongings on the street."

"Lynn and I went to see her two old maid aunts, and spilled our guts. I tell you, Aubrey, if there is a heaven, Ruth and Sue are sure to go there. Never have I met two kinder women in my life. Never critical on what mess you are in, but how can we help. Yes, they had plenty of money. It was hard. The house was small, and sometimes the generation difference got to be a struggle. The week the bank was repossessing the house. I borrowed Dad's station wagon and moved everything we owned, myself. Must have taken 10 loads.

"We put all of our belongings in the aunts' garage. I remember the last day of our possession of the house. The day the bulldozer came and cleared the land, the smell of the fallen pines and fresh tilled earth. I walked around the house and remembered all my plans for expansion. Of how I painted the whole house myself. Walking up the brick steps, I thought of how I cleaned each brick, and bought the marble caps on the entry way. Aubrey, when a bank takes someone's home, to them it's just a number on a piece of paper. Some S.O.B. who was sorry and couldn't pay or just a scum bucket. Bankers never look at the human side of every brick, every brick of someone's soul, their hopes, their dreams. Sure, I know there are some scum out there to beat a bank, but I think the majority are like Lynn and me, just got behind the eight ball and needed some more time."

"I walked into our home and cried. Walked every inch of it. Rubbed my hand on every kitchen cabinet, the walls. I was angry. I wanted to burn it to the ground. No one else is going to have my creation. Instead, I went to the hardware store and bought railroad spikes. I came back to the house and took 2 x 4's and nailed every window shut, every door. As I swung that hammer, I felt I was crucifying the house. I exited through an upstairs window and got in the car and drove away for the last time."

"The next couple of years were rough. Finally we bought another house. Yes, there were more ups and downs, but Lynn and I always seemed to come out of the storm okay. We worked all the time. In later years, we just never talked about how we were doing. It was always, 'what's for supper, or 'so and so called'."

"I have always been an entrepreneur. It would drive Lynn crazy. I would come home some days and say let's buy this restaurant franchise, or let's move here. I wasn't really going to do these things, I wanted to vent my ideas. Lynn always said I would trade everything for a pipe dream. That wasn't so. I just wanted to vent. On the other hand, when Lynn would want to do something or just talk, cutting the grass or painting the house was more important. How stupid I was then. I paid a great price to know how to have a strong relationship with a woman."

"Lynn's family consisted of five sisters. I never had a sister, just two brothers. Lynn's mother, a big fat woman, was a chain smoker. I guess after having six kids that would make you fat and a smoker, too." Frank laughed. "Her mother always seemed like she wanted more from life. She aspired to have it, but she wasn't to the point of being engrossed with having it.

"Lynn's father, on the other hand, was an engineer by trade. He was, to me, one of the most self-centered men I ever met. He was short and slender with huge ears and big thick glasses. And let me tell you, although you had to make the man talk, he always knew more than you or anyone else. Critical, my God, I think if the man faced Jesus himself, he would ask God to line up Jesus' chair. I remember my friends talking about going fishing with their fathers-in-law. I thought, how funny if Lynn's dad and I went fishing. I wonder who would be overboard first. Lynn's sisters, every one of them looked different, but, boy, they were as moody as their dad. I loved them, but, buddy, they would call all the time and worry you to death about the stupidest things.

"I remember when Lynn and I divorced."

"Lynn and I were married for 12 years and never had any children. The pressure was on from family and especially friends. Our friends started having children. Everyone would say, 'When are you going to have kids?' It would drive me crazy. Kids screaming and yelling. You couldn't have a quiet conversation.

"Have children, have children, it was almost like, let's get married, let's get married. I didn't want kids. Being a dreamer, I wanted to pick up and go where we pleased. Children, I felt, were like pets; they tied you down. Lynn had been feeling sick with flu-like symptoms for over a week. I told her she needed to go to the doctor. I never will forget. I was sitting on the sofa watching T.V. when she came home and said 'I have something to tell you.' I looked her straight in the eyes, startled, worried something was really wrong.

"She said, 'Frank, we are going to have a baby. I am pregnant.' I blurted out and said, 'How are we going to afford this?' What a stupid asshole I was, Aubrey. I have tortured myself for years over those words. How can we afford this! Must I base everything on money and a deal?

Yes, I was shocked and amazed. The entire evening was cold between us. Finally, Lynn went to bed crying. I kept things to myself. Shit, what are we going to do?

"The next couple of weeks I had never seen Lynn so happy. Her family and our friends barraged us with calls of congratulations. Married all that time and finally a child comes. People would kid me at work and church about how my life was going to change. 'Frank,' they said, 'you aren't going to b e a free bird anymore, going to have to settle down.' Those words every time I heard them would just kill me. I really tried to put the whole thing out of my mind. Travelling more and more, I wanted to run as far as I could.

"Everything with Lynn was baby this, baby that. Aubrey, it made me sick. Lynn became my mother. She wasn't sexual anymore to me. Before we would make love, we talked about the baby and after we made love, we talked baby. Time went faster and I started looking for a stable job. One with a regular paycheck. I sent resumés out and made appointments. Every interview I would hope they wouldn't hire me. I guess I projected that 'cause none of them hired me. This stable job search was like a prelude to a prison sentence.

"Meanwhile, Lynn and I agreed that we should run all medical tests available to us at the time and we did. See, we both were in our 30's. Everything was so right, all the tests came back normal, everything was just fine.

"The baby's due date was in the spring and after several months, I came around to the idea that I was going to be a daddy. Well, Lynn and I hadn't even named this soon-to-be child. I had named every dog or cat we ever had. Even in my childhood, my brother would let me name them. Maybe I am a good name picker. I told Lynn, I wanted to name the child, if a boy, after my two favorite people in the world; my two best friends, Peter and my Grandfather Popo. Henceforth came Peter Lockridge Moss.

"Peter and I met in the 8th grade at Briarwood High, and there was just something about his bookwormish personality I liked. Peter lived down the street from me, and lived with about the same hellish family existence that I lived in. It wasn't his mother like mine it was his father, who was mean as hell. We compared many notes on the drunken state of my mother and the brutality of his father.

"I saw Peter grow from a bespectacled kid to a man, marry, become a great M.D. and have a child. I love him as if he was my own brother.

"November approached and Lynn and I, and Peter and his wife, Lisa, decided we would all pack up and go to Jamaica for a vacation. Lynn's doctors gave their approval and off we went. On the plane, I told Peter that if we had a boy, we were going to name the baby, Peter Lockridge Moss. Peter and I had been friends since 8th grade and we shared everything; from our home life problems to girlfriend problems. When I told Peter the name, I could see tears forming in his eyes. He was so proud. 'That is the least you could do after being friends for 25 years,' Peter said. We laughed.

"The Jamaica trip was so fantastic. The women folk got to spend time together, and Peter and I could walk and talk about everything that was going on, both business and personal. We swam in secret coves in that crystal clear water. Rode horses on the beach. My damned horse almost ate up the souvenir stand. Those Jamaican capitalists. They would chase you to the plane if you owed them a quarter. I don't think they would understand my horse at your inventory.

"What a trip. It took my mind off so many troubles. The thing that still sticks in my mind was when Peter and I were swimming in the ocean. We began to talk and Peter asked me how I felt about the new baby comin. See, he knew my feeling about kids. I unloaded both barrels on him."

'Peter,' I said, 'I have never been so unhappy in all my life. I am battling with bankers in Atlanta for money to expand my business, and the doors are continually slammed in my face. On the home front, the baby coming; Lynn is so happy. I haven't seen her this happy in years. Why can't I see the happiness in this? Why must I see this child as a burden?' We talked for what seemed hours in that clear blue ocean. Peter always made me feel better about myself and when all the words had been sifted out his words called home, 'Everything works itself out.' I never wanted that Jamaican trip to end. I have gone on lot of vacations, but that trip is always etched in my mind. We all had a safe trip back to our homes, and I think everyone of us carried some peace back.

"Thanksgiving came and went, always at Lynns' mother's house.

There were always two constants, food, more than Pharaoh's Army could eat, and talk of sports, which I never cared anything about. You might think otherwise, but to this day I would rather paint the house that watch a sports game. I was glad when Thanksgiving passed."

"As the Christmas season approached, I thought ahead to the New Year. How Lynn and my lives would change. One morning when I was taking a bath, a premonition flashed into my mind. Our baby was going to die. With the water splashing on my face, I never realized how many buckets of tears I would cry over that morning's premonition. Yes, I have had this degree of E.S.P. all my life. The first time I experienced it was when I was 16 years old. Peter and I had been swimming. I got out too deep in the river with my clothes on. The rapids took a toll on the muscles on my leg. I was drowning. I called out for Peter to help me, and as I went under several times, I could see my body lying on the murky river bottom and people on the bank looking down at me saying, 'What a shame. He was so young.' Then I saw the face of my long dead Grandmother. Before I knew it, Peter's arm was around me.

"About a week before Christmas, Lynn and I were lying in bed and Lynn started hurting. I said, 'Lynn, don't you think we ought to call the doctor?'

'No-no, I will be fine.' That night Lynn's pain got sharper and sharper.

Finally, I said, 'We are going to the hospital.'

On the way to the hospital Lynn kept saying, 'Frank, you think the baby is O.K., is it O.K.?' It was all I could do to keep from crying.

'Yes, Lynn everything's going to be O.K."

"We got to the hospital, and Lynn was doubled over in pain. I never will forget that room they put us in. It looked like a funeral parlor, blue walls with blue satin drapes and lighted with what seemed like tall lamp torches. I felt I was in Hell. The nurse came in. Lynn's doctor came in.

"It was like this happened just yesterday. The doctor came in and said the baby is going to die. It was an incompetent cervix problem. Nothing they could do. That day, December 13, 1992, was a thousand hells for me. The nurse asked if we wanted to hold the baby before it died. I lost it then, I burst out and Lynn and I cried together. I got up from the chair where I was sitting and knelt at her hospital bed and hugged her and pressed my face against hers, and out tears joined each other; just as we had made the child, we joined. Before you knew it, the doctor was in the room, and we heard the baby scream life. The nurse cleaned him up and wrapped him in a little, white blanket and gave him to Lynn. Lynn asked if I wanted to see him. At first I said no, but I got up from the chair and looked at him and saw his legs were long like mine and long arms and hair like me. I kissed his head. He was so soft but becoming cold. Soon the nurse came in and took Peter away; never to see him again until I am dead and gone.

"That night, I crawled in the bed with Lynn, and we cried all night. We blamed ourselves, that I never wanted him. Now God saw fit to take my unwanted child and give it to someone who was deserving. Lynn said, 'No, Frank, you were just afraid.' Lynn blamed herself for going on the Jamaica trip. 'All those bumpy roads. Why didn't I call the doctor sooner?' I said, 'Lynn, none of that is your fault.' We cried all night and into the morning. During the hospital stay, we hadn't called any family and friends.

"When we got into the car to drive home, all we had to bring home was a hospital packet of how to overcome grief in the loss of your child and a little set of footprints. We didn't say a thing on the drive home. When we pulled into our driveway, I hated that house. I don't know why, I just hated it. We unlocked the door and made it as far as the sofa, and we both collapsed and hugged each other and cried some more. Composing ourselves, we had to call people. The onslaught of well-meaning family and friends arrived. Down the driveway you could see them coming bearing food and words of sympathy. Some not thinking, saying 'You can have another child,' as if this child was a broken item that could be returned for a good item. They kept coming.

"One day, Aubrey, I couldn't take it anymore, and I got into my truck and drove and drove and cried by myself. I think I went to South Carolina. I got back home late that evening and, in the driveway was still another family member's car. Even Lynn's old still-faced daddy came, not offering a word of encouragement, but he showed up. When the family left, Lynn and I sat on the sofa and gazed at an undecorated Christmas tree. I said, 'What do you want to do with that?' We both agreed, 'Let's throw the damn thing out in the yard,' and we did. I would decorate the store at Christmas time, but I never put a tree up in my house until I married Leacy.

"Lynn and I talked of what to do about the 'happy holiday season.' We agreed to go to the beach. I had been lobbying for years; 'Let's got on a cruise, get away from all those kinfolks. At least one Christmas.' Our decision was made, but it was greatly disliked by family and friends. We packed and headed for Grayton Beach, Florida, our favorite get-away place. Grayton was a private fishing village. We rented a cottage right on the ocean. You're not at the beach unless you can see if from your window and smell the salt air and walk out the back door and feel the sand between your toes.

"Christmas at the beach. It was a different experience. So deserted, the only footprints on the beach were Lynn's and mine, and some beach birds.

"Lynn and I talked a lot those few days. I said, 'Lynn, let's sell out and move to Texas where nobody knows us. A fresh new start. That damn house we live in now is a bad memory for me. Let's sell it.'

Lynn said, 'Frank, all you want to do is jeopardize what we build on a pipe dream as usual. My family is here, our friends.'

'I know, but we can make new friends, and your family is always your family even if you live in Texas.' With this conversation, I could see Lynn and me drifting away like a piece of driftwood. That Christmas beach trip, Lynn and I talked more than we had in years. We talked during the day and wept at night.

"Over the next couple of months, Lynn and I became engrossed in our work. We became cold to each other. Talking only to the point of 'What's for supper' or 'Have you paid this bill?' Sex between us was the same, cold nothing. Lynn started going to a therapist, and she asked if I would go to one. Sally Burkshire. We had several talk sessions. On my first visit, Sally had all kinds of toys on the floor. I said, 'Oh, let's play.' Wrong thing to say to a therapist. You know, those folks don't joke. I still remember one statement Sally made, 'Frank, as tragic as your baby dying was, the baby freed your soul to not pretend anymore.' She was so right.

"All through my life to this point, I have pretended everything was great, fine, perfect. On the surface everything to everyone else couldn't be better. From that point, I told myself I was going to be honest with my feelings.

"Those first few months in 1993 were so hard for me. I was overcome with guilt. The baby and Lynn. I felt it was all my fault. That's really how I found Eatonton. Riding, just riding to get away from the pain.

"I rode into Eatonton one Wednesday afternoon and found the antique store. God, that place was a wreck. The outside of the building was painted a puke green. Windows were boarded up with plywood. There was a poison ivy vine growing up the side of the building that one woman claimed to be the biggest in the county. Holes were knocked in the bricks as if left over from Sherman's march. Inside, the walls were painted to match the outside. Water stains on the ceiling and more. It looked like all anyone did was to prostitute the grand old building and not put one cent in its repairs or well-being. The store was piled to the ceiling with high-priced yard-sale merchandise. Three lights burned in the building. How anyone could see what to buy is still a mystery to me."

"The proprietor was a little old lady with a high-pitched, screechy voice. She had dyed red hair and eyes like a snake. They look like a marble. You can never focus in on them. Pinpoints of light going in every direction. Yes, Eunice, she would study you like a snake coiling her head back gathering information on you until it was time to strike. Always mumbling to herself. Probably new plans to strike out at someone. Yes, she produced a baby snake also. I'll tell you about her later.

"Eunice was overweight, and she sat coiled like a snake in the bag with her one eye scanning the dark lit store just daring you to try and shoplift. Looked like she would probably have a .38 in the desk drawer. I said hello to her and she responded back. Chit, chat, about what's the price on this or that.

She says, 'What brings you up this way?'

'Oh just traveling today, Do you know of any business for sale in the area? Restaurants, hardware stores?' I asked again.

She cocked her head back and said, 'No, but I will sell this place. I'm thinking about retiring.'

'Could the building be bought also?' I asked.

She said, 'That' the only way to sell it.'

I asked, 'What kind of money?' I couldn't believe it. It was nothing compared to Atlanta real estate. I bid the lady good-bye and went to check on another town close by.

All my business life to this point, everything, had been based on greed and money. How I could leverage this piece of real estate, how much I could make on the antiques; there was something more in Eatonton. I felt I was supposed to be there. I came back the next day to check further on the town of Eatonton. I had always wanted to live in a small town. The second time I went to Eatonton I felt the same, I was being called there.

"God, I had fought bankers in Atlanta all my life. They just weren't the visionaries I was. So my guns were raised when I went into Mark's office. Aubrey, you won't believe this. Mark was the only banker I had ever known that had an open Bible on his desk where the customer could see. I was impressed. We chatted about the old building in town and Ms. Eunice that owned it. Mark said, 'You are a Godsend, Frank. We have been wanting someone to fix and paint that building for 40 years.' Showing Mark my business plans, he said, 'Yes, we would lend you the money.' I couldn't believe it. It was too easy.

"Everything fell into place, but I wanted to make sure, so I left Mark's office and went down the street to the town's Baptist church. The door was open and I walked into the sanctuary. I felt God was there. I prayed in that church. 'Is it your will I be here?' I prayed for just a few minutes then I looked up and on the stained glass window was etched 'Faith-Hope-Love.' From that day forward those words have been my guiding force, through all of my pains and trials and tribulations. It made such an impression on me. I have instructions in my will that those words be inscribed on my tombstone. I felt good when I left that church, but the drive home to tell Lynn was a different matter. My gut feeling was that this decision of mine would end Lynn's and my marriage. I was prepared for that, I thought. For years, I thought I traded Lynn for a business deal."

"That night, I told Lynn I had bought a building where we can run the business and renovate the upstairs for our home. We could save money. Have a new life away from Atlanta. Lynn looked as if she had seen a ghost. She said, 'You are going to do what you want, Frank, but I am not going to Eatonton.' I knew the answer before the words came out of her mouth."

"The next day I did what I wanted; I saw Mark at the bank. We talked. Mark is the best Christian businessman I have ever met. He was 10 years younger than myself, but wise beyond his years. Mark looked like the kid on the cover of Madd Magazine. The kid with the freckles, reddish hair and devilish grin. What a guy. Built like a little tank. Mark was no wimp; no sir, not by a long shot. For sure, God made that Mark breed of a man. I wish I were more like him."

"Mark was more than a banker. He was my friend and still is to this day."

"I started working on the building and the business. The place was piled to the ceiling with yard-sale stuff. I painted and cleaned 'till I thought my hands were going to drop off. At the end of the day, I would travel back to Atlanta. Lynn and I would sleep in the same bed, kind of like friends. It was so hard to face Lynn with my true feelings. See, I still pretended so much. My guilt over baby Peter's death, and Lynn's guilt was becoming more and more overwhelming. I thought she hated me and wanted me to leave. Sure, you can read all the literature you want on a woman's mental health after the loss of a child, but until you live with them, you don't really know. It was hell."

"At the store in Eatonton, I found out how the old red-headed bitch Eunice made money on me under the table. God, she could be so spiteful some days."

"Time went faster. I saw less and less of Lynn. Some days when I was too tired to drive home, I would stay at the Eatonton Motel. It burned down about a year ago. Talk was that the last group of pine straw bailers got drunk and set it on fire. "

"That weekend, I remember it as clear as if it was yesterday. We sat on the den floor in our home in Atlanta and we talked. I looked straight into Lynn's green eyes, and said, 'I am not coming back to Atlanta. There is nothing here for me anymore. I belong in Eatonton.'

Lynn said, 'I am not going to Eatonton. Atlanta is where I belong.' We could never forget our baby. Lynn said, 'Do you want to call Sam, your lawyer friend?'

I said, 'Yes.' Then, we walked through our house just like an estate sale and divided up all of our belongings. Finished, we both laughed that we paid too much sometimes at auctions for some of the antiques. Our bed where we made countless hours of love, where we made our baby. Photos of friends and family. Gifts that people had given to both of us for Christmas or birthdays. Some things, like the box of all Peter's things, neither of us could bear to open. All the shower gifts we received before Peter died; toys, little shoes and clothes. All those special little things. Lynn and I boxed all of that because neither of us could bear to look at them. Lynn has that box. Like a coffin sealed for God only to see. Item by item, with no argument and an occasional joke or two, we divided it all. I always thought when two people got a divorce they clawed each other like game cocks. Lynn and I to this day are still friends. Friends of ours ask what happened? Could we have worked through the death of Peter? I don't know. I just didn't love Lynn anymore. Don't get me wrong. I loved her, but not as a husband should love a wife. Sometimes I feel guilty about the whole thing. What could I have done differently?

# PART TWO

Arriving at the Atlanta airport, Frank and Aubrey rented a truck. After a 30 minute drive, Frank asked:

"How about let's pull over and get a soft drink?"

"Sure"

"Tired of hearing my life story?"

"It just scares me."

"Scares you? What are you saying?"

"You and I are so alike."

"God help you, Aubrey. I wouldn't wish being me on anybody."

Frank and Aubrey got out of the truck and walked toward a weather-beaten old country store.

Opening a pair of colonial screen doors, Frank said, "These old stores are a thing of the past. Aubrey, most of these old fellows started up and bought someone out after World War II. Now they are all gone. I go to a lot of store auctions. It's sad Aubrey, selling a man's livelihood. Think of the many hours the storekeeper put on the linoleum. Yes, I wonder if the auctioneer really knows what he's selling. Think of what the storekeeper had to face after World War II. Price fixes, inflation, and the big discount chains running them out of business. Because of 'buy for less.' The voices...Aubrey, can you hear them?"

The only voice Aubrey could hear was his mother screaming on the linoleum floor. Aubrey quickly says, "Yes, Frank."

"Over fifty years of voices of a morning greeting, of a thank you. I miss my store."

"I know you do, Frank." Aubrey puts his hand on Frank's shoulder. Reaching in the red ice box, Frank and Aubrey get a cold drink.

"Let's drink it outside," Frank says. "Here's the money. We will take the bottle with us."

"Yes, sir," replies the storekeeper.

Sitting on the squeaky bench outside, Frank said, "Aubrey, look at all those pretty poinsettias in the pots over there. That's what I brought to Eatonton when I came. Paint, flower pots, and a new look at what had always been there. It was just common sense to me. I joined the Chamber of Commerce right off. I loved being a big fish in a small pond. Yes, small towns do have their advantages. In Atlanta, I never could make a difference. In Eatonton I could."

"A small town is like a rose — beautiful petals, that's the kindness of folks. Them helping you and you helping them. Then there is the stem, beautiful green with thorns that can prick you and leave a pain that can last a lifetime. I loved living in Eatonton. Eatonton's beautiful side and ugly side. I have experienced them both. I guess I am well-rounded in a small town."

Aubrey took a breath and said, "I have experienced it all too."

"When I first came there, people would come into the store and say, 'Frank, we are so glad you moved here—it's like you have been here forever.' Oh, I met some characters there. Sitting at my desk and looking on the sidewalk was like looking into a time machine. The blacks of the town were straight out of the old south. Take, for instance, Robert Mitchell. The blacks called him Wildman. Did you ever know Wildman?"

"Yeah, I know Wildman."

"Wildman is the best brickmason in Putnam county. Sheriff Billy LaSurre would lock Wildman up on a D.U.I. charge just to get him to work around his farm for free. Old LaSurre would get the judge to set Wildman's fee so high it would take him 6 months to work it off. Wildman was nothing but a modern day slave, as were the rest of the blacks that were picked up on bogus charges so they could be free labor for the town. If the free labor tried to escape I heard tales of how they were shot down like dogs trying to escape or beaten to death with a claw hammer."

"I always like to check on folks I hire, so I asked J.C. LaSurre in the office across the street. Boy, was he a character also."

Aubrey's face twisted with hate, but said nothing.

"J.C. looked like a 70-year old glutinous slug. A big fat round man with glasses that seemed melted to his sunbeaten face. His pants were pulled up so far you could see the print of his balls and dick. His eyes were bright, reminded me of killer eyes in the old movie days. He always wore cheap polyester pants and a knit shirt in the summer. None of his outfits matched.

"He had perfectly combed reddish hair that was stuck down with some sort of gel. Always boasting of how much money he had. He would preface every sentence by 'You know what I mean?' and, boy, you better agree with the almighty J.C. He was slick, a smooth operator. In the newspaper, he was always giving money to the Dairy Association or some worthy J.C. cause. When he smiled at you, it was unnatural, as if he were baiting you in a rabbit trap. Typical of his family genes, his mouth dropped in a sour, frowning way. His voice was much like his brother, Sheriff Billy LaSurre. The Sheriff was another story." Aubrey looked at the ground. "What another pig! Both men grunted like a pig when they spoke.

"J.C. had an austere office across from my building. Everything in it was cheap and functional. Political maps hung on the wall and a rotary black telephone sat on the desk. Piles of stock reports and timber booklets littered his desk. J.C. told folks he managed estates. J.C. was not a stupid man, rather, very intelligent. Of course, he let you know how smart he was.

"When I would visit him across the street, I would study him. He was such a vile man, someone from hell. I never quite encountered anyone like him, nor do I wish to. Looking at him while I was sitting next to his desk, I wondered how he really made his money. 'You know Frank, we have got the nigger race where we want them in the nineties. Hell, they talk equal rights, but we got them again. They think they can outsmart the white man; hell, we've got the niggers by the balls again. In the forties we sold them shine, in the nineties we sell them cocaine.' I saw J.C.'s picture in the paper once telling of him being in the Army in W.W. II. I wonder how many innocent civilians he maimed or killed. I wondered about the drugs that were sold down on Jones Street, the street J.C.'s office was on. They called it "The Strip." Seven days a week drugs were sold. Sure there were mock raids, but like J.C. said, cocaine replaced shine, got to keep up with the times. I always wondered how much cocaine money it would take to make a respectable mutual fund portfolio.

"I speculated how many blacks had been thrown down wells or buried in unmarked graves on LaSurre land. How many black scalps hung from his belt? J.C. loved to make love to black women. How many children did he father?

"Oh, and the women he got in bed to make a deal. Patrice, Eunice's daughter slept with him so she could sell the county a worthless building for $400,000."

"Yeah, I knew J.C.," said Aubrey sarcastically. "He slapped me in the face when I was ten years old. All I asked the S.O.B. was if I could have the coke bottles he threw in the trash. He said, 'Niggers want you to give them everything. Don't want to work for nothing. Equal rights, hell, I'll show you what equal rights are.' Then he slapped me so hard my ears rang as he knocked me to the ground. He said, 'Slap me, Nigger, that's equal. I am the richest man in Putnam County. Don't you want to slap me, nigger?' He didn't just slap me that morning. He slapped all of my people for 150 years of LaSurre tyranny. As we walked away, I told my mother I wanted to kill J.C. LaSurre. She said, 'Aubrey, vengeance is the Lord's, and don't you ever forget that. The Lord knows what J.C. did to you this morning. Let him take care of it.' I buried my head in my mother's bosom and cried, 'It's not fair.' 'A lot of things in this old world isn't fair, Aubrey.' My mother hugged me. When I was in the Army, during training or on the battlefield, I saw J.C. as the enemy. Every time I fired my rifle I aimed at him. Probably killed the S.O.B. a thousand times. That S.O.B. - He..." Aubrey cut his sentence short. "That's when I left Eatonton, to live with my Aunt in Atlanta. Mama figured it was best for my safety.

" I lived on the Southside of Atlanta known at East Point. My aunt lived not too far from where you grew up Frank. Aunt Lillian finally got to live in a good brick house only because you White folks were scared of black folks. I remember my Aunt telling me how the Atlanta Realtors scared the white neighborhoods with talk of decreasing property values, poor schools, and the greatest fear of all God forbid living next door to a black family.

"White flight as it was called gave white Atlantians about what they paid for their homes, many lost money. What white flight gave black folks was a chance to live in a decent home with central heat and plumbing that worked. My Aunt Lillian was a middle aged widow woman when I came to live with her. She had taken Uncle John's insurance money to buy her home. Uncle John had died young of a heart attack working two warehouse jobs. They had one boy who drowned in a bucket of water when he was two years old. Aunt Lillian treated me like I was her own child. She used to call me her "Angel Child". Aunt Lillian had known some hard times growing up with my mom and five brothers and sisters on a farm. Her great granddaddy was given the land after the Civil War. I guess that's why Mama never wanted to leave Eatonton, save that damn farm. Aunt Lillian could cope with more pain than anyone I ever knew.

"It was funny Aunt Lillian worked in the Activity Department of a Southside nursing home. There she played childlike games with the well to do old white folks. Often times she would tell me the demented old folks would blurt out "You ole black nigger, I ain't playing this damn Bingo?" Aunt Lillian would just smile and say "Now you know that's not a nice thing to say."

"God, Aunt Lillian was worse than my Mama about church meetings. Every Sunday without fail I had to put on a white starched shirt and bow tie and sit on those hard benches and listen to that old preacher.

"Waving his arms like a conductor, and sweat pouring off his face proclaiming the day when judgement would come to the whiteman and the black man.

"It's Gods vengeance on our enemies, not ours," the preacher would shout.

"While you were becoming Student Government President in High School Frank, I was in R.O.T.C. learning how to be the best marksman in all Atlanta. J.C. LaSurre and his brother Billy marked my target everyday, every year. Swing Low Sweet Chariot might of hummed in my ear every Sunday but rifle fire filled my soul. G. damn the LaSurre brothers.

"Aunt Lillian and Mama begged me not to join the army seeing my Daddy came home in a wood box. Aunt Lillian was as tight as Dicks hatband, and had a college fund saved for me.

"Give it to that damn church you love so much," I told her one day.

I was so damn sick and tired of hearing about how to forgive my enemies, and how the Lord would take care of the white man. I stormed out of Aunt Lillian's house and left for basic training.

"I never dated in High School I was always afraid of women, seeing as what J.C. did to me. When I was in Germany I met Francis Phillips. Francis was a nurse, and had to be the most understanding woman I ever met. She was from Beafort South Carolina, so we both understood the Southern way. I told her what J.C. LaSurre did to me, and she held me and loved me. After about 4 years Francis and I married and I signed for another tour. I thought I could make 20 years in the army, then retire and live on some golf course somewhere. Well, I hurt my back and that ended that plan. Francis and I adopted James my boy when he was just a baby. I love James so much. Francis and I split 5 years ago about the time we met Frank. Francis was tired of being tied down as she called it and she was sick and tired of hearing my hatred toward the LaSurres.

Aubrey threw his coke bottle on the ground and stood up. Looking at the sky, "My curse in life Frank, the LaSurre brothers, and Eatonton Georgia. Eatonton, Mama wanted to die in her own bed in the house her great granddaddy built. That's why I came back to Eatonton to take care of two unfinished things. Take care of mama till she left to be with the Lord, and settle an old score. Today is a milestone for me. I haven't been to Eatonton since they ran you out."

"Did your mother ever tell you how the LaSurres got so much money?", Frank asks.

"There was a man that came into my store one day and we got to talking. He told me he used to run the local beer joint. I got to asking him about the LaSurres, how they made their money. 'Frank,' he said, 'Old man Tom LaSurre, that's J.C. and Billy's Daddy, had a good deal of land. But, being the greedy bastards they were, they wanted more.' There was this fellow named Fougerty. His big white two-story house is on the Madison Highway. One of my old lawyers from Atlanta bought it.'

"You mean Phil Fougerty?"

"Yes, that's him. Anyway Tom LaSurre had a daughter he wanted to marry off to one of Fougerty's sons. One morning at the breakfast table, Tom and old man Fougerty got into an argument over how much land the new couple should have. Tom LaSurre pulls out a gun and kills Fougerty at the breakfast table. Thus, LaSurre gets control of Fougerty's properties."

"How did he get away with murdering Fougerty? That's a stupid question for me to ask, after all it's Eatonton."

"It depends on who you know. I think a new attorney named Franklin Anthony got LaSurre free of the charges."

"Frank, was that Doris Anthony's grandfather?"

"One and the same. Remember a while ago you were telling me about how J.C. slapped you in the face? Well, my first couple of weeks of business in Eatonton, I had a little black boy named Brock work for me. Brock was probably 13 years old. He would call me Mr. Frank.

"One day I was in the store scurrying about and the high and mighty J.C. came in. In the background, J.C. thought he heard Brock say 'Frank.' J.C. said, 'Frank, let me tell you something. Don't you let that little nigger call you by your first name. Let them do that and they will get away with anything. Remember, Frank, we white men are above the nigger race.' I looked at J.C., for this was the first time I saw his true color. I expected a Klan robe to burst forth from J.C.'s pocket.

"I looked at him with such contempt. 'How dare you come into my place of business and berate one of my workers?' J.C. knew from the look on my face I was not happy with his racist comments. 'He can't say Moss, J.C. He calls me Mr. Frank.' J.C. gave me one of his stare downs and said good day. I think he knew I was not a push over.

"Little Brock one day came in to ask for an advance on his pay. I said, 'Now, Brock, I have paid you real good. Where did all of your money go?' He began to rattle off all of his expenditures. From time to time I would comment on how he couldn't afford this or that. 'Brock you need a savings account,' I said, and after much discussion I said, 'I will put $25.00 in to start.' Off to the bank we went.

"All down the sidewalk Brock asked questions. When we got to the bank Brock asked Linda, one of the girls that worked there, 'When can I get my money out?' Again Linda and I explained how a savings account worked. 'You aren't going to take any of my money out and buy a new dress are you, Miss Linda?' We both laughed. 'No, Brock, we can't do that.' Brock said, 'I'll have to think about that one' and we left.

"I bet it was a month later the phone rang and Brock said, 'Mr. Frank, will you still help me open a up savings account?' 'Sure will if you don't chicken out on me again,' I said. 'No, I am ready now, Mr. Frank.' So we opened Brock's first savings account. About a week later he calls and says, 'Mr. Frank, I got wondering if I should die who would get my money?' I laughed and said, 'Brock, what you want me to do now? Help you make out a will?' He was concerned, Aubrey. Later I learned that Brock's mother and father had gotten into a gun fight and the mother killed the father. Every so often Brock would tell me of some more family members to die.

"Brock would call me up or drop by to see me. Sometimes I think he just wanted the companionship of a man. We went to the movies and shared a lot of good conversation.

" To make J.C. feel important, I would drop in to ask his advice. 'J.C., what do you think about Robert Mitchell?'

'Oh, he's alright to work. He's a good boy, been in jail,' said J.C.

I asked J.C. 'What for? Did he steal anything?'

J.C. said, 'Hell, all niggers steal.' What a character."

Aubrey looked Frank right in the eye. "How could you ask any thing of J.C.?"

Frank snapped back, "It's just politics. Robert was a great brick mason. Did a lot of work on my building. He looked like he was of the earth just as the bricks he lays for a living. Robert is what I imagine slaves looked like during the Antebellum South. His eyes were red yellowish looking. His clothes were torn and tattered. Usually a red flannel shirt with oversized pants and a rope belt. Robert was muscular in build. Always polite, he had probably done everything in the book.

"One day I was contracting with him to do some more brick work and I asked when he could show up to work. He said he was supposed to finish a carport.

'When will you be done with the carport?', I asked Robert.

He replied, 'Oh, soon. I will take care of your bricks first, Mr. Frank.'

'Well, what will you tell the man on the carport?'

'Well, Mr. Frank, I guess I lied 'bout being there tomorrow on that carport.' We laughed.

"Ghosts live in Eatonton."

"Oh now, come on."

"No, it's true. A guy that looked just like Elvis Presley lived a couple of streets down. I swear, Aubrey, when that guy would dye his hair black and dress in a '70's suit on a foggy morning, you would think Elvis himself was hitching a ride." We both laughed. "There is one tale that probably ties to my love life in this town." Frank got up from the bench and began giving directions with his hands.

"If you go down one block and take a right, where the old brick building is on the corner, does that say Bank? Well, turn there, go down a short way, past the first block, then look to the right. There's a big house with white columns, that's where Sylvia the Ghost lives. The way the story goes, on her wedding day, Sylvia, who had long black hair and a white wedding gown on, went up to the attic to get something out of a large trunk and fell in and suffocated. Everyone searched and searched, thought she ran away. A few days later, a servant found her in the trunk. She is known as a snooty ghost, only appearing to those of her social status."

"Have you seen her?" asked Aubrey.

"No, I haven't seen her, but felt her. When I first came to town, a lady came in the store and said she was the caretaker of the house. I begged for a tour. She said, 'Sure.' That day Aubrey, it must have been 100 degrees outside and hot inside the house. When I walked up the stairway to the landing, I had forgotten about the ghost story. Just the hair on my right arm stood up. Folks said that's how Sylvia introduces herself to new men in town. Sometimes I wonder if Doris Anthony was really Sylvia walking the planks of that old house."

"Oh, there were strange things that would happen in my old store, like pictures would not just fall off the wall, but rather slide down the wall. One night I was asleep and awoke and felt someone had broken into my house. You know the feeling? When you feel a presence in a room with you. Well, I looked to the side of my bed and there in a translucent form was an image. I don't know if it was a man or woman, but it grabbed me around my arm. I extended my arm out and grabbed its arm. It felt like a skeleton arm. I repeated over and over, 'Who are you and what do you want?' After a while, I woke up and was scared to death. The appearance of that ghost was the prelude to the Eatonton holocaust. The building was used as a confederate hospital during the

Civil War. I imagined what it would be like during the Civil War with dying folks all on the floor and upstairs where I lived.

"Oh, Aubrey, it was a grand home, at least in my mind. The only way you could get upstairs was to go to the outside of the building. Kind of like old Doc Adam's office on Gunsmoke. The ceilings were tall, probably 15 foot. The plaster walls had cracked, and I spent many hours patching and filling in holes. Around the walls was a beaded wainscotting. The millwork around the doors was something to behold. It all was so Greek Revival, kind of like a temple. The windows were 10 feet tall with those incredible fluted surrounds. Each window was like a doorway. The entire floor plan was laid out like an old Greek Revival house. A wide central hall with three rooms flanking either side. I had two fireplaces up there. The wood plank floors echoed as you walked on them. Streams of light poured through the windows, and the view of the courthouse dome and town square was surreal.

"In the morning, I would lay there in bed and look out at the courthouse clock dome and think of how it looked like a picture of Florence, Italy. You have been there, Aubrey, you know what it looks like. The pigeons would fly around the dome as the sun slowly rose. It took Brock and another little boy a week just to haul off the debris that was upstairs. I was only able to complete one room of my dream home before Doris took it all away."

"The building was built as a hospital?" asked Aubrey.

"Oh no, built as a meeting hall in 1849. Known as Temperance Hall. I guess the haints got used to my intemperate ways. I thought they would fly out the window when I opened my first bottle of wine or bedded down my first girlfriend upstairs. Finished with your drink?"

"Let's go."

Leaning on the truck, Frank said, "Hey, Aubrey, look at that pack of dogs over there. There was a girl in Eatonton that used to walk down the sidewalk; a pack of dogs would follow her all the way. That whole family was different. The mother, when she was driving either a car or a truck, would make that turn at the corner, and you could see her whole body turn with that curve as she turned that steering wheel. It was funny to see. The daddy would ride this vintage bicycle up and down the street always wearing a white Panama hat.

"I remember Beth Roberts. She was a tall woman with blue grey hair, a beautiful complexion and dark brown eyes. She must have been a knock-out in her day. She came into the store one day and said, 'Frank, do you buy pistols?' I said, 'Well sure, depends on price, Ms. Beth.' Out of her purse Ms. Beth produced a .32 pistol and said, 'My late husband got this from a drunk who owed him money. Now Frank,' she said, 'It's not registered, which is good because that Yankee government of ours can't take it away from you. But I'll swear last night I was checking the gun for bullets, and I cocked the hammer back and the gun went off.'

"'God, I thought I had murdered myself. I always heard that you go numb when you are shot. I wiped my face with my hands but, God, what if I had shot myself in the back of the head and I can't see the bullet wound. So I went to the bathroom and looked and couldn't see any blood. Then I thought, what if I have really killed myself and I am a ghost like Sylvia? You know they didn't find her for days. What would people think? I have sold this house, and I couldn't stand the thought of leaving and killed myself. What would my church friends think? Well, I finally I came to my senses and saw a bullet hole in the ceiling, and, Frank, I have sold the house. I got a piece of light colored chewing gum to put in the hole. Frank, do you think that's okay?'

'Yes, Ms. Beth.' I burst out laughing.

'Frank, you just have to buy this gun.'

'Okay, I'll buy it.'

"These older women of Eatonton. God, I miss them; like Virginia Ralston. Virginia was a retired school teacher. She was short and a little overweight with a dynamite personality, even in her 70's. Virginia would storm into my store with the most profound things. You never did know what to expect.

"My first meeting with her, she came in and introduced herself as Virginia Ralston. Out of respect, I would say hello, Mrs. Virginia. After about three or four times of 'Hello, Mrs. Virginia,' she said, 'Ms. Virginia is what my maid calls me. Call me Virginia.' Wow, then I started calling her Ms. Ralston. Then after three or four times, she said, 'Frank, Ms. Ralston is my husband's mother.' Henceforth from that time, I called her Virginia.

"One day, I was sitting behind the desk and Virginia comes racing into the store and says, 'Frank! You have got to help me.'

I said, 'Anything Virginia.'

'You know where the library is?'

'Yes, Ma'am,' I said.

'It's a disgrace all those card files all over the floor. Frank, you just have to find us an oak file cabinet.'"

"The funniest time, though, was one day I was getting into the truck and Virginia came running up to me, 'Frank, you are probably going to hear this story from someone sooner or later, so you need to have the correct facts. My husband, George, do you know him?'

'Oh yes, Virginia,' I said. 'He's a lawyer in town.'

'Yes, that is correct. 13 years ago, George ran off with a pretty young thing. When George got lung cancer from smoking all those damn cigarettes, she dumped him and George came back to me. I should have put a pillow over his face then, but no, I took care of him. He is better now.'

"Living in Eatonton, was like a stage play, all those characters. All those people, characters in my play."

"You saw Eatonton like a play. I saw it as a bigoted town. When I was a boy skipping down the sidewalk, white folks that would pass me on the street would say, 'They all have rhythm, don't they.' Every racial comment you ever heard of Frank I heard as a young boy. How would you like to grow up knowing that you are inferior, never good enough because you happen to be black. You had your white birthday parties and maids, you lived a privileged life Frank. That's all you see is glitter and gold and the gallant past of the South. How about folks like me just because our skin happens to be black, I had to step off the sidewalk because white folks had the right. How would you like to always be in the back of the line? You see the people of Eatonton like through a mirror, only a reflection, I saw them in real life."

"When I bought the building, the newspaper did an article on how my wife and I were going to move here and renovate the building and live upstairs. Boy, folks thought that was so neat to live over the store. It is an old concept; I created nothing new."

"Frank, let me ask. I thought you and Lynn were divorced when you came to Eatonton?"

"Wait, Aubrey, I don't understand?" asked Frank.

Aubrey responded, "You were saying that the newspaper article said you and your wife were going to live there."

"Oh yes." Frank chuckled. "What can I say, I am like Robert Mitchell, I lied. It was like this. I had always been a marketing man. I have always loved women. God help me!" Frank laughed. "I guess another reason, I didn't want women after me. I just wanted to be left alone. Let's get back to my building. When I started renovating the outside of the building, a black man came to my doorstep looking for work. This black man was named Bill. He had a neat appearance, about my age with a short haircut. Bill always looked tired and always worried. He had eyes of the past also, like Robert Mitchell. One time Bill said he was just drawn to my store and me. He said I brought happiness to this town and this store, a ray of sunshine. Boy, he sure did make me feel good. Bill was very articulate but sometimes he would mumble. I would say, 'What did you say, Bill?' Then he would switch back to his articulate manner."

"Maybe he was cussing you out in mumble, Frank," Aubrey laughed.

"No." Frank's eyes showed a serious side. "Although Bill never met me before, he knew all about me. I could read his soul. He knew me. Strange, uh Aubrey?"

Aubrey responded, "Eatonton is beginning to sound like a time warp."

"Could be," Frank said. "Anyway, back to Bill. He was dirt poor. I know he worked two or three jobs. He went to school also. Studying to be a preacher. Bill was a man of God. I asked him one time if he was my guardian angel.

"Talking about Bill preaching, Bill helped me paint the building, and I told him one time the painting crew I set up for him was the biggest witness program since Jesus. I had one guy that was an alcoholic, one guy a high school dropout and one guy just got out of prison for killing someone."

"All of that motley crew showed up, and I was late. Had to go get paint, a ladder or something. All of them wanted me to pay them for the time they waited. I sat at my desk with all their eyes looking straight at me as if to challenge me. I said, 'Let me tell you one damn thing. I am the boss and never, never question my authority. Work starts when I get here, not before. Got it?' They all nodded their heads and agreed.

I said, 'Look, if I tell you to go kill someone, then question my authority. Got it?' They for sure knew I was a strong contender. Can't mess with nice Mr. Frank.

"Later that day, Robert, the man who was in prison, asked me to take him home. I said yes. Robert was about my height, fat and had a patch over one eye. He claimed his cousin shot his eye with a BB gun. Riding back to his house, I asked him why he was in prison. He said, 'Mr. Frank, I killed a man.' Boy, did I shrink up, after my comment that morning about authority. But I didn't let Robert see my fear. 'Stabbed the guy 20 times in a bar. We were all drunk.' Boy, what a painting crew. But, you know, Aubrey, that damn paint job still looked good the last time I saw my building.

"Aubrey, look out the window. See that three-legged dog? Folks in town call him Tripod.

"Aubrey, there used to be two retarded men in town. Both about my age. Matter of fact, they still live there. One was Steve. Steve's body build and general physical appearance are normal. His speech and inflections are normal also. Overweight, he has eyes that look in a dead stare when he looks at you. Kind of like a Down's baby. Steve loved his mother and father more than any grown person I ever met. I asked him one time, 'Have you ever thought about getting a place of your own?' 'No, Mr. Frank. I love my mother and father so much. I just want to spend as much time with them as I can. You know, you don't have them for very long.'

"Steve was always friendly and seemed preoccupied with sex. I doubt he had ever been with a woman. He used to hang around me like a fly. It aggravated me when I was dealing with customers. He would be right over my shoulder. Drove me nuts! To this day Steve can't drive a car. Sometimes, I think that might be a blessing. Steve always rode a bicycle. He left school in the 10th grade. The principal, according to Steve, wanted to put him in a special education class. Boy! Steve told me one day at the store when I asked him if he finished high school. He said that 'damn principal wanted to put me in the retarded class. Hell, I told him where to go and walked out. Never set foot back in that school.'

"How did Steve manage?"

"He lived with his mother and father. I never met Steve's brother, but folks in town said he was a genius. Steve used to do yard work for a living. Steve was kind and generous. Often times he would say, 'Frank, I am going to the store, need anything?' 'No, I am fine, Steve.' He still would bring me a candy bar or soft drink. He never let me pay him. Steve was a far cry from another retarded man named Warren.

"Unlike Steve, Warren was crazy. Pretending to be a disc jockey, he would stop folks on the street and interview them. Drive you crazy. I'll tell you, Aubrey, if I saw Warren coming down the street, I would get up and go hide in the back of the store. I think about Steve. What would it be like not to be educated and all you have to worry about was riding your bike to the next yard to be mowed? Loving your mom and dad so much you didn't want to leave. How simple."

"Aubrey lets pull over here. Look at that grand old house with all of those columns. Built before the Civil War I bet. Look at the mill-work around the windows and doors."

"Yea, Frank, probably built that with slave hands. I wonder if the "MASA" issued sunglasses to all of the slaves so the big white beast wouldn't hurt their eyes. You and your old South Frank."

"See that little shack in the backyard that's where my people lived. In a weather beaten shack with rusty nails protruding out of the planks. One grungey stone fireplace that filled your lungs up with so much smoke you felt as if you are a smoked turkey. Everything is so green and manicured Frank, everything so perfect. Yet that little shack in the backyard isn't all that perfect. Hide the blackman in the backyard like he's a lawnmower or a ugly ladder. Pull him out when you need him, then praise him for a job well done and tell him he's just like a member of the family. I have heard folks say a cat or a dog is a member of the family. Fetch this nigger dog, fetch the ladder dog, and if you don't, because you are a member of the family we have a right to cuss you and beat you, and cut you..."

"Aubrey, I am sorry you feel this way. I don't know anything of the Plantation way of life. Just what I learned in history books or what my kinfolks told me. Hell, you and I were little boys when Civil rights came, I barely remember when Kennedy got shot."

"Yes Frank, but you told me your people owned slaves."

"That's right they owned I think eight slaves, but we are talking about the 1850's not the nineties. Just because Eatonton is some white racist town from hell doesn't mean all white folks are devils."

Aubrey looked out the window in disgust.

"Tell me about that damn optometrist office you rented."

"That optometrist office is a strange story also."

"How's that, Frank?"

"I had owned the building for about six months. See, I actually bought the building from the old eye doctor, Dr. Gordy.

"I thought you bought it from Eunice?"

"That's where Eunice the snake and I parted company. She represented she owned the building. All she owned was the business. Eunice the snake made $10,000 under the table on the building, and she didn't mind telling folks how she took the Atlanta boy for $10,000. What a bitch! Eunice slept with Dr. Gordy and conned him into giving her control of the property. After six months of owning Temperance Hall, I was renovating and fixing up. Dr. Gordy walked in one day to pay his rent. He looked pale and bad. He was bald and wore heavy glasses, demos, I am sure, and had the rottenness teeth I ever seen and reeked of tobacco smoke; but he had the kindest heart anyone would ever know. Treated many a patient at no cost at all. Really lived a poor life helping others.

"He dropped the check off without many words. I thought it was strange. We usually joked and laughed. I saw him walk out that door and down the sidewalk as I had seen him many times before.

"That night, I went to bed early. Bored, I had nothing else to occupy my mind. I awoke at 3:00 a.m. and lying in my bed, I peered out the window. Looking up in the sky, being in town you can't really see the stars for street lights. As I lay there on my pillow, I saw the clearest, brightest star I believe I have ever seen. I put my glasses on so I could see clearer. Surely, I thought, this time of year, January, the earth must be in line with some planet. I got up from my bed to look closer. It was fantastic.

"I thought of Peter, our baby, how he must be with Jesus looking down. Maybe that's him. I got back into bed and kept looking. The bright star moved past one window pane, past the other and then it was gone. This probably lasted 15 or 20 minutes.

"The next morning, when I was unlocking the door to the store, Millie Hawkins, Dr. Gordy's secretary said, 'Frank, did you hear? Dr.

Gordy died last night.' I was totally shocked. I told Millie, I had just seen him the other day when he left his rent check. Puzzled and amazed, I asked Millie about what time did Dr. Gordy die? 'They said it was around 3:00 a.m. or a little later.' A cold chill ran up and down my spine. The bright star I saw at 3:00 a.m., could it have been? Strange, uh?"

"Talking about a bright star Frank. Do you remember that good white woman that used to come in your store?"

"Why Aubrey, I thought all white folks were devils." Frank pokes Aubrey in the ribs and laughs.

"Yes, that was Millie Hawkins."

"Millie Hawkins, what a dear kind soul. The first time I met her was those few days when Eunice and I were working together. Millie, by some strange coincidence, reminded me of my mother. She was about Mom's height and had this hairsprayed-to-death hair. Fair complected, she had the sweetest eyes. Millie was always apologetic for interrupting my time. I loved to see her coming down the sidewalk. She was always bringing me a piece of pie or a homemade lunch. 'Like a little newspaper?' she would say. 'I probably shouldn't say this, but did you know...' and she would burst forth with some good local gossip. Good old Millie. She sent me so many letters and cards when the Doris deal came to pass.

"Millie was the one that introduced me to Eve. Eve was another Millie. Eve was in her late 70's, but folks in town said she could dance the legs off those old men at the V.F.W. Club. Eve was tall and so skinny, she looked like a bag of bones. Later, she told me she was diabetic, and that working for me was good for her blood sugar. Her son died around Christmas time, and she invited me for a Christmas dinner at her home. She said, 'Frank, I want you to cheer up all these sad folks with one of your stories.' Eve had this witch-like laugh and her face would brighten up, like she was under a spotlight. She had outlived three husbands and had served her time in Eatonton.

"She told me how Clay Langhorn, who was the magistrate then, had her arrested for shoplifting at Discount City. Eve told me the story many times.

'Frank, you wouldn't believe Langhorn sent the cops to Humphrey Aluminum where I was working the production line and arrested me. I told them there was another woman in town that had the same name I had. Shoot, you think they listened to me? I told them I was always getting this woman's mail and phone calls. Frank, if I had the money, I could have sued the city of Eatonton for everything they had. I got out of that mess. Cost me some money though.'

After the Doris Anthony ordeal Eve told me Sheriff LaSurre interrogated her on the street and said, 'I don't think it would be to your best health to run Frank's store.' Eve later apologized for not being able to keep the store open. She told me LaSurre asked if Doris came into the store regularly. Eve said, 'Yes, Frank's got a lot of women that like him.'

"People would come into the store and say they were drawn here. They don't know why but they felt as I did. I was supposed to be there. How different my life would have been if I had never come to Eatonton. Hell, I might be a lot richer that's for sure. Yes, Aubrey, maybe it's our karma we met.

"Do you really believe that nonsense?"

"I have all my life, but you know, lot's of people think you are nuts if you talk about it," said Frank.

"Do people in Eatonton believe in this karma thing?"

"Yes, a good number do. Some won't admit it because they are afraid. When I first came there, I met a couple that really believed in karma and destiny. Helen and Brian McCannon were their names. When I first bought the store from Eunice, Eunice kept telling me about Helen. Said she was a wonderful customer. Bought a lot of antiques because she was opening a bed and breakfast inn. Every day when I finished painting and working on the store, I would be black as a tar baby and too embarrassed to meet Helen because I was so filthy. One day when I was half-way clean, I drove up her driveway and knocked on her door. The house. We will pass it down this street here. Its about a mile on the left. The house was a Victorian masterpiece with towering brick chimneys. Huge gabled roofs with trim and fret work all over. It was painted white with Charleston green shutters. Before Helen and Brian bought it, two old maids owned it. They built it when their father told them to come home from Europe. Old money, but they say these old women were rich as Croesus and lived life as paupers. When Helen opened the front door of that house it was as if I had known her forever. See, she and her husband used to come to all the antique sales I had in

Atlanta. From the first time we said hello on that front porch, we were friends for life, I thought. Helen was tall and thin with a short blond haircut. A muscular face and determined eyes. She looked a lot younger than her age. Raised up north, I delighted her with my Southern accent. We soon became friends and I stopped by more frequently.

"Helen's husband, Brian, was a jolly sort of fellow. Medium height with a striking handlebar mustache. A fun man to be around. Brian had a dry sense of humor.

"It was becoming apparent after Lynn and I had separated, I was going to have to find a place to stay. Helen cut me a good deal at her B & B. It was a grand house. Tall ceilings and antique furniture. Not like a museum house but real homey. Helen had great decorating skills. She and Brian worked their hearts out painting and fixing up that old house. They always had some sort of project going on. With all the laughing and carrying on we all did, I would look in Helen's eyes and wondered if I could trust her. I needed so much to share my feelings about Lynn and the baby loss. Would Helen understand? One Friday evening, Brian was there. See, he got up every morning and drove to Atlanta, left about 5:00 a.m., hard worker. Helen gave orders one night to "her boys" to go to the store. On our trip, Brian wanted to show me some of the sights of Eatonton.

"The majestic old homes and who occupied them, and ghosts that wouldn't leave some of the old homes."

"Do you have any ghosts Aubrey? Those living in the attic or the basement that terrify you and give you the worse of nightmares?"

Aubrey looked into Frank's eyes and wanted so desperately to tell him what the LaSurre brothers did to him and his mother. Never trust a white man, even a man as good as Frank Moss, Aubrey's conscience kept telling him.

Frank could tell his friend wanted to say something. "You can trust me Aubrey, you can tell me of your ghosts when you are ready?"

"Well, Brian showed me the towering brick chimney of the Tannery, which Sherman burned during the Civil War. He got excited telling of how Sherman's troops surrounded the brick tower and threw ropes on it and blasted it, but to no avail. It wasn't coming down.

As we rode to another sight, I asked Brian, 'What brought you to Eatonton? Had it been a dream to always own a B & B?'

Brian said, 'No. It's an interesting story. Helen's only son died about a year ago and we both felt we had to get away from Atlanta. All those memories, the house — you know.' How well I knew. It seemed as if Brian was looking into my mirror. Only difference is that Helen and Brian were still married. Brian mentioned the stress of traffic and the sea of fake people in Atlanta. People who seemed not to care. 'When we left the driveway of the Jones' place and drove through the square of Eatonton, for the first time in both of our lives we felt this is where we both belonged. The bank lent us the money, everything fell into place,' said Brian. As I sat on that truck seat with Brian, I couldn't believe all I was hearing. When Brian and I got back from the store, Helen asked me if I was okay. I said, I guess, I am just tired. She read my face and Helen and I were to become the closest of friends.

"As I told you, Brian worked and stayed in Atlanta all week. When he was in Atlanta, he stayed with friends. I had Helen all to myself, of course with the exception of overnight guests. The hours Helen and I sat on that front porch, not solving the world's problems but our own. Helen rocked in the chair next to me on her front porch.

"I can see the pain in your face, Frank, tell me why did you and Lynn divorce?"

I looked up at the old beaded blue ceiling of the porch. I saw part ceiling part night sky. "We just grew apart, we had a baby to die, I just wanted to run and escape the pain, maybe that's why I am here."

Helens eyes teared and I could see the pain in her face. "I had only one son Frank. He contracted cancer when he was 24 and for two years he struggled to live. God, he went from a robust young man to a sheet of a paper. He was married and had a baby. " Helen reached over and squeezed my hand.

"I held him in my arms when he was born and when he died. Did you get a chance to hold your baby?"

"Yes, Lynn and I held him until be became cold. He had long legs and arms like mine."

"In the evenings when I came home from the store whether it is on the porch or the kitchen I would learn of Helen and Brian's life.

One night I was helping clean up the kitchen and Helen seemed real talkative. "You are going to make some woman a real fine husband again Frank. Its okay to be married again, Brian is my second husband. I guess I am the older woman."

"I stayed for about a month with Helen and Brian. I felt so strong staying with them. Helen was so particular about the house. Sometimes I felt like a cat creeping up the stairs to my room. Studying how she made the bed with all it's frou-frou pillow shams and covers. I made it up exactly every morning. Like a criminal, I covered all my tracks. I felt as if I was imposing. I don't know why. I was paying for the room. Night was hell, I was so tired from working at the store. I just couldn't go to sleep. I starred at the ceiling. Probably, I slept three or four hours a night. At sunrise, I was up again. God, I thought about everything, Lynn and the baby. Did I make the right decision? Over and over, I heard the voice of Helen telling her tragic story and over and over I heard Lynn's words and the little tiny crying of our baby Peter.

"Aubrey, I don't know how you fared after your divorce, but it was hell for me. I felt like I was plucked from one life and placed into another. Strange, all my friends, or 'quote' friends, when Lynn and I were married, none of them ever called to ask about me. What killed me was the friends who sat next to me in Sunday school and church just didn't seem to care. People whom I prayed with, not a one called me. Here it was eight months after Lynn and I separated before our old preacher called. Atlanta, land of a multitude of caring folks. What a joke. To this day, I have never seen any of those folks. Not a one has ever come to see my store or me. It just killed me to think about them."

"I was dying to talk to someone in person about all my problems. I had, of course, my best friend in Arizona, Peter, but I needed a female, a sympathetic person who had been through the same thing to talk to. Telling my story to Helen, it was as if she really cared. We both agreed we were supposed to be in Eatonton. Night after night of sharing, I went to bed really feeling I had a friend I could trust. Whatever turmoil in my life, I could go to Helen for advice, but above all she would listen.

"The days at the store brought more stories of different people stopping in. I would ask, 'Where are you from?' 'Oh, Atlanta, Ohio' or wherever. 'What brings you to this part of the state?' I heard so many times. 'Everything just worked out. House sold in Atlanta and we bought here. Guess it was meant to be.' I got so good, Aubrey, I could almost pick out those that were time travelers.

"What a movie this would make, Aubrey. Those days I would be working at my desk and look out onto the square. I'll swear sometimes it was as though I saw dirt roads and carriages going up and down the street. People that walked past my store window, they were right out of the 1870's or 1930's. It truly was like a time warp. Take a look when we roll into town. Maybe Eatonton is a land where you must find your path again, a direction center. Boy, I found Frank Moss here, let me tell you. What did I find out living here in Eatonton for one year. Well, if you are not born here or have some family name that goes back to General Putnam, you are nothing. Oh, yeh the people would be gracious and hospitable to your face, then soon as your back is turned their either slandering you or seeing how far they can plunge a knife in your back. I learned what small towns in the South are all about. A beautiful facade, but if you delve too far and ask what's behind the facade, death could be your answer. A person in this town that has a secret will go to any lengths to protect it, even kill...so much for my lifelong dream of living in a small Southern town. Aubrey, do you believe in God? You have to know," said Frank.

"I believe, Frank; you aren't going to start preaching, are you?"

"That's not my style, Aubrey," Frank said. "The reason I bring it up is I always thought Eatonton was a spiritual place. Helen really believed in it. Matter of fact, when she would introduce herself at meetings, she would say this is a spiritual place. It took lots of guts to say something like that. I never had those kinds of guts."

Frank and Aubrey entered Eatonton's town limits. "Look out the window, Aubrey. See that church steeple down there?" Aubrey squinted to look.

"Down there, Frank?"

"Yes, see that white steeple and cross on top. That's where I started going to church when I first came here. It was Eunice the snake's advice. She said, 'Frank, you work six days in this store. If you can't make it in six, no need to try for the seventh. The seventh day is the Lord's.' Good advice from a snake, uh, Aubrey?"

"I would like very much to see your church, Frank. If you have time, why don't we pull over and walk down there?"

Frank looked at Aubrey. "You want to walk down there now?"

"Yes, if you feel like it."

"Come on, let's go."

Frank pulled the truck over to the side and they walked down the street. Leaves danced at their feet and the sun was still hidden. All was quiet that December day. No cars, no people, like a ghost town. Pointing to trash cans and flower pots, Frank said, "Look, they're still there." Frank pointed out, "That's so and so's store," never criticizing the individual, rather, "I don't see why he doesn't paint that door." Rounding the corner, they came to Frank's church. A tall clapboard church with a bronze plaque stating this building was built in 1859. Fantastic stain glass windows towered to the sky. Huge Corinthian columns soared skyward.

Frank and Aubrey opened the double doors and entered the narthex, then the sanctuary. The doors closed with an echoing sound. The sanctuary had a ceiling which must have been 100 feet high. A round stained glass of Jesus commanded the pulpit. The glass was probably 25 ft x 25 ft. In the center of the glass was a picture of Jesus sitting on a throne with a crown of thorns on his head. His arms were outstretched and beckoning all to come forward. The colors were so vibrant, even though the sky was grey. Blue, red, yellow, purple, all the colors of the rainbow.

Frank grasped one of the pews and slowly sat down. Aubrey followed. "Aubrey, I have prayed many prayers here in this church. On my knees, and sitting here in this pew. Some prayers were answered, others were not. When I first came here, we had a great preacher, Rev. James Weldon. James was a big man. He made about three of me. He was balding and had a beard. His eyes, Aubrey, were deep blue, kind eyes. I think James, in another life, must have been an apostle. His voice was deep and, boy, could he sing. All those Atlanta churches I went to, none of those preachers sang, hired a music director. I still can hear James singing How Firm a Foundation. That was Robert E. Lee's favorite church hymn and James' also. Don't discount his sermons. They were fantastic. You knew he was talking to you when he spoke. James wasn't fake like a lot of people in Eatonton. He was real.

"He was not only my preacher, but my friend. He helped me so much, especially with women problems.

"James sure did know a lot about women. He and I were so much alike. God, Aubrey, he was a great preacher. I thought so much of him and still do. I put him in my will to preach my funeral. Hope he lives that long. No other preacher knows me like James."

"What kind of preacher was he?"

"Oh, the best, not one of those bible thumping, Oh, God will take care of you or God wouldn't like that. Hell, he wasn't afraid to say shit or damn or S.O.B. He was a neat man. Oh and yes, he was a time traveler too. Brought to Eatonton for a purpose. James told me one time he got so disgusted with the church that he left the ministry to work in a warehouse. James talked to God the way I talk to God. Tell it like it is. Of course, with reverence." Frank sat silent for a long time and stared out in space. Then he said, "I miss James. I miss him so much."

"Do you ever see him, now?" asked Aubrey.

"At least once a year. We're still great friends. I miss a lot of people, Aubrey." Frank looked toward the round stained glass of Jesus on his throne. He put his hand on the pew in front of him and pulled himself up. "Let's go. Aubrey, before someone see us."

Walking down the same sidewalk as before, they both saw Temperance Hall. Aubrey looked like he saw a ghost. Temperance Hall commanded the corner with its painted brick facade. It was Greek Revival in design. Six huge windows hung above the glassed-in store front. Everything was balanced, symmetrical. The pillars on either side of the structure were painted a light grey and the body of the building was painted a deep red. Charleston green paint trimmed the window casings. A large detail molding made of brick wrapped the building like a ribbon.

"I sold all of the lace curtains to Alice down the street so the place would look vacant. So they'd remember what they did to me," Frank said. "See the front store window" Frank points, "that's where my Christmas tree stood for months till that bastard from the bank, Smith, took it down. Look now, it has a For Rent sign in the window." Clasping his hands to the sides of his face Frank looks in the window of his old store. "I called it UNCLE REMUS ATTIC. I bought the name from Eunice the snake when I bought the business from her."

Aubrey stood on the sidewalk looking around to see if anyone would see them. He refused to look inside the window.

"Well, my old mural of B'rer Rabbit tricken B'rer Fox is still on the wall. See B'rer Bear and B'rer Fox caught B'rer rabbit sleeping under a big oak tree and they captured him and tied him up on a stick. The next picture is B'rer Fox and B'rer Bear going to bar-b-que old B'rer Rabbit. B'rer Rabbit tricks both of them telling them if they let him go just for a little while he would show them where the laughing tree is. The next picture is B'rer Fox and B'rer Bear looking down a hollow in the oak tree and bees are stinging them. Kind of like Eatonton isn't it Aubrey? Not much to see of what my old store used to look like. Remember when we moved that big English shipment in Aubrey? Remember Doris Anthony...I put everything I had into that building just like my first house and those bank bastards took it all. That's why I hate banks and bankers."

It commanded the square. "A most impressive building. It had permanence."

Aubrey stared at Temperance Hall with hatred. He could hear his mother screaming, 'No, No! Don't rape me...don't hurt my boy...please...Ever seen a white man castrate a hog boy?' The echoes of J.C. and Billy LaSurre filled the air and covered the plate glass windows of TEMPERANCE HALL like a film. "G. Damn this place!, " Aubrey said outloud.

Frank was silent as though he was in deep thought. He looked at the ground and the leaves. "I never liked the winter, Aubrey."

"Why, Frank?"

"It always seemed the end of everything. It makes me melancholy. I sure loved the antique business. I miss this old store. It was a challenge to hunt and find some rare object and buy it for little or nothing, then sell it for a profit. Those days of finding for little or nothing are about gone." Frank laughed. "Let's get in the truck and ride some more. Aubrey, do you like antiques?"

"Sure do Frank. My ex-wife Frances and I used to get up every Saturday morning when we were married and hit all the local sales."

"Find any good deals?" asked Frank.

Aubrey's face lighted up and he said, "One time, we found this 1840's table for $100. What a deal," said Aubrey. Before Frank could speak, Aubrey waved his arms in excitement as he told how they had a hard time getting it in their small car.

"What did the table look like?" asked Frank.

"Probably mahogany with a really intense grain pattern and folding top," described Aubrey.

Frank laughed with his hearty brand of laughter. "Really, do you like that Empire period of furniture?"

"Sure do, have all my life. I always felt comfortable with that period," Aubrey says. He turned to Frank with a confused look on his face. "Now, Frank, you say the table is Empire?"

"Yes, it was made before the War of Northern Aggression."

"The what?" asked Aubrey.

Frank looked seriously into Aubrey's eyes, not grinning as he had been doing. "Somehow I always thought I lived in that time and someone upstairs lost my file and put me in this century. Aubrey, do you know much about white Southerners?"

Aubrey stumbled around because in his mind all Southerners had just fallen off the turnip truck or were racists like J.C. LaSurre. Trying to avoid the issue, Aubrey looked down. "Uh, Uh, No, I don't know much about 'The White Southerners.' Just the poor exploited Black Southerner. I just never divided America in two halves, North and South."

"You don't think much of the South do you?" asked Frank.

Aubrey could feel a confrontation coming. " I will be honest with you, Frank. I didn't want to come on this trip. Matter of fact, I told my girlfriend last night, I dreaded this trip because I had to deal with all these rednecks here, all the bad memories, the way they talked." Frank listened intently. Aubrey defended his ground. "Frank, I have never met a Southern gentlemen like you. All I have ever encountered are racists and uneducated people."

"Yes, you are right, Aubrey. There are two worlds here, especially in Georgia. A racist factor that would hate some color of frog that crossed the road because they are not all green, but, Aubrey, there is another old South like me and I appreciate your compliment calling me a Southern gentlemen. I try to be."

"Hell no, Aubrey. In Eatonton truth reigns. Don't try to cover up the way you feel. That's what's wrong with society today. People don't say what they feel. Always afraid they are going to hurt someone's feelings. Hell, tell it like it is. I just told you there are some quality

Southerners. Aubrey, there are only a handful of people like me left in the South. We are a dying breed. With the advent of mass communication, T.V., computers. Most of my friends with children, you would never know they were ever raised in the South. Leacy's kids you wouldn't know they are from the South. The Southern accent is gone; I am not talking about the uneducated accent you have been exposed to. I mean the refined accent. It's gone. You would think my friends' children grew up in the North.

"A true Southerner is a person you never can force any ideas on. We are stubborn to the core of our soul. When integration came to the South, forced on us by the Federal Government, it could have been so much easier on the blacks and whites if the Federal Government had just known the southern race of people. Don't try to force anything on us. You think Southern men are stubborn. The women are the worst. A southern man loves his woman. He brings her flowers and puts her on a pedestal.

"I guess what hurts me the most about the loss of the race, Southerner, is a southern compassion for other people. Not to brag, but I would do anything for anybody if I could. A lot of times, I have gotten into trouble with folks in this town for trying to be nice. See what I am saying, Aubrey? The qualities of a true Southerner are about gone. It makes me sad. You ask why so many of us talk about the Civil War? Because it was our race's last remembrance of an ordered society, of how we believed in a cause and were willing to fight to the death for our way of life and our society. The Civil War was a battle, not to lose our slaves, but a people. Never was a black-white issue."

Aubrey looked at Frank. "I-I never looked at the Civil War in those terms. I always thought history was a boring subject. Having to remember all those facts and battles, boring, boring."

"It was my favorite subject because I was there. You see, Aubrey, history is imagination. Being on that battlefield with those troops. Standing next to Robert E. Lee, what kind of man he was , and how about Sherman, who was he? All imagination, Aubrey. History is being there."

"You should have been a history teacher."

"So many people said I should have been. Always thought I would go nuts in the same classroom for eight hours. See, I like to be a free bird, to come and go as I please. Good thing I went into business for myself."

"Did I ever tell you about my Great grandfather J.A. Knight? His daddy owned a big plantation in North Carolina. J.A. hated his step-mother so when the Civil War came he was eager to join the Confederate forces. J.A. had grown up with a slave boy named Sammy." Aubrey rolled his eyes.

"What are you going to say I remind you of Sammy?"

"Hell no Aubrey, quit bashing the white folks and hear the story. 'J.A.'s daddy said the only way you can go to war is to take Sammy with you. The both of you know how to live on the land and take care of each other. So, J.A. and Sammy go off to war. The story goes J.A. and Sammy were camped out somewhere in North Carolina and Sammy couldn't sleep. Sammy walked over to the next ridge that's where he saw the Yankee camp. Sammy snuck up by one of the officer's tents and heard plans of an attack on the Confederates the next day. Sammy went running back to tell J.A. what he heard. J.A. didn't at first believe Sammy, finally convinced J.A. went and told his commanding officer what Sammy had told him. The Confederates were ready the next day for the attack, thanks to Sammy."

Aubrey cleared his throat. "I bet your white grandpa got all of the credit."

"I don't think life is who gets the credit."

"Aubrey, life has just a few moments of true happiness and just a few moments of unhappiness. Everything else is in between.

"Moments are all that we have, Aubrey. Then you are gone.

"I will tell you the secret of life this afternoon, Aubrey. If you do not make time to take in everything, you will never have a fine relationship with a woman. Because you only have a few moments of happiness with her, then it's gone. Your business is the same thing. Only a very few great victories, then it's just a memory. My old Sunday School teacher, Mr. Donny, God, he was 92 years old when I first came to Eatonton, and he taught Sunday School. One of his favorite sayings was, 'To have a great victory, you must have a great fight.' True, isn't it, Aubrey? Life is such a battle, then if you have just a few victories along the way, it makes life that much more bearable. I don't know your background, Aubrey, but I never really had to worry about money.

My family was never rich, but we were never poor. My battle with life never was with money, although many times I thought that to be the case. No, my battle was in my head. Understanding what really matters in this world. Those few precious moments of happiness. You never know, Aubrey, when they are going to come, never can plan for those moments. Just as you can't plan for the bad moments."

"Talking with you, I think, has been a good moment for me, Frank."

"Frank, do you have any brothers or sisters?"

"Sure do, I have two brothers . Mike is my middle brother, I am the oldest, and Kevin is the youngest. Mike is a commercial photographer. He loved to take pictures. Hell, every picture I ever took, the store would put a red sticker on the photos of how to improve my photos. I told Mike one time I was bad for his reputation. Mike always seemed to have his act together. Still married to the same woman. They have two girls. I love both of those girls. They love to come see Uncle Fry. That's what they call me. They never could or wanted to say Frank. It's the stubborn streak in them, runs in the family, you know. Mike is a perfect father, good provider, great husband. I always thought the oldest child in a family was supposed to be all those things. I envy Mike sometimes, seems like he has had such a happy life."

"You say you have another brother, Frank?"

"Yes, Kevin is my youngest brother. His first marriage he was young, early twenties. They were married less than a year and his wife came in one day and said, 'I don't love you, here's the bills I owe, here's what you owe, I want a divorce.' The next thing Kevin knew, he came home from work one day, and she had a moving van out in front of the house and loaded up all the furniture and even took the toilet paper and paper towels off the rolls. Can you believe that?"

"Pretty incredible," said Aubrey.

"Kevin always fooled with computers. That machine drove me nuts and Kevin did, too. I love Kevin, but, boy, I can be in the room with him ten minutes and I am nuts. What's so funny is Kevin and I are so much alike. He got his divorce the same day I did. He got married for the second time. I think he's happy. Kevin and all of his women. I guess that's why Kevin went into computers, to keep all his girlfriends' names and addresses straight." laughed Frank.

**ii**

Aubrey looked out the window of the truck and saw a big peach on a mailbox. Frank turned and looked at that big peach. "Oh, that's where April Preston used to live. Not long after I bought the Antique store, I met her. She was small in frame and stature. Looked just like a Barbie doll, Aubrey. Long blond hair that glistened when the sun shone on her long strands. April had that California look about her. Still looked like she was 15 years old and in high school. Oh, but, Aubrey, those blue eyes. Eyes that seemed to sparkle like a blue kaleidoscope. I'll tell you, I was in love with her looks at first sight. April looked like what an angel must be.

"She came into the store a couple of times and I was hoping she wasn't married. I found out she married into one of the richest families in Eatonton. April and her husband Dan were building a new home down the street. April was a flight attendant and traveled a good bit, so her visits to the store were quite infrequent. I looked forward to the day when she did grace my presence. Such a pleasant voice, such warmth. We laughed and joked around, just loved it. Never once had she mentioned opening a store in Eatonton. Then, to my surprise, late one September night around 9:00 p.m., I saw her car, a convertible. So I went to investigate.

"April was up on a ladder painting cornice near the ceiling. She looked funny, a dusk mask covering her face and eye goggles over her eyes. I laughed and said, 'Why, April, have you taken up another profession—late night painter?' We both laughed.

April said, 'I have always wanted to open a gift shop all my own. Let me tell you, Frank Moss, of all the support I have gotten from the Queen Mother, you know, Dan's mother, Ms. Cadillac. They all are against me, claim this is below the family's standard. If I need money, Dan could ask for more draw on the trust fund. Can you believe that, the sorry S.O.B.'s.'

"I made a couple of jokes to snap April back to a positive mode. Carefully plotting my words, not to offend anyone, I said, 'They don't like the store because it wasn't their idea first.' We both laughed. I said, 'April, get down off that ladder and let me finish that up.' Finally, she gave in when I started painting and shaking the ladder out of fun.

'Frank, you have got to be tired.'

'Hell, I am not tired. All I have done all day is run my mouth trying to sell antiques.'

"'April,' I said, 'Why didn't you come to me with this store idea? How long have you been working on this place?'

'Oh, Frank, she said, 'for about a week now. I have been here every night till 2:00 a.m.'

'My God, April. Why didn't you come recruit me?'

'Oh, Frank, I didn't want to bother you. You are trying to renovate your building.'

I said, 'April, if a friend is in need, my business can wait.'

'Oh, Frank, you are too kind.' 'No, April, I am glad to help.'

"Later that night April tells me, 'Eunice wants to be a partner.' April said, 'Everyone is telling me don't get involved with Eunice, she is a crook.' I wanted to confirm those statements, but I kept my mouth shut. For more than a week, I would go down to April's store and help paint or haul off trash, anything I could do to help. Plus I loved being with a female my own age. Sure I had Helen at the Bed and Breakfast to talk to, but I needed someone else.

"What a great time April and I had. I have got a photo of us somewhere at the house. What a great time in my life. One of those moments, Aubrey. A moment to remember. April was due to open the next week. Frantically moving merchandise in, also display shelves. It was coming together with no help from Dan's royal family. April did all of it herself with my little help. I encouraged her everyday. 'You can do it.' Just a positive outlook. Who cares what other people say. This is a model that you can build other stores on. Maybe that's all I am good for is to encourage others.' As Frank leans back into the seat, 'Things were going all right for April, but she was always arguing with the landlord over fix this, fix that and now. Well, in small town, U.S.A., you don't get anything done that way. See, April was not from Eatonton. She was originally from the Midwest, Kansas. Dan's people, they were the land barons in this region for generations.

"One rainy Saturday, I was in the store and we were packed with customers. I looked out the window while ringing up a sale and saw April across the street in front of her store. She was on the sidewalk waving her arms at Mr. Thompson, the landlord. Things didn't look like she was telling a big joke. Soon after the arm waving, Thompson ran over and got into his car and April chased after him. The next thing I saw was April banging on top of Mr. Thompson's car. Mr. Thompson drove off with April standing on the sidewalk. After a couple of minutes, she walked rapidly toward my store. I busied myself as if I didn't know anything had just happened. April walked in the door and tears were streaming down her face.

Sobbing uncontrollably, she said, 'It's all over. He gave me back my rent check.'

April approached me and I hugged her and said, 'I am sorry. I am so sorry.' Her tears touched my cheeks. I hugged her what seemed like hours. Customers milling about the store were forgotten. I felt so bad for her.

"I said, 'April, here sit down. Let me get you a washcloth and some water.'

"She said, 'Frank, you are the only one that has stood by me. The only one that cared.'

"Those words made my day, Aubrey. It was so refreshing to know I was worthwhile. Bringing back the washcloth and water, I said, 'Tell me what happened.'

April said, 'All I told that S.O.B. was I wanted a written lease. What's so wrong with that, Frank?' More tears came rolling down her face.

'It's all right.' April blotted the new tears with my handkerchief.

'Then he handed me back my rent check and told me to get out. Frank, what am I going to do? All the money I have is tied up in merchandise. We are supposed to open in a week. What am I going to do, Frank? It's just like Dan's family said. This business is a money loser. Just a waste of money and time.'

"'Now stop that kind of talk right now, April. You can do it. We just have to come up with another plan. Do you want me to talk to Mr. Thompson? That's what I am good at, negotiating deals.'

'No, Frank, you have done too much already.'

'It's your business, April. You call the shots. If that doesn't work, how about Mr. Parks' building across from mine? Might be a better location. We could send customers back and forth from our stores. More money for both of us. Mr. Parks is a nice old man. I'm sure he would work with you.'

'Oh, Frank, you are my best friend.' April hugged my neck. It made me feel so loved. She stayed for hours that day and when she left, she was ready to face another day.

"That night when I was lying in my bed looking out at the moonlit sky, I thought about the day and April. She had tried so hard at that business. I hope I had given her faith and encouragement. About 10:00 p.m. that evening, the phone rang and it was April. I could tell by her voice she was crying.

'Frank Moss,' she said, 'Dan just cussed me out and told me I was stupid as Hell for ever trying to open up a business like mine in Eatonton.' Sobs start again and April tells me, 'Dan said I disgraced his family. The God damn Royal Family. What am I going to do Frank?', April asked.

I responded, 'April, you have to believe in yourself. When you are down you have to pull yourself up by the bootstrap. Try again! Believe me, you must try again. The idea of the Victorian Peach will work. You just have to believe.'

'Oh, Frank, you always know what to say,' replied April.

'April, what are you going to do about Thompson and the store?', I asked.

'Frank, I have been thinking about what you said. I could rent Mr. Parks' store across from yours. It would be great and that Thompson can take that piece of shit of a building that he's got and if he doesn't want to fix the bathroom, maybe he can rent the store and customers can piss right on the floor.' We both laughed and laughed.

"I tell you, Aubrey, April could cuss more than anyone I ever met, male or female. How such a little woman could come up with the analogies and cuss words. It was damn funny to me, still is. We both hung up the phone laughing.

"The next day, April negotiated a deal with Mr. Parks. Now mind you, by herself, we started moving her store across the street. The Victorian Peach has survived one blow, now on to victory. I again poured my time into the store, painting and fixing and most of all, encouraging, 'You can make it.' Her store had this big window that faced my building. Oh, maybe you could see from here. Anyway, April would beat me to work every morning. Sitting at my desk, I loved to look at her hair glistening in the sun. Her desk was catercornered to the window, so her back was always next to the window. I could see her laugh when passersby would stop in for the latest opening update. I was so proud of April. She had really built the business on her own with a little help from me. Somehow, I felt it was my business, also. I was proud of the Victorian Peach.

"Opening day was coming and April had planned a Grand Opening, the night of my auction."

"I thought an Auction would be fun, stir up some activity, and get rid of some of Eunice's inventory. Let me tell you, Aubrey. What an auction! We had a band that night and Helen and Brian catered the food. A sandwich six feet long. Wow!" exclaimed Frank. "Before the auction preview night, I called Pat's, a florist down the street. He was the best and most expensive in town. I told Pat I wanted the most elaborate flower arrangement he had sent to April's store and say on the card, 'You made it. Much success in your business, signed Frank.' Aubrey, that arrangement was so damn big. I could see it from across the street. April deserved every stem. Before opening day, Dan and the Royal Family graced the doorstep and gave April their blessing. Of course, not to have a junk dealer outdo them, they sent flowers, too. Not as good as the ones I sent, though. Hell, they were too cheap."

"Tell me about April's in-laws," said Aubrey.

"Dan, her husband, looked like a punk. A kid like April. He had thick brown hair with sideburns cut up to his ears, short and trim. The thing I remember most about Dan was he strutted his ass like a peacock. Really, Aubrey, he looked just like a peacock. Dan had this nasal Yankee type voice, so negative. I'll swear you would think he was in his 80's. According to Dan, 'Everything was going to hell. Eatonton was such an armpit of a place to live.' He would go on forever. I tell you, I never could stand the man. He reminded me too much of my ex-father-in-law. You remember me telling you about Mr. Perfect, Lynn's father."

"Yes, Frank. I think you and Mr. Critical did a lot of fishing together," said Aubrey.

"Yeah," Frank laughed. "The bottom line on Dan, he was a spoiled asshole. He probably got his attitude from his mother. She drove around in a big cadillac. Got a new one every year. Always bought a white one. Dan's mother looked like a corn cob got stuck up her ass."

Aubrey said sarcastically, “Frank, I can tell you really were fond of these people. Do they still live around here?”

“Oh, I am sure they do. Money. It’s funny how many people worship it and become it. It’s their personality and when the money’s gone, the person of money has no existence. That’s all they lived for, just a facade with no dept. Let me tell you more about auction night. The band arrived at my place. Hell, Eatonton hadn’t seen this much action since the troops came home from the war. The band was great. After a few hours, I saw the lights at the Victorian Peach turn off and April came over to listen to the band. I remember it as if it were yesterday; April standing in the doorway of my store. That night was magical. April standing there, those tight blue jeans. Wow, if she just wasn’t married.

“After a few minutes of mingling, April approached me and hugged me and said, ‘Frank Moss, those are the most beautiful flowers in the world. You shouldn’t have. I thought you got flowers like that when you had a baby, or hell, died. Frank, I took a picture of them. They are so damned beautiful.’ She whispered in my ear, ‘Thanks for everything.’ I was on top of the world that night and my problems seemed to go away.

“As I looked at April Preston’s face that night I wished a genie would grant me just one wish that I could have a April Preston in my life. Oh, if she just wasn’t married to that damn peacock. I could of made love to her standing in that doorway. I wanted her so much that night. I wanted her to leave her husband and the both of us make lots of children.

“The auction the next day was a success and during a break, across the way I could see April laughing and customers carrying off packages. The Victorian Peach was alive and prospering. Two of my friends from Atlanta came up, Casey and Lynnette. They were to faux paint my metal columns in front of the store. In exchange, I was to put them up at Helen’s B & B. Lynnette told me later that night she and Casey snuck off like two teenagers and went to the Wild West. Lynnette said J.C. and his hunting buddies were there.

“J.C. hugged Lynnette around the waist and fondled her breasts. Lynnette pushed J.C. away. “You getting a little too personal.”

‘Where you ladies from?’ asked J.C.

'We are from Atlanta. We are here to paint Frank's store.'

With his face getting closer to Lynnette, J.C. said, 'Frank's a fine boy.' His breath reeked of liquor. 'I am the richest man in the county,' he said. 'Why don't you ladies come stay with us?'

"We better get back," said Lynnette. J.C. then lunged at Casey. Grasping Casey around the waist he felt her breasts.

Casey slapped J.C., "Mean hellcat."

"We better go," and both of my friends left.

"That evening, Lynnette and Casey met John Pinkston, the former theater owner. I met John when I first came to Eatonton, one of my first real friends. John was probably in his '60s. He had married a local woman who had inherited some of the Johnston fortune. John reminded me of an absent-minded professor. He was color blind, and I tell you he could come up with some of the damnedest outfits you ever saw. Usually, he would have a pocket watch chain sagging in his front pocket. The chain had a watch fob with the faces of theater. John probably shaved every other day, and had a mildewed smell to his breath. His voice was that of an old Southern gentleman.

"I really liked John despite his eccentricities. We would philosophize on all subjects from love to politics. He could talk the horns off a billy goat."

"More than you, Frank?" asked Aubrey.

"Sure enough, Aubrey. John's the one that got me in the Kiwanis Club, where I met Doris Anthony. Anyway, Lynnette told me John gave her and Casey a tour of the Eatonton cemetery. 'Lynnette, a man in this county can kill his wife and get away with it, but you mess with his cows and you have bought the farm.'

"About a week passed, and one night I was working late at my desk down in the store and the phone rang. It was April. I said, 'April, what's wrong?'

She said, "That God damn Eunice set up a table full of junk outside the Victorian Peach while I was gone on a trip. I let the God damn bitch run the store while I was gone and there is money missing." April's sobbing got worse.

"It's all right April. Calm down."

"I should have listened to everyone in town, about how crooked Eunice was," cried April.

"I learned when I first came to Eatonton, don't talk about anyone. It always comes back on you. A small town is a beautiful rose but the stems have lots of thorns.' I told April that night, 'You have to tell Eunice that you are the boss. You are the one paying the rent." April agreed, 'And once again, Frank Moss' in her words 'saved the day.'

"A couple more weeks passed by. Fall was approaching. One day I went across the street to see how April was doing and she said, 'Frank, I am going to Atlanta to the Mart. Do you want to go?'

I said, 'Sure.'

We got into April's convertible and off we went to Atlanta. The air was cool and crisp that morning when we departed Eatonton. At a stop at the family oil distributorship, April popped out of the car to assist the attendants and joke with them. April had a great personality. I heard her while I was sitting in the car. 'Frank's going to show me what to buy in Atlanta for my store.' It was a good line so the help wouldn't go and think April found another man, and she was going to Atlanta to find a hotel room. Small town gossip, you know.

As we headed out of town, April pointed very proudly, 'That's Dan's uncle's house, that's where his aunt lives, that's where Dan's grandfather died last year.' She rambled on and on about how the Prestons made their money and how eccentric they all were.

"How did you and Dan meet, April?" I asked.

'We were on a flight from Atlanta to Houston. He was one of the youngest pilots that the airline had. The first time I met Dan, I thought he was a pompous asshole.' I wanted to agree, but I kept my mouth shut. 'We dated a couple of times. He really treated me like shit. We got married and moved to Eatonton, his family's turf. Frank, how about you? What brought you to Eatonton? I have to know what brings a good-looking man like you from a big city like Atlanta to Small Town, U.S.A.'

"'Well,' I said, 'when Lynn, my wife, I should say my ex-wife...'

April interjected, 'But I thought the newspaper article said you and your wife had bought Temperance Hall and were going to renovate it and make your house upstairs.'

'Well, April, a lot of that was marketing. Lynn loved Atlanta and I loved Small Town, U.S.A. We had a baby die, which caused a great gulf between us.' April wanted all the details. Women love details of relationships. It seemed, riding in that car that October morning, my soul was free of some of its pain. I felt some of my energy connecting with April. I trusted her. I spilled all my guts to her.

April said, 'Frank Moss, not a soul knows what I am about to tell you. Marriage is hard, it's damned hard. When Dan and I first married, Dan would beat me. I would go to work black and blue. Other pilots would say, What happened, and I would come up and say, Oh, I fell or some damn stupid thing. Dan's temper was incredible. He put his fist through the wall in our first apartment, and we had Christmas guests coming in an hour. Cover-up, Cover-up. I got so sick and tired of it, Frank.'

"'Why didn't you leave, April?' I asked. 'I was afraid. Dan's family is so rich and powerful. They would stop at nothing to see Dan come out on top. They would destroy me.'

'April, I can't believe.'

'Believe, Frank' said April.

'Does this wife beating still go on?' I asked.

'Dan agreed to go to a therapist with me. Things have been better this year.'

'Are you still afraid of him?' I asked.

April said, 'Only when Dan is under a lot of stress. I know when to go.'

'You know you always can stay at my place, April, if you need to.'

'Thanks, Frank Moss. You are my friend.'

"It seemed in no time, we reached Atlanta. April and I were affectionate people, always hugging each other and laughing. I remember walking up the sidewalk that day with April laughing, wondering when the laughter would end. 'Capture the moment,' I said to myself, and I guess I did like a photo on my mind cause I still remember and can tell the story. That day at the Mart was so much fun. Taking the elevator from floor to floor, buying merchandise for the Victorian Peach. April constantly asking, 'Frank, would this be a good seller?' Always reaffirming the Victorian Peach is a store that could be duplicated.

"Had a great lunch that day. April and I laughed about the different characters in Eatonton. Funny how we made fun of Eunice, the snake, slithering through town in search of gossip. We shared stories with each other, of different customers that came into the store. Oh, Aubrey,

I remember to this day April's face and voice.

"Like all wonderful days, it must end. We headed back to Eatonton. We both were tired, but continued on talking. April taught me a valuable lesson in that car, that day. Always lay your cards on the table with a relationship, always come clean. I never could do that with Lynn until April taught me that lesson. I think I taught her that day never to cover up.

"On the way home I hugged April with my head on her arm and I said, 'I am so glad you came into my life.'

"As the weeks went by, everyday I would walk across the street and see if April needed lunch or whatever, and got the latest sales scoop. Sometimes I had to motivate her because Dan was negative about her business. Somedays I could see heavy makeup around her cheeks, and I wondered if Dan had started the beating again.

"As Thanksgiving approached, April and I went to a wholesale place to buy Christmas decorations for our stores. Like the time at the Mart, we talked all the way there and laughed. At the store, we had a great time.

"On the way back to Eatonton, April was upset about her mother and father coming for Thanksgiving dinner. 'God damn,' April said. 'We got to stop by the grocery store so those folks can eat that damn turkey.' April told me of how she always felt her father, who was a tile contractor, never could express his love.

I said, 'April, some people just can't express love. When your father came into my store the other day, he was telling me about the time you and your mother had done a tile job, better than he could. He loves you, April. He just couldn't express it. It doesn't mean he hates you. Your daddy told about the time the duck chased you in the yard and you thought the duck was going to eat you up.' We both laughed.

'Yeah, I remember that!' said April.

"When we got to the grocery store, we got a buggy and hit the isles. I felt like I was ten years old again. I hadn't had that much fun since my brother Mike and I threw meat stickers on people's butts, the stickers saying boneless, fat free."

Composing himself, Frank cleared his throat and said, "Yeah, what fun. That night I told April in the car, I hope I could find a companion like her. I loved her as a friend. April seemed shocked at the statement.

She immediately said that she loved Dan. I meekly said, 'Now you have two men that love you.' What a mistake to say those words. What a mistake.

"Aubrey, most folks don't understand what love is. Hell, I love a lot of people. I never wanted to entice April to get in bed with me. I just needed a friend, someone to talk to besides Helen at the bed and breakfast. God, Helen heard enough of my problems. She needed a break.

"After that conversation, April and I were quiet on the way home. The next day, I continued my usual routine of walking across the street and asking April if she wanted a lunch plate. She treated me coldly that day. I felt something was wrong. I could call tonight. I could see April from my window. Something was wrong. Later that afternoon, April appeared in my doorway with a sign that said peaches, and a peach crate. I had bought both items for April to sell at her store, but I told her if she didn't think these items appropriate bring them back.

"I spoke up and said, 'You didn't like these things, April?' Very coldly, she put them on the floor and said 'No.' The way she did this reminded me of the time a girl in high school broke up with her boyfriend and handed him a cigar box with all the letters and gifts he had ever given her. I though how cruel. The ultimate insult. I felt that same way when April laid those items on the floor and walked off. Tonight I will call. What's wrong, I wondered all afternoon. It was hard to eat supper that night thinking about what to say when I called.

"I planned to call April around 9:00 p.m. The phone rang and I knew it was April before I answered the phone. I remember that conversation like it was yesterday.

'Frank, I wanted to call you.'

'Well, April, I was going to call you. Why did you bring the peach sign back? Did you not like it?' I said, 'you could have sold it, you know.'

'Frank, I don't want to see you anymore.'

I blurted out, 'Why, what's wrong?'

'I feel uncomfortable around you. Dan is my husband, even though we have had our share of problems. I still love him, and when he is 30,000 feet in the air, I don't want him to worry about me.

'People are talking, Frank. When Dan's gone on a flight, they think we are in bed together.'

'What!' I said.

'I am just telling you, Frank, what's going on. The other day when we were in the car, you told me, at least there are now two men in this town that love you.'

'But April, I meant I love you as a friend. I needed you. I trusted you with my feelings.'

'I know, Frank. But I have too much invested in five years of marriage to jeopardize that. A man like Dan comes along once in a lifetime. I can't loose him. His family is rich and powerful. Frank, this situation is not good for you or your business. I am asking you not to come to the store anymore.'

'All I did was ask if I could get you some lunch. I knew you were by yourself, and, like myself, couldn't run out to eat. April, I don't understand.'

'I am sorry, Frank' and she hung up the phone before I finished talking.

"I stood there holding the phone, pounding the receiver up to my chest. What in the hell have I done? What have I done? I mumbled to myself. Sure, a guy like Dan only comes around once in a lifetime. Sure does, you can only find a wife beater and all around S.O.B. through a lot of searching. I went to bed that night, Aubrey, and I cried. I had trusted that woman with my feelings, my inside thoughts.

"As I lay there and stared up at the ceiling, I thought of how April and I worked on the Victorian Peach, how we laughed getting on and off the elevator at the Mart in Atlanta. All those good times. Then I thought of the stories she trusted to me about how Dan would beat her and how her father didn't love her. The phone conversations when she would call me crying, help me Frank, what am I going to do, Frank? Frank, you are my only friend. All that danced through my head. I wondered if April ended our friendship in fear she might fall in love with me or vice-versa. Who knows.

"Some of April's personality scared me, and it wasn't until later I found out how she protected her friends. There are some things April told me that I still recall. One day we were talking and she told me what she would do if she caught Dan messing around on her. 'If I found out who it was, I would take a razor and carve her face up. No one would look at her again.' April's face contorted as she told this macabre scenario. It really upset me, Aubrey.

"I continued to think, about my childhood. I remember my grandfather telling me, 'Frank, never trust a woman.' I don't believe I slept a wink that night. Before I knew it, the sun rose and birds were dancing around the courthouse dome.

"The next day was hard for me, Aubrey. I thought all day how I came to Eatonton to find peace and contentment. I hurt. I hurt bad. I felt the happiness and joy had been taken once again from my life. Adversity had added another gift on the platter.

"When Christmas rolled in that year, I looked through the large green bow wreaths April had made for me."

"Frank, you are a lot of fun at Christmas. I bet everyone would want you at their Christmas party," said Aubrey.

"That's true; Frank Moss, land of laughs. When I was a boy, I loved Christmas. So exciting, I remember being in the room with my brother, Mike. Those old blue candleholders in the window, always smelled like melting plastic. We would talk for hours. 'Do you think Santa Clause might bring us...'

"Of course, I told you about our baby, Peter, dying on December 13th. There have been lots of blows to me at or near Christmas. Don't get me wrong, Aubrey. I love Christmas for the celebration of the birth of Jesus. I do believe in God. It's the only hope I have of seeing all those I love and miss, one day. Christmas,... oh, Christmas that first year in Eatonton, I couldn't wait till it was over. I would see April on the sidewalk and she would pass by me, my greeting her, 'Hello' and she saying nothing to me. I still could see her across the street in her store.

"Early in January, I saw a bunch of trucks out front of her store, loading up. I felt sad as racks and displays were loaded one by one. Dan triumphantly pulled down the Victorian Peach sign out front of the store like a victorious general. I was so mad, Aubrey. All that I had done to help that business survive. The hours of motivation for April, 'You can make it work.' The death of a good business. Pictures came down off the wall. Why, why is she doing this? So she doesn't have to see my face everyday. Am I that much of a problem? April never said goodbye or thanks or I am sorry, just packed up and left.

"The next thing I heard, April had opened a store at the mall in the next town. About a month later, I went on a mission to go look at the new and improved Victorian Peach. It was no doubt first class and funded by Dan's family. I noticed flowers in the window. Congratulations on your new business. There were not a lot of flowers and nothing as grand as the Frank Moss arrangement. April wasn't there. Funny, she had another girl working which I recommended. No thanks to Frank Moss. As I walked down the mall corridor, I thought I helped that business, and I was glad it still lived.

"I didn't hear from April until months later. She called out of the blue one day and said, 'Frank, do you know who I am?'

'Yes,' I said very humbly. I complemented April on her new store.

'Frank, I want to tell you how sorry I am for what I said. Eunice had told folks around town we went to bed together; I had to do something. My mother-in-law asked questions and Dan began to wonder, and you know how I am afraid of his beatings. I am sorry, Frank.'

'I understand, April,' I said.

'Anyway, Frank, the man that I was using to put antiques in my store has pulled out. Do you have anything I can use?

"Like the fool, I said 'Yes.' April and I became friends again. My preacher, James, told me when I shared the April problem with him, 'Frank, don't worry about April. She is an emotional woman. She is immature and jumps to conclusions.' That day April and I talked. It was a conversation on edge, but it was conversation.

"I would see April maybe once a month in my store, and she would wave at me in town. I guess the curtain was lifted on my banishment."

Pulling up in front of a yellow clapboard house, Frank stopped the truck. The house sat back from the road with a long lawn extending to the street. The grass was brown and the ferns on the front porch were dead. Leading up to the house was a straight gravel drive. Around back of the house was a carport shed with a metal roof. Under the carport sat a wine-colored Chrysler Le Baron convertible. The top was down. The carport was visible from Frank and Aubrey's vantage point. A commercial security light hung from one of the trees. Leaves blew across the high-gabled roof; the house looked dead.

"There it is, Aubrey. Doris Anthony's house. A house it was, never a home. She rented it, you know. Doris never knew what a real home was and never will."

"Frank, is it safe to be here?"

"Probably not," responded Frank. "Ever been in love, Aubrey?" asks Frank.

"Yes, I guess I have," responded Aubrey.

"Maybe it's the Southern blood that makes men down here romantic fools. How did this story start? One Thursday, I went to the Kiwanis meeting down the street. Every Thursday we met and ate that God awful Chinese food. Business men and a lot of the men from my church belonged to the Kiwanis Club. Even James, my preacher, was a member. We always laughed about James always going on a diet. Yes, Mr. Donny, my 92-year old Sunday School teacher was a member. Mostly men belonged.

"One day, I went and I saw a woman that would change my life forever. Sitting at the table, I saw a woman. Aubrey, she had to be the most beautiful woman I had ever seen. Long black hair, pulled back from her face and a hair barrette clasping the long silky strand of hair from behind. Her face and complexion were so smooth and olive colored. Piercing black eyes that looked like black marbles. The first thought that popped into my head was Charleston.

"I had seen her before, long ago. She looked like the woman I had seen in an oil portrait when I would roam the roads when I was in college. The oil portrait over the fireplace, in that old home I visited, that was her. She was from the past, from my long ago past. The energy was incredible!

"I could hear her voice. Soft Southern accent but with a feisty twist. She had large breasts that she tried to conceal with a tight fitting bra. It was as if she was trying to hide her sexuality - Victorian in a sense. She was dressed very businesslike with a jacket and skirt.

"She didn't belong in that meeting room. She seemed so out of place. Almost like a Southerner in New York. Very professional and articulate. She looked just like Scarlet O'Hara. Her dark eyes talking, expressing themselves like one would talk with their hands. She had such a presence about her, like a movie star or celebrity. I thought to myself, surely this woman must be a visitor or maybe the guest speaker. I looked and didn't see a wedding ring, only a silver ring in an old setting on her olive hand. I tried not to stare, not to appear to be a fool. I just couldn't keep my eyes off her.

"When the meeting adjourned, I wanted to meet her. She got away from the meeting room and I raced to say 'hello' on the sidewalk. Standing at the street corner, I said, 'I don't believe we have met. My name is Frank Moss. I own the antique store,' and I pointed there.

'Yes, I have heard of you,' as she threw her head back in a cocky position. 'You and your wife are going to live upstairs.'

'Well, that didn't work out,' I chuckled. I looked down at the ground then back up at her. 'We got a divorce.'

'Ah, how sad,' as Doris' eyes met mine with the pleasure of hearing the divorce news. 'My name is Doris J. Anthony. You can remember my name like Cleopatra and Anthony.'

"We laughed and I said, 'I think I can remember that name. Maybe we can have lunch sometime.'

Doris said, 'Sure, I would like that.'

I couldn't get her face out of my mind. A couple of days passed and we had lunch, February 4th. We got a plate from a local eatery and we picnicked, even though it was cold outside. Sitting there on that picnic table eating with Doris was indescribable. Wind blew through her hair. It was like a dream. Doris had to be the most beautiful woman I had ever seen in my life."

"Well, Frank I haven't heard anything negative about you from the town folk."

"I can't believe we have never met." Frank added.

"Well, I have been working on my house. Mother says all houses need painting inside before you move in, and of course I had a lot of business to wrap up at my old law firm in Macon. That's where I am originally from, Macon, Georgia. I have been busy with the house and setting up my new practice.

"Oh where is your office?"

"I have space leased from Patrice, Eunice's daughter across from the courthouse."

"At first, I didn't know if I liked Doris J's personality. I called her that, Doris J. A lot if times she was quick and to the point, almost cynical. Then she would squint and twinkle those black eyes and make you feel comfortable again. We talked a long time that winter afternoon. Doris told me she was engaged to a man for five years in Macon.

'He said I was afraid of a commitment,' Doris said. 'I broke off the engagement and moved to Eatonton. I came to Eatonton as a child and loved going to my aunt's house and playing.

'What's her name, Doris?' I asked.

'Martha Anthony. She lives in my grandfather's old house down the street from your building. I hope when I am old, I am just like her, independent, Frank.' Doris looked defiantly. Doris puffed up. 'I drew her will up one day. That house will be mine. My grandfather was a judge here long ago. He was an attorney also, so I guess I am following in his footsteps.'

"I couldn't believe a woman as beautiful as Doris J. had never been married. Later I learned she was 44; of course she looked 35. No wrinkles on that woman. No scent of a favorite perfume or hairspray. She was scentless.

"'Doris, are you seeing anyone?'

'Oh,' she said, 'there is this guy from Charleston, a romance three years ago. I don't know, he wants to get back together.'

'Doris, have you ever been married?' I asked.

'No,' she said defiantly.

'I find it hard to believe a woman as attractive as yourself...never been married?'

'At parties, those boring legal events, I remember a guy coming up and saying, You must be a lesbian. I told him, I beg your pardon?' Doris looked at me like someone had complimented her. 'I have nothing against anyone's sexual preference, do you?'

'Oh, I agree with you.'

"That statement puzzled me. 'Frank, now tell me about yourself. You are divorced.'

'Lynn and I haven't finalized things yet.'

'Frank, it's the same as being divorced a long time. Usually I don't see anyone until they have been divorced a few years. They are so screwed up, you know?' Taking a sip of her tea, she swallows and says, "Frank, you seem pretty much together.'

'Oh, I am getting along pretty good. I love Eatonton and all the wonderful people I have met.'

'Well, there could be something wrong with you.' I waited to hear the rest of her sentence to see if I had offended her. 'You did pick Eatonton to move to!' Doris laughed.

"Tell me about your family. Your mother and father," she said.

"'Mom has been dead almost ten years now. It's strange how my mother and father ever got together. See, my mother came from a rich family.'

Doris interrupts and says, 'I suppose you have a trust fund.' She really insulted me with that statement, but I continued, laughing it off.

'No, wish I did. Granddaddy married a second wife and she cleaned the estate out.' Doris looked disappointed at that revelation. 'Mom was from the city and Daddy grew up in the country. Daddy never remarried. I think he really loved her, even though they fought like cats and dogs all their married life.

"I wouldn't put up with that," Doris says throwing her head back where the wind would put her hair back in place. "I suppose if I had married, I would have been divorced long ago."

"'My daddy is real sick these days. Daddy is like one of those T.V. dads. Sure do love him,' I told her. Doris sort of smiles.

"Frank, do you have any brothers and sisters?"

"Yes, as a matter of fact I do. I have a brother named Mike. He is married and has two little girls. Also, I have a brother named Kevin and he is married to a girl named Teresa."

"Why do you like all this antique stuff so much?"

"I don't know. I just feel comfortable with old things. I just always loved the past."

"I have a few antiques. I like them too,' Doris says. 'Have you ever been antiquing in Macon?"

'No, can't say I have.'

"Well, there is...," and Doris rambled on and on about this shop or that shop.

"Maybe you can draw me a map, so I can find all those places."

"I will be glad to," Doris says.

"I thought to myself, maybe I have a chance with this woman. That lunch; I wish I could relive that lunch. If I had one wish, I wish I could relive that first lunch with Doris J.

"A few days passed and on Saturday, Doris called early one morning and said, 'Frank, I was wondering if you got my note on finding the Macon antique shops?'

'Yes, I did. I was wondering who put that under my door.'

'Well, I did. If you are not busy today, maybe we can go antiquing.'

I said, 'Sure, it's raining outside. Probably a bad day for business.'

Doris said, 'That's great. I like these quick decisions. Let me dry my hair and I will be over and pick you up.' I hung up the phone and thought, wow, she wants to pick me up.

"Doris had this convertible, a deep wine color. That's it under the shed. She said, 'Once the yardman said it was the color of my hair.' Off we went to Macon. Doris was a small woman. I think she only wore a size five shoe. In the car I kept looking at her legs in those tight jeans she had on and a wonderful winter sweater. Still she tried to conceal her breasts, as if ashamed.

"We told stories and laughed and stopped at all the Macon antique stores. While visiting The Iron Horse, I saw a couple that frequented my shop.

'Where were you today, Frank? We came by and you were closed.'

'Well,' I said, 'This beautiful woman came in and...' I was so proud to have Doris J. at my side. I kept thinking what a beautiful woman, and she was, and she wanted to spend the day with me. After we had hit a good number of shops, Doris said, 'Let's go by and you can meet my mother and father.' I will tell you, Aubrey, I was a little uncomfortable on a first date meeting a girl's parents. But after all, Doris was not a conventional woman. Doris made an opening statement.

'Now Frank, Jeanette and Ken don't live in a large house or anything like that. Once daddy gets settled in he just doesn't want to leave. They have lived in the same house for 30 years. It is paid for. Daddy's very conservative.' With that tour of homes opening statement I thought we were going to a tar paper shack.

"We drove in the driveway. The house was a typical brick ranch house. Wrought iron danced across the cornice of the house and the brick was painted with an understated elegance. Inside, I met Doris' mother, Jeanette. She was a small woman quick in every movement and action, almost as if she were directing a movie. I could tell where Doris got her beautiful skin and looks from. Her mother had those same dark eyes and her hair was greying. Ms. Jeanette busied around the house showing me all of her antiques. 'How do you like this blue, Frank. Doris and I liked the blue in our Doctors office so much we both agreed it was the perfect color to match the oriental rug. Ken liked to have died, as Jeanette whispered 'when he found out how much it cost.'

"Of course, me touching each piece saying, 'Oh, I really like that. Oh, how beautiful.' Ms. Jeanette couldn't wait to tell me the story of how each piece was acquired and how much she paid for it. The house was laid out like most 30-year old ranch homes. A tiny kitchen with out-of-date appliances, of course, the usual bend of a modern countertop to keep up with the new houses. Somehow, the updates looked pretentious, out of place, like you were trying to be rich, rich, rich, when you are not, not, not. The long narrow living room was Ms. Jeanette's pride and joy. The walls were painted with a thousand coats of paint trying to hide the past. A beautiful old empire secretary desk was positioned against one wall. 'Ms. Jeanette,' I exclaimed, 'you have got my style of furniture.' I rubbed my hand on the surface of the piece. 'That came from.. and I am going to leave it to...' I felt I had encroached on Anthony's territory of what is mine and what is yours. Quickly, I got the drift and moved on about the room.

"Doris' father, Ken, was sitting on the sofa. He seemed a very quiet man. Ken didn't look at all like Doris. He was bald-headed with a little paunch of a stomach. Very soft spoken, it was as if he was trying to warn me about the other side of Doris. I guess with a wife like Jeanette, he was probably worn out from all that woman's hustling around.

"We sat in the living room for about half an hour. As if I was being checked out to be a suitable friend or husband for Doris. Doris would go on and on, 'Frank has done so much for Eatonton. He is going to take Mr. Sid's building and make an antique mall out of it. Frank ordered this container of furniture from England.' As Doris went on and on about what a fine fellow I was, my eyes moved about the room in search of answers. What went on in this house? Why did Doris never marry? Were none of her suitors rich enough for Ms. Jeanette? What about Ken, as I looked at him? How much money had he had to dish out to cover up Doris' mistakes, or did he just do his job and go on? I felt there was no love in that house. Just things, things acquired through 'I deserve to have this, I worked hard all my life.' I don't know why I didn't see it then. Everything in Doris' childhood was pretend.

The mantle clock ticked and Doris was in one of her trance like states. Doris's eyes glazed over. "Daddy, no it hurt last time, not again, I hurt." Doris quickly snapped back into the present. "Frank, let me show you my old teenager room. Mother has redone it. Ms. Jeanette looked uneasy at Doris's invitation, but then rambled on about the antique be she bought from an old colored women.

Her room looked like make believe movie set having the only hint of its former resident's presence from a photo of Doris in high school. "Wow, I love this picture of you!" Doris ran her finger through her hair "High school, what a long time ago." It seemed like Doris stared at her bathroom for a long time.

*"Doris, are you sure your parents won't be home for the entire weekend?" "Quite sure, Jamie. Now, here drink some of this crown. It's Daddy's favorite."*

*Both girls in their early teens propped up on pillows in Doris's bed. Doris could smell liquor on Jamie's breath. "I love the smell of whiskey. Don't you Jamie? Kiss me I want to taste it on your tongue." "Doris, that's kind of weird. The only one I ever kissed with whiskey on my tongue is Billy." Doris retorted "Oh, Billy is like all the rest of the boys in Macon. All they want to do is get us in bed. We are already in bed, so why do we need a guy inside us?"*

*"Doris, you really can be weird sometimes. My head is really spinning, how about you?" "I feel really good." Doris kissed Jamie and ran her fingers through her long hair. "Play with me, Jaime." Jamie hesitated, " I've never, well, you know with another girl before." Doris removed her top and her breasts soon were on top of Jamie Both girls slowly removed their clothes. "Doris, you won't ever tell that we played, will you?," whispered Jamie. Doris continued to make love, and soon both girls fell asleep in each others arms.*

*"Jamie, we have got to get up! Remember, we are supposed to meet Mary and the other girls at 10:00!" Doris looked at Jamie's nude body wrapped in her sheets and felt disgusted she had made love to her. "Doris I am getting up. Meet you in the bathroom in just a minute."*

*Doris was brushing her long hair when she saw the reflection of Jamie in the mirror. Jamie's nude body revolted Doris. "Jamie, I have poured some bathwater for you." "Doris, you are so sweet." "I'll swear that Crown did me in last night." Don't remember anything." Doris had the hairdryer blowing in front of the mirror. Still, she saw Jamie's body in the tub. "I don't remember anything either."*

*Doris's eyes became blackened and her eyes meet with Jamie's blue eyes. Then, Jamie knew... Doris threw the hairdryer into the bathwater. Sparks flew...*

"Doris, are you alright?" Frank asked.

Doris replied, "I am ready to go, Frank."

"Strange, when we entered the house usually a parent would hug or kiss their child. That never happened. Ms. Jeanette was a cold woman. I wonder if she taught her daughters the same coldness. Doris kissed the top of Ken's bald head, showed no affection toward her mother, and we left...

"We headed back to Eatonton. 'Doris, have you always lived in Macon?'

'Gracious, no,' Doris said.

'When I finished college here, I lived for a short time in California.'

'Bet they loved that Southern accent of yours.'

'Yes, Frank, but after a while it becomes so trite.'

'What did you do in California?'

'Oh, I worked in a bank. It was so boring.'

'Did you meet anyone there?'

'Oh, a few men,' then Doris paused and looked at me. 'I did go out with this black guy, don't get me wrong, Frank, he didn't look like my yardman, or you know, he was very nice looking. I could never date a black guy in the South. His people would hate me just because I was white and my people would hate him just because he was black. Rules, rules, my mother is very fond of rules. The world revolves around Jeannette Anthony's rule book. Mother was so afraid of either of her girls getting pregnant that she insisted that we not date until our Senior year in High School. Mother never missed a chance to berate a young woman who had a child that looked the least bit a "half breed" as she called it. She was fond of saying, 'Look that child is a high yellow.' Doris paused again, turning away from looking at the road. 'My parents would have killed me if they knew I went out with a black guy!'

'What happened after California?'

"'I came back and went to Seminary.'

'Seminary?" I looked surprised. To study to be a preacher.'

'For heavens sake, I taught school. Those children drove me crazy! I guess it's a good thing I never had kids, probably would've killed them. I left the having kids up to my sister Kate; she's got three. After I burned out on teaching, I started working at a law firm in Macon. I was a legal secretary; one of the lawyers there said he thought I should go to law school. Well, I thought how granddaddy was an attorney, so maybe I could follow in his footsteps. This lawyer helped me.'

Aubrey, Doris would go into these trance-like states and pause, like she was remembering and wanted to tell me one thing more, then quickly composed her self.

'Want to know any more, Frank?

'Did you ever live with anyone?'

'Sure, if you are...' then she paused, 'well, if you are my age...sure in college I lived with a guy.'

"I suspected Doris J. had a lot of adventures in her 44 years of being single. We stopped at a Bar-B-Que place on the way home, and she bought my lunch. Independent woman, I tell you, Aubrey. When we got back to my store, I told her I had had a great time, and I rubbed her arm in affection and kissed it. 'My, aren't you the affectionate type, Frank.' She was cold to me, but I thought about her mother, Ms. Jeanette, and knew why. Maybe I could help her love.

"Another week went by and it seemed Doris would call just to chat. Always an excuse though. I was passing by and I thought of you. Every day she would call me. Made my day. I still can hear her voice. 'Frank,' she would say, like I was on the witness stand, 'This is Doris.' Then I would respond and say, 'I know who you are.' I loved it. Loved every minute of it. Doris J. was from the past, Aubrey. I had seen her before.

"One day she came into the store; I was sitting behind the desk. She looked just like she had gotten down off a horse. She had on riding boots and a brown corduroy coat. Her hair was pulled back. That beautiful black, silky hair blowing in the wind. Aubrey, I could have watched her for hours, standing in that doorway. A form with the light behind her. I hope when I die, I see her in that light again.

Doris said, 'Frank, what are you doing for lunch today?'

I responded, 'Same old thing.'

She said, 'Let me go get us some lunch and we can eat at your store.'

I said, 'Great, let me give you some money.'

In her typical manner, 'Frank, you can pay for yours, but you are not paying for mine.' I agreed and gave her my share of the lunch money.

"At lunch we talked about everything from life to politics. Doris was a very educated woman and loved to spout forth all she knew. 'How are the Halls of Justice today, Ms. Doris?'

'Nothing much going on. I am still waiting for those damn real estate folks to call back. You used to sell real estate, why are real estate people so slow?'

'They are just made that way,' I laughed.

'Doris, when you passed the bar exam, what did you do to celebrate?, I asked.'

'I locked myself in my room and got drunk on several bottles of wine.'

'You didn't want to party with any of your friends?' Doris paused and looked to be in a trance-like state.

'Didn't have any.' When she would cock that head of hers back, you knew you were in for a real tough one liner.

"That afternoon Doris had brought some mail-order magazines in to show me what she liked in the way of dresses. 'Oh, Frank, I like this one,' as she flipped from page to page. 'I beg your pardon.' That was her favorite saying.

"Oh, I remember that wine-colored convertible. She would drive that car up and down the oak-lined streets of Eatonton. Her hair blowing in the wind. Reminded me every time I saw her in that car, of Doris driving a carriage, those reins firm in her hands. Strange, isn't it Aubrey? How it seems you have met someone before, like another time and place. From the first time I laid eyes on Doris at the Kiwanis meeting, I knew her before.

"From the window at the store, I could see her walking on that hill to the courthouse. The horizon and the grass and Doris J., all three converging into one, walking, her dress blowing in the wind. Seems like the wind played a big part in me falling in love with this woman. God, those great times I had with Doris. She would call me, 'Frank, I am going to Milledgeville to the store. Do you want to go with me?' I couldn't wait to say 'Yes-Yes.'

"She was a strange woman. She always wanted to be in control.

Like she would always pick me up in her car. I suppose the strangest thing, every time I would attempt to kiss her, she would draw back like I was some sort of freak or something. Her black eyes would get as big as a saucer. I tried several times to kiss her and I got the same old response. Hell, I had been with a lot of women. I never had the problem they wouldn't kiss me. I didn't know what the reason ever was. It hurt me. Doris wouldn't let me show affection toward her. She exhibited a lot of coldness that her mother Ms. Jeanette displayed.

"One time when we had gotten back from the store, I tried to hug her in the parking lot out front of the store. She said, 'Frank, what will people think?' I said, 'Who cares what they think?' She was hard to understand.

"The next day she would call and leave a message. 'I was wondering if you were going to the Kiwanis Dance, but if you are going to take someone else, I am not going.' I called to say I would love to go to the dance and then she said, 'Well, I really don't want to go. Instead come over to my house and we can watch a movie.'

"I never had been to Doris J's house before. I arrived that night and Doris gave me the tour of her house. She was just renting the house, as I said. Typical of most old houses, you enter from the back door to a sloping floor; where the kitchen used to be, I am sure was an old back porch. Inside everything was decorated with an exactness. Everything had its place. I rubbed my hand over chests and furniture, exclaiming how beautiful. Where did this come from? Doris was shy showing me around. We tiptoed in the living room and spoke softly while looking at a grouping of small-framed pictures on a bookshelf. 'Who are these people?' I asked, and Doris would say, 'This is my sister and brother. This is me at my high school prom.' "Who is this girl?" She is so pretty." Frank asked. "That was my friend, Jamie. Stupid fool, she meet a tragic death. A hairdryer fell into her tub and electrocuted her." "God, how horrible!" Frank exclaimed. Our faces were close at that time. I should have gone for a kiss then but I didn't. Quickly she would spin around and say, 'Frank, I got this at...' I remember how her house was designed for one. She didn't have a sofa that would accommodate two, just one.

'Where's the T.V.?' I asked.

'In the bedroom,' Doris said.

“Her room was typical of the house with mix-matched pieces of furniture posed in spaces that seemed appropriate. She had a tall rice carved bed. The posts were real high, and I thought the bed was too large for such a small woman as Doris. I fantasized about who she had made love to on that bed. The groaning sounds of another woman, or the climax of a man. Somehow, I didn’t see Doris enjoying the sexual pleasure, rather that she was just an object for someone else’s pleasure.

‘Where did you get this great bed, Doris?’

‘I bought it when I had money; you know, when I worked for the law firm in Macon.’ The T.V. sat on a chest and a rocking chair was in front of the screen. Doris sat in the rocking chair, and I lay on the floor with my arm propping up my head. Doris said, ‘Here, Frank, take this blanket to rest your head on.’

I responded, ‘Why don’t you get down here on the floor with me?’

‘No-No, Frank, you know I had that back surgery. It hurts my back.’

I said, ‘O.K.’ I looked up from the floor periodically to gaze at her face.

“She starred into the screen motionless like she was in one of those trance states. We had bought a box of chocolates at the store. Doris loved chocolate.

“One time I drove all the way to Milledgeville, and went to a theater just to buy her a box of her favorite brand. When you are in love, Aubrey, you do some strange things.

“The movie was over and I said my goodbyes. I wanted more that evening, but I was afraid to ask. Afraid, so afraid, Aubrey, it would go away.

“Doris had a bunch of dogs and cats. When I was leaving, the dogs were whooping and hollering. Strange, the poor things were always caged up. I never knew Doris to take the animals out and play with them outside the cage. She had found the critters abandoned or lost. I think she liked that control, keeping them caged.

Pointing to the house, Frank said, “I have been in there a couple of times. One night Doris and I went to an auction that one of her clients was holding. ‘Frank, look at those bangs on that woman; how tacky. A woman’s hair should be pulled back like mine,’ as Doris runs her hand through her hair. ‘Look at that outfit that woman has on, Frank.’ While riding back in my truck that night, I put my hand on her leg and we started talking. 'Frank, you know Tim in Kiwanis Club?'

'Yes, I know him, and his wife both. They always are coming in the store.'

'What's his wife's name?' asked Doris.

'Laura,' I said.

'She is really cute. I would like to get to know her,' Doris said, looking out the window in a sexy, sensuous sort of way. When we got back to her house, 'Frank, are you thirsty?' asked Doris.

'Sure, could use something,' I said. Doris opened the refrigerator door and looked in.

'Frank, do you like beer?' No, beer is not for me. I am a wine drinker.' Doris then pulled out two bottles of beer and a cheap bottle of wine.

'Frank, I didn't like beer all that much till someone told me to mix it half and half.' Aubrey, you know what a big drinker I am; hell, I could sip on the same glass all night. The thought of a beer-wine mixture started to turn my stomach, but I would do anything she asked. Sitting at that breakfast table, my head started to spin. I became nauseated. 'That's enough for me, Doris,' I said. We said our goodbyes and I didn't even attempt a kiss for fear of throwing up in her mouth.

"Seemed like Doris was always coming into the store bringing her mother, Ms. Jeanette, or sister, Kate. Kate came in the store one day, and I had never met her before. As soon as this woman came in, I said to myself, that looks and sounds like Doris. Kate was about Doris' size and a very lively personality. Her hair was dyed a reddish brunette color. It looked horrible. Kate's hair was long like Doris'.

'So, you are the man Doris keeps talking about.'

'That's me.'

'Frank, I want you to meet my son. This is Jimmy.' Jimmy seemed shy as his mother put her arm around him. 'I have three children,' Kate explained.

'Now, Kate, who would ever guess,' I said.

'I am younger than Doris,' Kate boasted.

'And where do you live?'

'Peachtree City. My husband is a builder.' Kate proudly displayed a three carat wedding ring, as if to say, we are loaded. 'Frank, let me show you this wallpaper for my dining room. What do you think?'

About that time Ms. Jeanette came in the door. ‘I’ve been looking all over for you, Kate.’ Ms. Jeanette waved her arms and hurried off down the isles of my store. ‘Got anything new, Frank?’

‘Not yet, still waiting on my English shipment.’

‘Tell them to hurry it up,’ said Ms. Jeanette. Ms. Jeanette then raced back to the front of the store. ‘Kate, we have to go. You can talk to Frank later.’ Ms. Jeanette stood beside her grandson and patted him on the back as you would a pet. ‘Have you met my grandson, Jimmy?’

‘Yes, Kate introduced us,’ I said.

‘Kate and Jim are my children with children,’ she boasted as if to put Doris down for not marrying. Then Doris came in the door.

‘Here y’all are!’ yelled Doris.

‘We have to go, Doris. We are going to be late for lunch at Martha’s,’ snapped back Ms. Jeanette.

‘Couldn’t we stay just a little longer, Frank...’ Doris said in a child-like way.

‘Later, Doris’ and Ms. Jeanette walked out the door.

Doris looked at me and said, ‘Jeanette’s a good mother when she has her way.’

“Doris was always bringing some kin folk in to meet me. I felt I was being checked out to see if I was suitable for a husband. In the store, I would hear Doris say to her mother, ‘Frank is going to do this,’ or ‘Frank, this’ or ‘Frank that.’ Just like when she first took me to meet her parents.

“Aubrey, it was a dream come true, the girl down the street. I came to Small Town, U.S.A. to find my dream. What a dream; God, that February. I would give anything to be back to February of that year. I had just cut a deal with a guy in England on a whole container of furniture sight unseen. It was just like Christmas, waiting for the containers’ arrival. Doris would call and say, ‘Is it here yet?’

“One day she came up and took pictures of how the store looked before the arrival, and after it came, with boxes everywhere. The day it came, Doris came up and polished furniture right alongside me.

‘Now, Frank, this piece right here would be perfect in my office.’

‘Well, buy it,’ I said.

‘I would, Frank, if you didn’t have such a ridiculous price on it.’ Doris looks up with those black eyes. ‘Of course, you could just help out a poor starving attorney who is just getting started.'

'Why don't I lend you the piece till you feel comfortable about paying? How about that?' I said. Doris looked pleased.

'Can we take it to my office today, Frank?' Doris asked.

'Sure, let's go now and see how it would look.'

"Aubrey, it was a lot of furniture. A conference table one time, a wardrobe. I think I would have signed over the store to that woman, I was so mesmerized by her. "

"Aubrey, but I really thought I would marry Doris. Bring her love and affection, what her family could never give. I would have been a good husband to her. I could have helped her.

"Those times it seemed she wanted to be around me. I savored every moment. I knew I was falling in love with her and I didn't want to. Often I would come back from lunch and Doris would leave me little notes tucked in a crack in the door. 'D. 11:30 Fri. Call & leave message on home phone if you'd like to go Exercise Walking this eve. D.'

"We would walk together at night. I remember saying "those little feet can't keep up with me."

'"Those little feet just can't keep up, Doris J. We are going to have to get you some bigger tennis shoes."

"I will show you, Frank," and Doris would competitively race up the hill.

"We walked past all of our friends' homes and businesses.

"Jan Ramsey has bought the old Patterson home, and she is going to open a B&B. Let's go up and look in the window."

"Are you sure, Doris?"

"Come on, Frank. Don't be a chicken." We both pressed our faces next to the stained glass on the doors and peered in.

"Look at that molding, Doris!"

"Yes, Jan is going to give your friend Helen a run for her money. This house is a lot neater than Helen's," Doris said vengefully.

"We walked and walked, pretending. 'Oh, Madam, look, this is where that fine antique establishment is.' 'Oh and yes, Mr. Frank, here is where that exceptional attorney is located.' Laughing, we would both comment on the white house next to the Chamber of Commerce. 'That's the house I want!' 'Me first,' Doris would say.

"'Frank, you know the house that you said was painted an aqua green. Let me remind you my aunt went to considerable trouble to research that color and it is a historical green! I drew her will up, also. I am going to inherit that house, too.'

'Doris, tell me about Kate. She is married to the builder in Peachtree City?'

'Yes, that's her second marriage. She was married to a football coach the first time. He didn't have anything, but Howard is loaded,' Doris exclaimed.

'Those kids, they are from her first marriage?'

'Yes.'

"Your brother, Jim, he's married?'

'Yes, second for him, too. His first wife was a real bitch. I never could understand her. Did you know, Frank, Jim and that woman had a little girl, and when Jim divorced her, she took the child and refuses to this day to let Jim see her. It just broke Mom and Daddy's heart.'

'Why did they take her away?'

'I would rather not talk about that, Frank.'

"Aubrey, we walked a lot of nights, and shared our lives. Some nights Helen would invite me over for supper and we would talk on the front porch.

'Helen, I think I am falling in love with Doris. I just don't know, some times she seems like she really wants me, then she just cuts me off. A lot of times she is like a child, 'Frank, can you help me', or 'Frank, can you cover for me at a meeting.'

'Frank, let me tell you something,' Helen would look me in the eye with her muscular face. 'Doris is 44 years old, almost my age. She is a professional woman, you can't push her. Women like myself and Doris like to go after our man, in our own way. If you force us or threaten us, we won't have anything to do with you. Give it time, Frank. If she really wants you, she will come after you. She's scared, Frank. Listen to me, Frank. You are a good-looking man. You have a lot to offer a woman, so don't put yourself down. You have been through so much, your baby dying, your father sick, your divorce, moving to a new town, take it easy. You look so thin, so tired. Take a break. I know you're lonely.'

"'I feel like some sick high school puppy in love,' I said.

'Personally, I don't like Doris. The time she came to the open house and wanted to open every door, even our private quarters. Watch out, Frank. Doris may not be what you think.' I have remembered that last sentence many times, that starlit night on Helen's porch.

"One day I ran up to the local hamburger place to get lunch and I saw Doris and a little girl. 'Why, Frank, I want you to meet Kate's little girl, Emily J.' I shook her little hand and shyly she turned away. 'Come sit with us, Frank.' Sitting there, I looked at Doris talking to little Emily, and I thought what it would be like to have a family again. I knew Doris was too old to have children, but I thought for a moment what it would be like, to be normal again, have a wife, again. After I left, it wasn't long until Doris pulled up outside my store where I was washing my truck.

'Mine is next, Frank.'

'It will cost you, Doris J., and just where are you and Miss Emily J. going?'

'To Aunt Martha J's, her name sake. Little Emily, stay in Aunt Doris' car like a proper lady while I go and talk to the car washer.'

"In March, things started to go bad. I remember at the Kiwanis Club Pancake supper, me asking Doris to 'let's go out to dinner,' and she said, 'I can't Thursday night. I have a dinner date with a stranger.' It hurt me when she said that. I thought she cared about me. You see, Aubrey, I had never been on a real date with Doris. Never took her out to a nice restaurant. In the weeks after that, I would call, probably once a day just to see how she was doing. Then I started getting the ice cold treatment. 'Frank, I have got to do this, so many deadlines, you will understand I am sure.'

"I remember being in Atlanta once near a pet store. I called and said, 'Doris, can I pick up some dog food at this pet store? It's pretty cheap here.' 'No Frank, mother can get some, what you would buy the dogs won't eat.' I shook off the cold treatment as problems in building a law practice. I wouldn't call for a while, then she would show up at the store with her mother or sister and all would seem fine. I missed her everyday that I didn't talk to her.

"The Riverwood auction was coming and everyone in town went to this event. It's purpose was to raise money for the private school in town. I asked Doris one day if she would like to go in halves with me, and we donated a vase I had. I said, 'It would be great publicity for both of us. Also, they are having a dinner. Will you be my date?' She agreed. I was so happy. I thought things were back on track.

"Doris I am going to the beach for a week, why don't you come with me? The only house that's available is big enough for a brass band. You can have your own room."

"I'll have to think about it."

"Cocktail hour was to start at 6:00 p.m. Although I am not a big drinker, I wanted to say hello and meet some of the big shots in town. I called Doris about 4:30 to check on the time I needed to pick her up. She said, 'Frank, I have got to work late and why don't you go on ahead of me.' I tell you, Aubrey, I was hurt and mad and I sensed something was wrong. Being a good salesman, I said, 'We don't have to go to the cocktail hour.' So, we agreed on a time as to when I was to pick her up.

"I drove up her driveway and walked to the door. Then Doris J. emerged. God, she was so beautiful. Black pantsuit with a gold neck band, hair pulled back with a gold braid. I never had seen her dressed up like this.

"We got to the V.F.W. club where the auction was to be held. Entering we were greeted by all those wonderful friends and soon-to-be friends of Eatonton. We chose a spot near some of Doris' kinfolks. She was kin to everybody in town. I would ask, 'Who is that?' and she would respond, 'That's Uncle so and so, that's Aunt so and so.'

"I remember Roy Sims coming over to our table and saying, 'Frank, I like your choice in women.' I was on the top of the world that night. My date was Doris J. Anthony, the most beautiful woman in all Eatonton. Doris' cousin was to do the auction and that damn vase brought $500.00. In the brochure it said, Chinese vase donated by Uncle Remus Attic and Doris J. Anthony, Atty. I was so proud.

"Doris wanted to leave early because she had a deposition early in the morning, and I was to leave for a much needed trip to the beach. I drove up in her driveway and was getting out to walk her to the door and she said, 'No, it's not necessary. The dogs will start barking.' I knew I wasn't getting a kiss that night. I said, 'I will miss you at the beach, not too late to change your mind.' She said nothing as she went in the house. I went home half happy, half sad. I just didn't understand that woman.

"I left early the next morning for the beach. I decided to go to Grayton Beach, that's where Lynn and I used to go to get away and solve problems. That's the place I told you we went when our baby died. I needed to think. The ocean always renewed my spirit. My mind played the Riverwood affair over and over. Why wouldn't Doris let me walk her to her door? Why wouldn't she let me kiss her? Over and over, I thought, mile after mile of road.

"Soon, I reached the beach. Hell, I rented an eight-bedroom house, that's all they had, same price as a cottage. Aubrey, I never in my life had been on a vacation by myself. It was so strange. Every morning, I would walk the beach at sunrise. Oh, the ocean is so grand to see once again, I thought as I walked. The ocean never changes. It's always a constant. It's the same, tide in and tide out. The birds that walk the shore, the same little birds when I was a child. The footprints look the same. The old people, the young people, all the same. Nothing was changed there but me. I have grown older. It saddened me, peering out beyond that horizon. Wishing my life was as constant as the ocean.

"My every day was the same. I walked the beach at moonlight one night. How I wished Doris was with me. I could imagine holding her hand. Running my hand through her black, silky hair. Caressing her back and telling her I loved her. I saw a couple in the moonlight doing just that and it made me jealous. The next morning, I took my float and floated out to a private part of the ocean. I was mad that day, mad at God. I remember saying, 'God, do you hear me? Do you know I am still here? Why have you taken so much from me? Why? What more sacrifice do you want? You took Peter, you took Mom, are you going to take Doris, too? What have I done to You? I am not a scum. I pray to you. Where are my answers? Why God? Why? What more do you want? Are you going to take Doris also? I love this woman. Why won't she respond to me?'

"At this point, Aubrey, I was yelling over the waves and tears were streaming down my face. Waves lapping up against my float. Dead quiet. All I remember thinking was everything will be all right. I don't know to this day if that was God or me saying those words.

"Leaving the beach, I came back to Eatonton suntanned and relaxed and ready to face another day. Coming home, I passed through a little town in Alabama. There in the town square stood a monument to the Confederate dead. A simple wreath with flags surrounded the stone. I thought, today would have been Lynn's and my anniversary, if we had made it. I couldn't wait to get back to Eatonton to see Doris. I called her as soon as I hit town. 'Let's go have dinner where I can tell you all about my trip.' She was cold to me on the phone like 'I don't care if you drowned in the ocean,' that was the impression I got and it hurt me. That was nothing compared to the hurt that was to come. I called several days later and always a put off.

"I talked to Helen about Doris and me. Helen could always give me straight talk. She said, 'Frank, Doris is just like me. A career woman. Totally independent. You have got to lay off and let her call you.' Helen said, 'I know how hard it's going to be, but you have got to, Frank. If it's meant to be, it will be; if it's not, it won't.' As the words poured out of her mouth I knew she was right. Helen had been through a hell of a lot of adversity herself; she knew. I knew she was my friend and would never hurt me.

"For two weeks I thought about Doris J. Anthony. The only one I could turn to and trust was God. Those two weeks had to be one of the toughest in my entire life. I thought on Sunday at my church, as James, my friend, was preaching. The only hope I had in having a relationship with Doris was to ask God for his help.

"On Monday morning I went to Doris' church. A white clapboard church 175 years old. It was across the street from my church. It was the church of her ancestors. Walking into the sanctuary, I felt I had been there before. The green carpet, the smell, it seemed like home. Like my cousin Myra's house. God was there. I was embarrassed to be there and afraid someone might come in and see me. I got down on my knees and prayed at that altar. Tears streamed down my face. 'Please, God, please, God, don't take Doris away from me. I have lost so much. Please, God, don't take Doris away.'" Tears were rolling down Frank's face. "Aubrey," Frank said, "I have loved a lot of people in my lifetime. I loved Lynn, but never have I loved a woman to the core of my soul like I loved Doris J. I prayed and prayed on my knees. Standing up, I sat in one of the pews and looked down the aisle.

"Sure Doris had been a bitch toward me, but somehow I just knew I could help her love. Me, Frank Moss was sent into her life to help her.

Doris' mother was so cold toward her life. She never wanted her, never loved her.

"I imagined Doris with her father coming down the aisle in a wedding dress with the Prince of Denmark march playing. I saw my niece and little Emily J. as flower girls. I saw Doris' mother, Ms. Jeanette, and Doris' sister Kate, and the church just packed full of people. All so proud that things had worked out for us. A woman who had never been married, never known love from a man, finally she had married a man that truly loved her to the core of her soul. I can still hear the music; see her in that white dress. I figured Preacher Bill, the preacher then, who was also my friend, wondered why every morning I asked him to open up the sanctuary. I confided in him one morning, and asked him to pray for Doris. For two weeks, I knelt at that altar, heard that music and prayed. Aubrey, that two weeks, my faith was tested. I doubted, I hated. For the first time in my life, I felt the devil alive beneath my feet. I asked myself the question every day, 'Am I stupid? Am I Crazy? There are other women who would like to go out with me. Why torture myself with this one?' Faith. Got to have faith. I remembered the stained glass window when I first came to Eatonton. Faith, got to have that first, then you have hope, then hope will lead you to love.

"My biggest worry during that time was becoming some kind of religious freak. I knew God, but not like this. Was it my will for Doris to love me and not God? Every story in the Bible I recalled that had to do with faith I read. I would tell myself, how Jesus' disciples doubted when they were on the sea and Jesus said, 'Come, walk with me on the water.' God, I doubted. 'Do you hear my prayer, God?' I felt so stupid some days coming to that church. For what? Do other people in love do this? I have always been so impatient. I hate waiting.

**iii**

"The days were awful. It was all I could do to keep my mind on the business. The nights were even worse.

"Every afternoon I would walk to think. Passing by Doris' law office, I hoped I could catch a glimpse of her. Sometimes I would, and I wondered if she saw me. I constantly looked for her car in town. My walking trail passed by her house and I looked for her car. I wondered if she had found someone else when I didn't see her car. The pain was so great.

"I took to walking in late evening. One night on the streetlit sidewalks, I saw a shadow near the church. It was James, my preacher. I asked him to pray for me. Telling him sketchy details, I told him of a woman that was afraid to love. He knew, I felt, who it was. In those shadows that danced on James' face, I could still see those blue eyes. 'You are a good man, Frank.' That evening meeting let me cope with another day.

"Two weeks had passed, I had counseled with many. Mark at the bank. Mr. Donny, I remember what Mr. Donny said, that wonderful old man, 92 years old then. He said, 'Frank, there must be a show down. You must know where you stand. Sometimes the will of God must be swayed a little, pushed a little.' Always at night, I could count on Helen's advice on the front porch of the Bed and Breakfast. Sternly looking into my eyes she said, 'Frank Moss, don't you call her.'

"Well, Aubrey, one sunny Sunday afternoon, I went walking. I passed all the familiar sights; Doris' law office, the courthouse, and the churches, and I thought and I thought. I must know, I must know where I stand. Rounding the corner, I was on the last street of my walk; I saw the yellow clapboard house of Doris J. My heart beat so fast. Aubrey, I thought it was going to jump out and run down the street.

"I saw her car, maybe she's home, I thought. Maybe we can talk, sort things out. Each step up that gravel driveway sounded why, why. I must know. I saw her taking a sunbathe. Her beautiful olive skin rubbed with oil and that two-piece swim suit. Wow.

Quickly she said, 'Frank, what are you doing here? Let me put some clothes on.'

I sat down on the gravel next to her lawn chair and said, 'Doris, why don't we talk anymore? What have I done to you? Have I offended you?'

Coldly and calculatedly, she said, 'I wanted to call you and tell you, this thing with us is getting out of hand.'

I quickly spoke up, 'What?'

'Frank, I wanted to tell you before you went to the beach, but I didn't have the time. Frank, I am not interested. I know you are an intelligent man. It was all I could do not to wear a T-shirt around town stating I am not that interested. See, Frank, I classify people, friend, good friend, romantic, non-romantic. I never saw you in a romantic class, Frank.' At that point she should have pulled a gun on me and killed me.

"You are a man, Aubrey, you tell me. How would you feel if a woman told you that?" Frank continued, not allowing Aubrey to answer. "She said that she and Buddy, the flame from years ago were seeing each other again. Every word that came from that woman's mouth hurt me. She stomped me to the ground as if I were a cigarette butt. She said I embarrassed her in front of the entire community at the Riverwood Auction. People came up to her and said, 'I didn't know you and Frank were so serious.' 'How dare you put our names together in a brochure. Everyone in town thinks that we are dating.'

"I pleaded, sitting next to her on that ground, 'What have I done? I would never embarrass you. You don't know what I have been through for two weeks. I was so excited to see you when I came back from the beach, and you just put me off, treated me like I was nobody.' The last words I said to her was, 'I am so alone, and I love you so much.'

"I stood up and brushed the sand from my pants and walked down that driveway. I felt like Doris had pulled all my guts out. Every step I took was like lead. Never in all my life since that time have I been so totally rejected. Nor have I wished so much harm on myself. With all the shit that had happened, I wished that day, a truck would have come up on that sidewalk and killed me in front of Doris' house.

"I was so drained. I didn't know if I could make it to the store. Somehow I did and I opened that door and sat in my desk chair all afternoon. Doris' words paralyzed me. Sitting motionless, I stared into space till dusk. No tears, no nothing. All I thought was, how could one human being be so cruel and heartless to another? No wonder she is 44 years old and not married. How many trophy heads hung on the wall because of this woman? How many have loved Doris and was executed? How many?

"The next couple of weeks, I tried to recover from the devastation. Yes, I would see Doris ride the streets of Eatonton, passing by my store, either on foot or by car. She never would acknowledge me. At the Kiwanis Club, she wouldn't even say hello to me. The Egyptians used to wipe the name of their enemies off all buildings and monuments when they had an argument with someone, really wipe their name off the face of the earth. That's the way this woman I loved treated me. It was nearing Mother's Day and one day at Kiwanis Club, I approached Doris and patted her on the back. She turned in shock. "Why, Frank,' she said. I responded, 'Doris, I've got a card for your mother.' 'Oh, Frank, you shouldn't have.' That day I looked straight into her black eyes and said, 'When are we going to talk?'

"Aubrey, as I looked into her eyes, I saw a figure of a man floating, aimlessly floating in her eyes. Just a shadow of a man. Strangest thing I had ever seen. Of course, the typical response to my question, 'We'll see.' About a week later, Doris' mother, Ms. Jeanette, and Doris' sister, Kate, came into the store. Believe it or not, with Doris. All acted like the old days before the backyard talk. I really didn't know what to make of it. Probably Doris didn't say anything to them about what was going on. Always the front with Doris, always the cover up.

"I met some of Doris' girlfriends. One, I remember, was Cindy. Cindy was, I guess, around Doris' age, an ugly woman, fat with grey stringy hair. Doris used to tell me how Cindy got a divorce from a man who was such an authoritarian. 'I just wouldn't have put up with it,' Doris would go on and on. Cindy looked scared, frightened. I'm sure that gave Doris a lot of power.

"Bill, Doris' preacher, confided in me once, of meeting Sue, one of Doris' other girlfriends. 'She was so negative about the church, Frank, and, Frank,' Bill continued, 'she sounded like a lesbian.' Sue was from Alabama and while I was gone on a trip, Eve told me several of Doris' friends came in the store. 'They just went on and on, rubbing each other's back. Frank, Doris might be queer,' Eve said.

"In April I was to do a play at the Community Theater. That was probably the hardest stage play I ever did, not because of the lines, rather I was so torn up over Doris. I remember announcing the play at the Kiwanis Club meeting one day. 'Y'all come on down and see me.' Doris spoke up and said, 'Well, there's not much to see.' Every night of that performance I looked for Doris in the audience. She never came. One of the lines from that play was, 'Once you find the one you love, you must never ever let her go.' 'Depends on one's point of view,' the other actress said.

"Doris got where she would call maybe once a week. For some stupid question about when the Beautician committee would meet or something. When I would call and say, 'Let's go out to dinner and talk,' it was always some excuse. Another knife, another blow. I was still in love with her.

"One day, she came into the store. I was sitting behind the desk and she entered the door, white linen dress blowing in the wind and black hair tossing back and forth. I thought, what a photograph. She approached me and said, 'Frank, you have got to help me get some furniture for my office. All those real estate closings. Can you help?' 'Yes,' I said. So I took a loss and sold her furniture at my net cost. When she was leaning over my desk, I could see the little girl Doris trying to get out and say, I'm sorry. But the steel facade Doris closed in rapidly. For a moment I thought we could get back to old times. We both were Chamber of Commerce members and the committee I was on met on the first Wednesday of the month. Well, that Wednesday, guess who showed up? Doris. It was chairman election time and all voted for me with Doris seconding the motion. That afternoon, I got a letter from Doris under the door, congratulating me on my appointment. Naturally, she outlined how the committee should work.

"Let's drive down the street. I want to show you the Chamber of Commerce office. I spent a lot of time there. The Chamber was run by a mouse of a woman, Arlene Ray. She was a skinny little thing with a face that looked like a weasel, and she had two beady eyes. She had these God-awful braces on her teeth. Looked like some acne-faced teenager. Arlene had been married before and had an older son. Arlene married Sammy Ray. What a pompous ass! I never could stand him. He thought he was better than anyone. He always had this frown on his face.

"Sammy would have made a perfect cover for a preppy magazine. Neatly combed short hair. Arlene was a lot older than he. They never had any kids. I guess Sammy might mess his hair up if he made love." Frank laughed, "Hell, Arlene married him for his daddy's money. Old man Ray owned the furniture store in town. Sammy used to tell me, 'If you need a reference on any black in town, let me know. Daddy knows all the boys and their families. I can tell you who steals, who you can trust.' Sounds like J.C., doesn't it, Aubrey?"

"Sure does," replies Aubrey.

"In July, that's when I met my life long women friends. I never knew who I would be with, but I liked the way my karma turned out. Way back when I first started having auctions, a woman came into my store; her name was Anastasia Hudgins. Anastasia was a short woman who probably didn't weigh more than a hundred pounds, but what a bundle of energy. She had this waist length brown hair."

"You like long hair on a woman, don't you,?" commented Aubrey.

"Love it. I don't think a woman should ever cut her hair. Anyway, Anastasia had this long hair and tight ass. God, she was a knock out. She always looked like she was dressed for a party. Anastasia used to say her friends would say, 'You are a decoration in this town' and Anastasia surely was. Anastasia decorated my store and things sold like hot cakes, that female touch, you know, Aubrey. She always had a sequin hat on and stylish shoes and an outfit to boot. I had inquired from another friend about Anastasia. I was hoping she wasn't married, but turns out she was. Just a short time, though. We made plans for an evening drink one night at the store. Sipping our wine, Anastasia and I started to share our life. She was so unhappy with her new husband, James, and I shared how Doris had ripped me apart. 'Get a life,' that's what Anastasia would say. From that point that hot July night till this day we are the best of friends. Love my Anastasia Baby, that's what I call her.

"I just wanted James to really want me. Not that I want him to need me. We went to a party the other night, and I was dressed to a T. James flaunted his Southern aristocracy around the room like he was a overseer of a Plantation. That's what mama calls him 'The Overseer'." Charming those other women, but did he tell me once how pretty I looked, hell no!"

I wanted to passionately kiss Anastasia that night. Her lips were so wet and her brown eyes sparkled. I knew she was married, but I wanted her. Men have needs and so do women I told myself.

"You are so beautiful, and you have made my store such a great success. How can I ever repay you?"

"See Frank, you always complement me. You make me feel I am a real woman. I wish I had the guts to leave the S.O.B. He tricked me out of my lake lot saying he was going to buy back Windward Hill, my childhood home. My daddy died of a heart attack on the back steps of that house when I was 16. James played me for all I was worth, and mama too. Hell, he came from a cotton mill village, never had a damn thing."

"Then came Samantha Gold, another friend for life. I met her at the same place I met Doris, the Kiwanis Club. Samantha was my age, and she had these big brown eyes that had a story to tell. The first time she came into my store we were talking and James Brown, a friend from town said, 'I think y'all like each other. I saw both of your eyes. I can tell.' Samantha had brown shoulder-length hair. I would tell her she looked like a film star in the 30's. She had this deep Betty Davis voice, real sexy. I never knew that Samantha was Jewish until much later, after she left Eatonton. One time I asked her, and she said, looking up with those big brown eyes, 'Frank, these small towns in Georgia, being a Jew, I guess I am still afraid.' I thank God she didn't tell anyone in Eatonton, or LaSurre or Hugh Bixby would have persecuted her.

"Samantha was part little kid, part grown woman. When she would laugh she looked like a little girl. Samantha had never married. Oh, don't get me wrong. She wasn't another Doris. Samantha had the usual relationships, men had used her for money, sex, typical male barbarism. She traveled all over the world, a lot of neat adventures. Samantha was an artist, Aubrey. Her theme was from the darkness to the light. A neat concept, I thought. Matter of fact, you know that watercolor of a boat in Leacy's and my bedroom. That's an original Samantha Gold work of art. That picture has been on a lot of trips with me, both mentally and physically. I consider that picture my prize possession.

"Samantha came to Eatonton on a grant from the National Endowment for the Arts. She couldn't get anyone in that stupid town to help her. Eatonton folks like to talk a good game, but when it came down to actually doing something — forget it. I helped round up art objects for the school. Samantha had planned a project, a massive block of concrete with little pieces of junk the kids rounded up. Through Helen's B&B, we sponsored an open house to introduce Samantha to the community. That was a great success, even Doris came, naturally opening every private door in the house.

"Samantha and I would take evening walks and philosophize on all subjects. Sometimes she would put her arm around my waist, and tell me everything will be okay. I opened up more and more to Samantha.

I felt she was a time traveler like myself. She shared with me probably the most profound concept of life I have ever known. 'Frank, in everyone's life comes a woman dressed much like the scales of justice. She is blindfolded and she carries a silver platter. On that platter is your adversity. In your case, your baby's death, divorce, and now the issue of Doris. Out of that adversity, Frank, you must look for the good the adversity has brought you. It's a gift, Frank, the gift of adversity. Sometimes you can see the good, other times it may take years. Sometimes you will never know, maybe when you die, I don't know that. All I know, Frank Moss, is you are a spiritual person, a good man. If Doris Anthony can't see that, then you are too good for her. She never could appreciate you.'

"Those words from Samantha that night, that hot humid night in late July, I never will forget. Later in the week Samantha gave me a composition notebook. In the cover it said, 'Dear Frank, May this be at least a beginning for you in your path toward resolution...I care very much about you and for you. I want & wish for you only the best in growth, love & happiness. May you find strength & peace of mind in time w/ your writing. Much love always, Samantha.' I still have that composition book. The Georgia Bureau of Investigation didn't get that during the raid.

"Through that book, Aubrey, I came to deal with a lot of adversity. Through Samantha's teachings, I gave many others a composition book just like that. I gave Anastasia one and Leacy, some folks I have known for a short while that were put in my path."

"Sounds like you should have married her, Frank. Maybe you should have become a Mormon, Frank, and married them all," laughed Aubrey.

Smiling Frank said, "I probably would have married Samantha, but I wasn't Jewish, and Samantha wanted a Jewish husband. I still love her, and she still is one of my best friends."

"How did you and Leacy come to meet?" asked Aubrey.

"For sure not the Kiwanis Club," laughed Frank. "It's funny, my Sunday School teacher from Atlanta, where Lynn and I went to church, once told me, 'Frank, one day a woman is going to come through the doors of your store and bells are going to go off and she's going to be the one. It will be a day I predict when you least expect it.' Aubrey, he was right.

"One day I was sitting at my desk doing paperwork and I looked up and here came this angel. She appeared as if she had just got off a plane from California. Suntanned, long blond hair, she swayed like the wind when she walked. 'Hello,' as we exchanged greetings. My usual sales system was to let a customer look a while, then I would start idle talk and see if they were interested in anything. I felt like a giddy kid, how to approach this woman. Leacy had brought her daughter Charlotte to the store with her. So I was thinking, probably this one is married. My heart was pounding in my chest, and the juices of fear and shyness were brewing in my stomach. 'Isn't this a nice piece' as we both rubbed our hands on an old English sideboard. 'This is great. You see,' Leacy said, 'I have just bought this house in Tucson, Arizona, and I want to take old sideboards and use them for my kitchen counters.' Wow! That's where my best friend lives.

'That's a great idea,' I said.

'Those Baker kitchens are fantastic, but they cost so much!' Leacy commented.

'They really are,' I replied.

"I couldn't take my eyes off her. The energy was unreal. Looking down, I didn't see a wedding ring, but, hell, these days who can determine marriage by a ring.

'Where are you from?' I asked.

'Tampa, Florida.'

'Isn't that something?' I said. 'I was born in Tampa, Florida. Maybe we were in the same nursery together.' We laughed. 'Not many of us real Southern folk are left.'

Leacy emphasized her Southern accent and said, 'There are a few of us left from the plantation.' God, I loved that smile, that voice.

"'I don't believe we have met. Hello, I'm Frank Moss. I am the head chief here at Uncle Remus' Attic. I extended my hand and shook her soft hand.

'My name is Leacy Ross, the pleasure is mine.' Before she left that woman spent over $1,000. 'Frank, I need to get some wardrobes, can you get any more?' asked Leacy. 'I have six children.' Let me tell you, Aubrey, my mouth dropped open. 'Did you say six children? No way,' I said, surprised.

'This is one of my daughters. This is Charlotte.' Leacy hugged her daughter. Charlotte looked at the floor like she had been embarrassed. 'Is that true, Charlotte, six of y'all?' She nodded her head yes.

'There is a great place for more English furniture in MacDonough, about an hour and a half from here. Maybe next week we can go.' I paused...'have lunch...'

'I would like that very much, Frank,' Leacy said very matter of fact. After she left, I felt mesmerized. Her scent of musk perfume permeated the air. I was so turned on by her. Recalling her face, she was so sensual.

"Looking down at the check she had given me, it said Mrs. Leacy Ross. My fantasies were shakened, another Anastasia, someone I couldn't have. It is always some barrier with women and me. With Samantha, it was the Jewish issue, Doris, God knows what, why does everything have to be so hard for me? That night as I lay in bed, I thought so much about Leacy. Something is there. The words from the day filled the night air of my room. I tossed and turned and fantasized about making love to her. Her scent still filled my nostrils.

"The next week I called, and Leacy and I went off to MacDonough in search of wardrobes. On that trip I learned about Henry, her separated husband, and his domineering control over her life and her kids. Leacy came from a wealthy family, so did Henry. 'He's trying to get control of my children and my money.' 'That money is for your kids, Leacy. Fight for it,' I told her. We blended so well. Leacy told me about this movie producer in California that she went with. 'I just can't live that lifestyle, Frank. Partying all night. I don't want my kids to grow up with that.'

"I shared with Leacy that day about Doris and the gift of adversity. We put a lifetime of pain and hurt and joy in that afternoon. One of those moments, Aubrey. It was like we both had been searching all of our lives for each other and finally found each other. There were many fun and exciting dinners and lunches during that time, but somehow I knew through my E.S.P. I guess maybe all of those moments were a prelude to a later happiness. We found each other, to help each one at that point of time, but through adversity we would be brought together.

"One morning, Leacy called and said, 'Frank, what's going on for lunch today?' 'Not a thing, Leacy, want to do something?' 'Sure, Frank, all the kids are gone off. Let me bring you lunch.' 'That would be great!' I said.

"That afternoon I closed the store early and Leacy and I went upstairs to my home for lunch. She had made a platter with strawberries and all sorts of fresh fruit, and little sandwiches, and, of course, a bottle of wine. For the strawberries she had brought powdered sugar. We sat on my bed upstairs and began feeding each other the wet fruit. I felt her tongue with my finger as I put the strawberry in her mouth. Then she responded likewise. Our mouths met, sucking on the same strawberry, then our tongues wrapped around one another and my head began to spin. The smell of her perfume and the feel of her hair, as I ran my fingers through the long silky strands, drove me to ecstasy. I unbuttoned her blouse and my tongue found its way to kiss every part of her. We sprinkled the powdered sugar on our bodies and tasted each other for the first time. As we lay there side by side holding each other, I ran my hand along the side of her face and said, 'Let's do one thing for each other.' 'What's that, Frank?' as Leacy whispered. 'Let's never hurt each other. We have been hurt so much in the past.'

"After that afternoon, Leacy and I would talk on the phone, but the problems with Henry got worse. He tried to buy the children's' love with money and the tactic of how sorry your mother is. Leacy once told me of how the S.O.B. knocked her down the steps when she was pregnant. 'I have been fortunate. I don't have to deal with the bastard anymore,' Leacy said. I thought, if he tried to lay a hand on her, he wouldn't be able to ever walk up or down any steps again. Henry was a lot older than Leacy. I think that's why she went with younger men. She dated younger men during this time I knew her, but, as she found, these young ones may have the long hair and slim physiques, but when it comes to wisdom and knowledge of what a woman needs, only a time traveler knows how to truly love. I wanted her so much during that time, but I was not going to make the same mistake of going after her too strong. Doris taught me that.

"During this time, Doris would still, for the most part, ignore me. On the 4th of July we had a big church Bar-B-Que, and I called Doris to see if she would like me to bring her a plate. 'Oh no, no.' Night after night I would see her car at her house. I would say, no date for Doris J. tonight. I dated a few women at this time, mostly from Atlanta. Every date, I would look across the dinner table with those flickering candles, and I saw Doris' face and heard her voice. I was in the sea of good and evil. Trying to live up to my granddaddy popos philosophy of, 'If someone hurts you hunt them down, look them in the eye and ask what have I done to hurt you?' Doris was so evil and Leacy was so good. The struggle just wore me out mentally. Doris would fade into my life, then out. Still she would basically ignore me at parties or meetings. I got so tired of it. The ignoring and running away from me.

"One August morning, I went to her office to see if she had done a lease for me. It was her part of the deal on that damn vase we donated for the Riverwood Auction. I had mailed her what I wanted included in the lease and wrote at the top of the letter, 'Re: business' and at the bottom 'Re: personal, When are we going to talk? You name the time and the place.'

" The door was open to her office that Friday, and I walked in. There she sat in her black dress working away.

I said, 'Doris, did you have time to do my lease?'

'No, not yet. See, I have been so busy.'

'Can you get to it in a couple of days?' I responded.

'I'll try. I can't believe you didn't make the party last night at the lake. It would have been good for your business.'

I said, 'Well, I had... let's see, what did I do last night? Oh, I had something. You need to say goodbye to Cindy at the bank. She is leaving today. I just can't believe you didn't hire her. She would have been a great asset to your business. I see you working so early and late every day. You need to be a lawyer, not a secretary.'

'I couldn't afford her,' snapped Doris.

'I would have helped you,' I said. Then I closed both doors of her office. 'Doris, when are we going to talk?'

Rapidly she responded, 'We have nothing to talk about.'

I said, 'Doris, I am so tired of being treated like a dog' on the street. You ignore me, don't come to meetings. You treat me like dog shit. Why, you don't care if I live or die.'

"She responded, 'Why, just the other day, I was telling someone what a neat person you are. What an asset to the community you are.'

'All I ever asked of you, Doris, was to go somewhere and talk. I am not trying to read anything into the situation. I love you, Doris. Don't you know that?'

"I remember her face to this day. She sat there like I was someone she never met. Coldly looking straight ahead, she said, 'You have been a great asset to this town, Frank.' Hell, a damn newspaperman could come up with a line like that. I was mad, Aubrey.

At this time, I said, 'All I have done for you, sold you furniture at my et cost, helped you, talked your name up, handed out your business cards.'

"'If you were a competitor of mine, I would have shredded up your business long ago.' I regretted saying those words, but, hell, I said them and she took them the wrong way. My last words were, 'If you can't do the lease, I will get someone else to do the job.' And I walked out. Walking up to the bank and waiting for the bank to open was James, my preacher. I looked straight into his blue eyes and wanted to tell him how much I hurt.

He said, 'Everything going all right with you, Frank?'

'Oh great, James.' Sunday I drove to church. I saw Doris' car in front of her office. Maybe she is working on that lease, I thought. I prayed for Doris that Sunday morning as I had done everyday since the backyard talk.

"Saying goodbye to all my friends and neighbors at church, I drove down the tree lined street of Madison Avenue and took the left turn to my building. There in front of my store was Doris' car. I pulled the truck around. 'Doris, wait,' I yelled out. 'Have you done my lease? Let me read it.' Before I could put the truck in gear, she placed a white envelope on the door and I yelled, 'Wait.' She got into her car and floored it. Like I was some raving maniac in the street. If she had a carriage a hundred years ago, she would have whipped up the horses.

"I got out of the truck and this letter...never have I received a letter like this in my life. I still have it. I want you to read it, Aubrey." Frank reached in his coat pocket and handed Aubrey the letter. The letter was word processed and looked like a legal brief.

"See the part where it refers to the other woman in town that I did the same thing to. That was Patrice Baites and her mama Eunice the snake deal. Remember me telling you about Eunice's little snake? That was Patrice. Patrice was about Doris' age. She owned the building where Doris had her business. Patrice was rather attractive in a slutty sort of way. She had class, don't get me wrong. Patrice got her class by laying on her back. I think Patrice would make a classy prostitute. The building she owned was built with the money she conned some old man out of. The talk I heard was Eunice sent Patrice down to work at the Eatonton Hotel, owned by Bill Stern. Eunice encouraged Patrice to be real friendly with old man Stern.

"Eunice has always been poor white trash, but she was smart and she could always smell money. She had slept with men to get what she wanted. Why not teach the 15-year old Patrice the same? Eunice had a valuable asset, a fresh young daughter that a rich old man liked. When old man Stern died, he left everything he had to Patrice. Patrice then cut a deal with J.C. to sell the hotel to the county for $400,000. Patrice slept with J.C. LaSurre to cut the deal. Can you believe that building?" Frank pointed.

"That's it, Frank?" exclaims Aubrey.

"That's it," said Frank. "Anyway, Doris goes to Patrice with the "Frank" problem, and Patrice, an old pro at conning men, told Doris of the fabricated story of April Preston and me in bed together. Patrice recommended Doris go see April at her place of business in Milledgeville. So off Doris goes. Remember the girl I told April to hire? Well, she came to me one day and told me what went on. 'April, I need your help with a person that we mutually know,' Doris says. 'Oh, who is that?' as April looked up from the counter. 'May we talk in private?' 'Sure, let's step behind these curtains,' April says.

"Passionately, Doris looked in April's eyes. The conversation went on about the "Frank Moss" problem. 'He knows some of my secrets, Doris.' April's tear-filled eyes looked at Doris' face. 'Frank is a different type of man, Doris. He is a real affectionate man, a stubborn man. You have to get right in his face and tell him what you feel. Frank is a nice man, he has a wonderful reputation in town. Dan and I want him to run for mayor. He's done a lot of good, Doris, but Frank is lonely. He needs a woman. Does he know anything of your secrets?' whispers April. Doris gently caressed the side of April's face and slowly pulled her blond hair back. April seemed startled at another woman's touch and slowly pulled back. 'He knows too much, April.' The fallout after that letter showed me who my real friends in Eatonton really were.

"April, I will pick you up here at 7:00." "Doris, I don't know.." "Get that girl who works for you to close up tonight. Frank told me about Dan beating you." April teared up and then hugged Doris.

When April arrived Doris had her housecoat on. "April, I am so glad you showed up. Forgive the way I look after dealing with this Frank Moss problem. I just wanted to put on something a little more comfortable. Come up here to the bedroom. Can I get you anything to drink?"

"I think I need a big G. D. drink." said April. "I've got some Crown that Daddy gave me for Christmas." "Great." "Come April sit up here on my bed, lets have a girl talk." April looked into Doris's black eyes. "I had a girlfriend in high school that had eyes like you, April. Those blue eyes." April took a good swallow from her drink. "Doris what has Frank told you about Dan and me?" Doris wrinkled her eyes and looked down into her glass "That he beat you. You know Frank is writing a novel about us" "A novel?" " Yes and if I know Frank Moss he's told all about dan beating you. What do you think life is going to be like for you and April, when that story gets out?"

"Doris you are a lawyer. Can't you figure out someway to stop him?" Doris ran her fingers through Aprils hair and down her cheek. "Doris kissed April and felt her nipples. "I know what you need" Doris whispered then ran her hand inside April's leg.

April didn't put up a fight but gave in freely to Doris's advances. "I want you to lay flat on your stomach April. I want to be on top of your back."

Doris brushed back Aprils long blond hair then grabbed a silk scarf from her nightstand drawer. "you will like this." Doris wrapped the scarf around Aprils neck. "Doris its too tight." April struggled , but Doris's strength was too much. April died wrapped halfway in a sheet.

I remember that night going up to Doris's house. The screen door was open and I yelled, "Doris, Doris are you home?" Doris's bedroom is to the right of the foyer, so I walked in. I looked in the bedroom and saw April Preston nude with her eyes open but she didn't say a word. Doris stood in the shadows of the far back hall also not saying a word.

The newspapers every week had a reward for information on the missing person, April Preston. The talk around town was that she finally became tired of Dan's beating and ran away. I never told a soul what I saw that night at Doris's house.

As Aubrey handed the letter back to Frank, he carefully put it back in his coat pocket. "Doris J. hurt me more than any human being on earth. That hateful letter, that cruel letter. My friend, Samantha, who read the letter, told me in the Jewish faith that letter was the same as murder. Yes, indeed, Aubrey, Doris murdered my spirit.

"I hurt so bad. I tried to find solace in my friends. Helen read the letter and front porch medicine was given. My banker friend, Mark, read the letter, and said he would pray. My attorney friends in town read the letter and several said Doris was trying to set me up, as the letter stated, she could be 'ruthless' because she knew the law. Mars Strickland, the County Attorney, who went to church with me, said go see Sheriff LaSurre.

"Frank why in the hell did you show that damn letter all over town?"

"I thought they were my friends, and could help me understand. Also I was scared like Mars Strickland said she was trying to set me up."

"Frank you white folks could sure use some common sense from black folks. You don't show nothing to nobody in a town like Eatonton. You can't even trust that's Jesus sitting next to you on that church pew, 'cause he's probably the devil. You went to see that bastard Billy LaSurre!!"

"Entering LaSurre's office was like entering a pig sty. Papers piled to the ceiling on a new desk. The Sheriff figured the county needed this monument of a building, naturally, built on LaSurre land. There he sat behind his desk. His belly lapping over his huge belt buckle. He looked like a grease mechanic. A cheap white unironed shirt with a pocket protector in his pocket with an assortment of pens and pencils, and an open package of cigarettes. His face was oily and his hair was slicked back with what looked like motor oil. His breath was foul. The stench of tobacco and eggs. His mouth drooped like his brother J.C.'s, and you could see the family resemblance.

"Stacked in piles on the floor and on top of file cabinets were flea market trinkets bestowing the attributes of being a small town sheriff. A fat ceramic pig with a star on its fat belly was on a shelf. I wondered how many gifts were given the Sheriff in order for him to protect them. I thought about what Doris had said in a committee meeting one time. 'LaSurre thinks women are good for only one thing.' I looked at him and thought what Wildman had said, 'If LaSurre wants you dead, he will find a way.'

"I prefaced handing him the letter by saying, 'I know you have had your share of women problems, Sheriff.' He grinned and said nothing. He read it and said, 'If I hear anything negative about this I will squash it.' Doris is and interesting women. Never did figure out what killed that girlfriend of hers back in Macon. Did she tell you about that Frank?" Frank nodded his head no.

"They found her girlfriend buck naked in Doris's bathroom. They claimed she was electrocuted by a hairdryer falling into the tub. " It cost Old Man Anthony a plenty to pull Doris out of that one!" I quickly left and never told anyone what I saw.

*Doris had dragged April into the backyard where the dogs had a pen. The wooden doghouse was on top of an old storm pit. Doris slid the doghouse off the door to the storm pit she threw April's limp body down into the pit. A splash of water was heard for it always leaked. Thinking quickly Doris ripped open some bags of lime which the yard-man had left and sprinkled them over April's body.*

"After I left the sherriff's office, I went home and took a bath to clean myself of his tobacco breath and stench."

**iv**

Aubrey's face became contorted with anger and his bottom lip started to quiver. "I would have killed him when I first got back into town, but not you, Frank Moss... all the shit had to happen to you."

"What are you saying, Aubrey?"

"That S.O.B. raped my mother when I was 10 years old...in your G.D. store, Frank! On your floor...Billy LaSurre ripped my mother open and even bit her nipples clean off her breasts." Aubrey poured tears and put his head between his legs, crying uncontrollably. Frank was stunned and didn't know what to say.

"When I was 10 years old, I was having a birthday party..."

"I don't give a damn, Frank, about your white world in Atlanta!" Frank looked out the window of the truck, then turned to Aubrey and put his hand on Aubrey's back.

"Both are dead now, Aubrey, your mother, she is with Jesus and the high and mighty Sheriff Billy LaSurre, he is in Hell. You can't kill him. Aubrey, he is already dead." Aubrey raised his head and unbuttoned his coat. Frank saw an army service revolver.

"Yes, Frank, one bastard LaSurre is dead and in Hell, and today the other brother, J.C. LaSurre, is going to join him. I didn't come on this trip to hear your life story, Frank. I have come on this trip to this cesspool of a town to kill J.C. LaSurre!" Aubrey finished his statement with crazed eyes.

"Put that damn gun up, Aubrey Harrison. You are not going to kill anyone! I don't give a damn if you are black or white or green, you are my friend and I am not going to stand by and watch you go to prison for the rest of your life because you killed a corpse."

"I'm going to tell you something this day, Frank Moss, and I want you never to forget it. On your 10th birthday, May 19, 1967, the day Billy LaSurre raped my mother and beat her and beat her, J.C. LaSurre threw me on Hugh Park's meat block and he cut me, Frank..."Aubrey covered his face with both of his large hands "...He cut me Frank...He castrated me, Frank...Took away my manhood..."

"My God, Aubrey!" Frank hugged Aubrey, and he felt the coarse hair of his head against his clean shaven face. A few minutes later, Aubrey composed himself. Frank said, "Why didn't you ever tell me Aubrey? That's why you never wanted to work in my store."

Aubrey looked out the window. "My wife left me because of all the pain and hatred, Frank, and today when they put that bitch, Doris Anthony, in the ground, tomorrow there will be another funeral for a hellion, J.C. LaSurre."Aubrey pulled the gun tucked in his coat pocket and firmly held it. Frank looked at him with compassion.

"J.C. LaSurre has been dead all of his life, Aubrey, like I'm telling you. You can't kill a dead man. I'll be damned if I am going to let you kill J.C. You are going to have to kill me, Aubrey." Aubrey, stunned at this statement, rested the gun in his lap. "Millie Hawkins wrote me a letter a few weeks back and she told me J.C. LaSurre is just eaten up with cancer. He lies in that bed down the street in that cheap brick ranch house he foreclosed on and screams constantly. The pain, Aubrey, you can't create such pain. Your method is too quick. Millie said he screams all day and night. The gates of Hell are opening for J.C. LaSurre. Aubrey, I am here to keep you from pushing him in before his time. I have come this day to forgive my enemies, Aubrey. If you kill J.C. LaSurre, he will finally have the victory over you. He would have won.

You see, Aubrey, J.C. turned you into the monster that he was. We're both in Eatonton, Aubrey, for the last time in our lives. Today, you and I are going to bury the dead.

"Where the hell did you get that damn gun anyway? You sure didn't pass through airport security with that thing on you."

"Wildman planted it at that old grocery store we stopped at," snapped Aubrey. "How would you like Frank to go through your whole adult life with half a dick. Aunt Lillian had to get special permission from the school so I wouldn't have to take showers after P.E. You know what the white boys said at my school "Nigger always smells bad, not enough sense to take a shower. Know what its like Frank when a woman reaches down to pet you and feels nothing but scars. Doc Wingate was a half ass Doctor, and sewed me up like a dog. Girls would laugh and tell their boyfriends at the bar that I had half a dick, and you don't think I should kill the bastard that maimed me? In the army I had to explain that I wasn't a rapist and the state didn't castrate me. My mother and I almost bled to death in your old store Uncle Remus Attic. My mama and I saw those damn B'Fox murals on your wall when we screamed for life. You know who was at the laughing tree on your birthday my mama and I. J.C. and Billy were laughing because they had sent all of the bees from hell on us. That's the last thing I remember "MR. FRANK" was that damn B'Fox mural when I passed out. The next thing I know I was at Putnam hospital and mama was in the next room. I thought they had cut mama too. I could hear her crying all night. I called, 'Mama, mama, I'll kill them if its the last thing I do, I'll kill them for you.'

"The Doctors told mama I could never have kids. I was there in the room when they told us. She burst into tears, and yelled 'God why? Why my boy?' Where was the great and almighty God my Aunt and mama prayed to. They told me Jesus loved little children, yet a devil cut me and ruined me for life. How I wish everyday J.C. and Billy killed mama and me that day. Mama died on her daddy's farm holding my hand telling me she was sorry. Sorry for what? Being born black and poor and being raped and her son castrated. I'll finish this day in my own way Frank." Aubrey put his revolver back in his coat pocket.

Frank pulled the truck over in front of the log cabin known as THE UNCLE REMUS MUSEUM. "Let's walk Aubrey." Frank rubbed his face and saw the picnic table where he and Doris first had lunch. Leaning against the concrete slab Frank looked at Aubrey.

"My God Aubrey I never knew, well, you have a gun in your coat pocket and I have a diary and a letter in mine," as Frank patted his coat pocket.

"The Royal Georgia Bureau of Investigation thought they got my letter, but the real copy was in my safety deposit box. Of course, I went on my knees every night to pray for the situation. God had become my dearest and closest friend. I would walk the sidewalks of Eatonton for answers. Looking at all the places I loved, my church, the buildings I helped repair and paint. The flowers I brought to town, the echoes of the many souls saying, 'Thanks, Frank.' I would pass Doris' house, look up the drive and wonder why everything went so wrong. Passing by her office I would sometimes catch a glimpse of her in the window sitting at her desk talking on the phone and I would think, 'How could you be so cruel to another human being?' I would blame myself for everything.

"For the first time since I came to Eatonton, I wanted to sell it all and leave. The business was going so bad then. I had let all of my sales techniques drop. The card mail outs, the calls of come see what I have new. All of it ignored. Money was so tight some days. I didn't know where the next dollar was coming from. I didn't care. I even listed Temperance Hall with a real estate company. Hoping they would just sell the damn place. One day I even applied for a job selling cars, and I got the job.

"What a crooked business! I went to work for Heritage Motors in Milledgeville, the next town over. All those old salesmen. Rocky, a tight-skinned 50-year old. He looked like a sofa with leather stretched over his face. Arrogant S.O.B. Keither who looked like an ex-con. I remember one salesman named Jim. I asked him one day, I said, 'Jim, what brought you into the car business?' He said, 'I owned a business in which I had a partner, and he had a couple of heart attacks. It was time to get out. Let me tell you, I am not here to do society any favors, just to make all the money I can.' I couldn't believe his attitude!

"The car business; I learned a lot that week. The sales manager was named Will Bull. That's a name, isn't it, Aubrey? I tell you, Will would have made a perfect devil. He had a little boyish grin, a stocky build. Always wore a long sleeve white shirt. Will had this rocking motion about him when he would talk. Rocking back and forth on the tips of his shoes. Aubrey, I think Will could sell you on all the good qualities of hell. 'Come on down, it's great. You are going to love it down here.' I can hear him now. What an experience! What a week! Never did sell a car, but I learned the car business was not for Frank Moss.

"Still questioning, 'Where would I go?' I asked myself on my evening walks. Arizona maybe, live near my best friend, Peter. What would I do for a living? Each footstep on those sidewalks, I searched for answers. A lot of my close friends read the Doris letter. I guess, Aubrey, I wanted to see if I was really as unstable as Doris painted me to be. I talked to Rev. James at the church. I said, 'James, tell me why I should stay here in Eatonton? I thought I had found sanctuary here. Why? I loved this woman so much.'

"Up to that time, I never told James who the woman was but he knew. He knew all along it was Doris. James looked me straight in the eyes. With his blue eyes, he said, 'Frank, you have been a tremendous asset to the community. Why do you want to run? You can't make a habit of running. There are probably six people in Eatonton that think I am the worst preacher in the world. I can never change their hearts to want me, but there are 6,000 other people in Eatonton who love and admire me. Only five or six people know about the Doris deal, then another 6,000, Frank, know you're the man that brought flowers and paint and regeneration to downtown with your enthusiasm.' James drew a piece of paper from his desk, 'Frank, I'm going to teach you what an old professor taught me long ago.'

"There on that paper he drew two circles. 'Frank, see those two circles. That's two people that have a conflict, but these two people will always say, no you did it, no I didn't do it, forever. Never a compromise. Draw the line between these two circles, Frank, and say I have no further business to discuss with you even if you are innocent and right. It's hard to do, Frank, but you've got to do it. Everyone is not going to like you. Life is a crock of shit, accept it.' As I looked at James, I thought, what a real man's preacher. What preacher would say shit or yell at God? No, that morning James didn't give me Bible thumbing verses, but practical living.

"His closing words were, 'Frank, you have been through so much the past three years. I look forward to the day when the sun shines on your life and the day that brings you to this office to say. James, I want you to perform a marriage ceremony for me.'

"Everyone that read that letter came to the same conclusion. It was not Frank Moss that needed help, but Doris. Along the advice trail, I learned who I could trust and who I couldn't. Doris' attorney friend, Alice, who later I learned was Eunice, the snake's, lawyer, what a pair, gave me the cold shoulder in her office one day. 'Yes, Frank,' she said. 'Doris has confided to me the situation. I don't wish to discuss it or know any more details about it.' Now, Aubrey, this is a woman that sat next to me in church and prayed along side of me. Lawyers, what a breed! Cold hearted and desensitized to human kind.

"A couple of months after the hateful letter, my life in Eatonton became so unhappy. I resigned from the Kiwanis Club because I couldn't bear to look across the dinner table at someone who hated me so much. While sipping my glass of ice tea, I'd look across that table straight into Doris' eyes and wonder how could anyone be so cruel. All I ever did was to love her. I'd always greet Doris when she would enter the room. She shunned me without saying a word. People, after the meeting, would ask, 'What's wrong with you and Doris?' People in Eatonton could sense things. I got so tired of it all. I wasn't myself at the club. I didn't joke or laugh. I was caught up in so much grief. I felt I'd lost the most precious thing I ever had.

"Finally, one afternoon, I went to see James. James had been elected president of the club. I went to see him in the church office. I said, 'James, I have come to resign my membership from the club.' James swayed back in his chair and threw his head back as if he'd been hit with a huge boulder. 'No, Frank, don't do it.' I relayed the story of how I couldn't enjoy myself anymore having someone who hated me so much. James said, 'I knew that when her name came up for nomination as Secretary Treasurer, problems would arise. When I talked with her she told me, 'You know Frank and I have had problems, but Frank took the friendship the wrong way. There was nothing there, James." I tell you, Aubrey, that statement hurt like a thousand spear thrusts into my heart. Nothing there! It just killed me. James pleaded, 'Please, Frank, reconsider. We were hoping you would be an officer of the club. You have done so much for the community.' Well, I stood firm and resigned.

I told James to tell the others I resigned because of personal reasons.

"Every Thursday when the Club met down the street, I saw all my friends walk down the sidewalk. I'd see Doris, her silky hair glistening in the sun. I missed all of them so much. I felt I was a child not chosen for a ball game, so left out. When they all came from the Chinese restaurant, I saw them on the sidewalk, going to their cars on business. Doris would walk back to her office. She looked in every direction at store windows, but never my way. Yes, I resigned, resigned from a lot of things that year. Arlene, who ran the Chamber of Commerce, said to me one day that I needed to choose between Doris or the Chamber. I chose Doris. Maybe I just wallow in the pain these days.

"October came and the nights became cool, and I knew my story telling event in Atlanta was soon to premiere. A tour of Confederate Ghosts at St. Mt. Park. I'd told stories there for five years. Old 'True' Southern tales. I loved it. Dressing in a frock coat and vest with watch chain, I felt I was back in a period of time to which I belonged. I began also that month to write my book about the characters of Eatonton. John Pinkston had lent me gratis the use of his old projectionist booth in his theater for a writing spot. The small room had concrete walls and smelled of projector oil. Every morning at 5:00 am, I would walk down the sidewalk in front of my store to the 'Show,' as John would call it, to write. I wrote from 5:00 am till 8:00 am Monday through Friday. I poured my heart out on my recollections of my love for Doris and my feelings for Eatonton as a land of Karma and destiny. The watercolor of the boat that Samantha painted was beside my legal pad. So too the sound track from my favorite movie - Forgotten in Time.

"My mind those days were filled with thoughts of my novel, and the ever increasing sickness of my Daddy. Daddy was getting worse in Atlanta, and I dreaded the thought of going to see him. The last visit to the hospital, he begged me to take him to the homecoming at the Methodist Church in Meriweather County. All my ancestors had gone to that church for 100 years. Mike and I got approval from the doctor for Daddy to travel. So, one Sunday, I picked him up from the home health care center. Daddy's feet were swollen like balloons and he had a grayish tinge about him. Many times in that truck I thought he was going to die. We had a good talk during the trip, seemed he wanted to stop at all the relatives' homes and close friends to say one last goodbye.

"At the church, I rolled Daddy to the front of the church in his wheelchair, and everyone that had sent him cards of get well were so happy to see him. The last song of the service was 'Stand Up For Jesus.' Daddy looked at me with weak eyes and said, 'Frank, help me stand up.' I steadied him by his belt, and he stood up for Jesus one last time."

"Sure you want to tell this, Frank?"

"I want you to know it all, Aubrey. Tell your grandchildren my story, and I will tell mine your story. I took Daddy back to the health center and as they rolled him in the doorway, I felt in my heart that was the last time I would see him. That night I got back home and started scribbling some notes and concepts for the eulogy for Daddy's funeral.

"The next morning, I went down to Pat's florist and got a white bow because I knew the end was coming. Every day I waited for a phone call. One Saturday, I got the call from the Doctor.

"Frank I have tried to reach your brothers, but I have had no luck. Your Dad is increasingly getting worse. Seems everything we can do for him counteracts another problem. We need to know what you feel about life support."

Silence fell on my end of the phone.

"Daddy wouldn't want it."

"Frank if we don't do life support pretty soon your Dad will expire."

"No life support," I said.

I hung the phone up and thought about when Lynn and I made the decision of no life support for our baby. I thought about Mama lying on the hospital table with her blue eyes bulging out of her sockets as a respirator pumped air into her lungs. Rising her chest up and down like some carnival freak, I never wanted to die that way. The high and mighty Miss Jo. All those high powered pills and drinking finally caught up with her at the age of 53. She suffered a massive stroke. I was there with Daddy as we talked to a nurse about turning off life support and how to donate her eyes and organs. I knew I should of felt sad with my mother's passing, but somehow I felt relieved that my brothers and I wouldn't hear any more drunken tirades. We never would have to cover our heads to drown out my mothers cuss words. I thought how before I was 40 years old both of my parents are gone.

"My Daddy had put up with so much shit from my mother, but he really loved her. I had the best Daddy ever lived, and I want to be that to Leacy's kids.

"My store was filled with Saturday customers, and with all of my might I said, "I must close early today because of a family emergency." When the last customer left I placed the white bow on the front of my door. The drive to Atlanta had lasted only a half hour when the Doctor called me on the phone and told me Daddy was dead.

"James preached Daddy's funeral and the eulogy I had written was read in front of 100 friends and relatives. I wondered many times did I do the right thing about the life support."

"Frank one time we were training in the middle east and a friend of mine Mark stepped on a mine. He was right beside me when the damn thing blew up. I remember holding him blood squirting like a fountain. "Aubrey don't let them hook me up to machines. How bad is it?"

"Your going to make it Mark, hang in there man."

In a slurred voice Mark said, "My grandma they hooked her up with machines, she lived 5 years that way. The bed sores ate her ass up man. I don't want to die that way Aubrey. How bad is it?"

"I looked and tore his shirt to see how it was. His whole guts looked like sausage. Then his eyes got wide and he died. I have seen men hooked up to machines, you made the right choice."

"As November approached, I became more interested in Doris' family for more stories for the book, and I just wanted to know why Doris hated me so much. One morning I saw Doris' Aunt Martha struggling with a car load of groceries in front of her house.

'May I give you a hand with those groceries, Ms. Martha?'

'If you want to,' Ms. Martha said firmly. Martha looked like what I would imagine Doris to look like in her '80's. She was small and had buck teeth and fine white hair. She wore a pair of tennis shoes and a rather modern looking outfit for an old person.

"Helping her with the groceries up the stairs she turned and said, 'Doris has spoken about you before.' I didn't know if that was in a good light or bad so I inquired. "I hope she told you all the good things?'

'She has spoken very highly of you.' Inside, the house was furnished with functional furniture, cheap chairs and very inexpensive bric-a-brac.

In one corner I noticed a hall tree, and I ran my hand across it and said, 'Oh, Ms. Martha, I like this piece.'

'It was from my father's family.' Now, let me see, your father was Franklin Anthony?'

With hatred in her eyes, she said, 'That was him.'

'Could you tell me anything about him?'

As I inquired, Martha paused like I had intruded on a family secret, and said, 'He was a lawyer, like Doris. He was a judge also.'

'Did he handle any really interesting cases that you remember?'

'No,' Martha quickly answered. 'Do you want to see the rest of the house?'

'Sure,' I replied.

"The house smelled of new paint. Martha explained how her brother had died and left some insurance money. What was so strange was on every conceivable shelf or cheap bookcase were photos of her family. Martha had volumes of picture albums and picture frames everywhere. The pictures were of children and other members of her family. Every photo I saw with Doris in the picture looked as if Doris was somehow etched in. Like she didn't belong. Always the same expression, a surprised look. She blended with no other family member in the photos.

"Martha showed me photo after photo of her father and Doris' daddy, Ken, when he had hair, as Martha put it. Somehow the old maid began to feel comfortable with me. She seemed so lonely and longed for company.

'Why, Ms. Martha, I can't believe you never married.'

'Never needed a man. I can fix anything a man can. I can climb up on the roof or fix the car. Why do I need a man to boss me around? My mother was my best friend,' as Martha raised her head in a dignified pose. 'Never needed a man, that's what I tell Doris. Don't let folks kid you about being an old maid. Who wants a man to put up with?'

"Somehow with that revelation I began to understand Doris a lot more. Folks in town used to tell me that Martha kept her mother's grave like a golf course. Manicured with scissors. Martha also would visit her mother's grave almost every morning and talk to mama.

"Inquiring around about Doris' grandfather, a lady in town told me, in the '30's Franklin ran off with a floozie named Jewel Bailey. Jewel seemed to be in every bed in Eatonton. Old Franklin fell for her and left his wife and five kids. Apparently the disgrace was so bad that Martha and her mother locked themselves in the house and became recluses. Mr. Durand, who owned the clothing store in town, said, 'Yes, I knew Franklin Anthony. He loved the women.'

"It was interesting to learn that Franklin got Don Hudson's daddy off a murder charge. Old man Hudson stabbed a lawyer to death with a screw driver over some land dispute. Don Hudson is the big rich man in town who owns the lumber yard. I went to the city cemetery and Franklin was buried all by himself next to another old maid sister, Julia Anthony.

"Doris came from some weird birds like her uncle, Ham Anthony. Ham would walk the sidewalk every morning. He dressed always in a business suit and fresh haircut. He looked as if he paced the deck of his former ship in the Pacific.

"I had just about gotten all the information I could on Doris' family. One day I went to her old law firm and, unlike the G.B.I.'s claim, I did not represent myself as a lawyer. I went there representing myself as Frank Moss writing a book with Doris being a character in the book. I met one fat ass lawyer there named Joe Sampson. It was like pulling teeth to get anything out of that bastard. He said Doris left on good terms.

"I really wanted to see Keith Barrow, Doris' real buddy. I suspected for a while he was the married man she couldn't have. Oh, Doris would have liked that. Destroy another man's family so she could have the country club lifestyle. On my way out I got to talking to the receptionist that had been there for years. 'Yes, I knew Doris,' as she looked like she wanted to tell me more, but couldn't because of listening ears. 'Maybe we can have lunch sometime," she said, and we exchanged business cards.

"In November, I was at the Eatonton newspaper office to pay my bill. For some reason, it was jam-packed with folks. I noticed Doris in the next office with her back turned, talking to Jerry Knight, the editor. Doris had on this below-the-knees red dress. She spun her head around like an owl. She looked at me with such hatred, such animosity. I think if she had her gun with her she would have shot and killed me on the spot. She gave me this stare down then threw her head back and stormed out of the office. I stood next to the door and said, 'Good morning,

Doris.' She didn't even look at me as she passed through the door and ran down the street.

"About an hour later, Jerry Knight, the editor, came to my store and asked, 'Frank, what's the problem between you and Doris?' 'We've a bad relationship, Jerry, ' I replied. 'I was wondering. She asked me if there was another exit from the building, other than the front door where you stood.' When Jerry said that, I thought of what Mars Strickland had said to me, 'She is trying to set you up.'

"I started to see strange things toward the end of November. Late one afternoon I was sitting at my desk, and I looked up and an old black man with his hands clasped against the front glass looked in at me with a grin. He laughed when he saw that I noticed him. He laughed like he knew what was going to happen to me. Aubrey, he was like one of those faces from the past. He was dressed in ragged clothes, like the brick mason, Wildman. He scared me. In a moment he disappeared. I got up to look down the street, but he was gone.

"In the late afternoon before sundown I saw Doris walking across the street near the courthouse. She walked to and fro like the devil in search of a new soul to claim. She turned and looked back. She studied me, watched me. I could see her long dress blowing in the wind. She wasn't a kind spirit, rather evil. Doris was like a poison wine. I had drunk a little of her. Thank God I didn't drink all of her, or I would be dead. The energy, the hold she had on me was incredible. Almost like being under some sort of spell. She was a ghost that haunted both my past and present. Just like Sylvia, the ghost of Panola Hall. She had come back to walk the earth again.

"I started making plans for the new year. I was determined to put Doris behind me and get rolling again. I visited Tennessee and got a great concept of opening a sandwich shop, combined with antiques. So I started to put my financial program together. I talked with Mark at the bank, and he agreed to lend me the money. That's when we met, Aubrey. Remember that crazy woman in Madison. We had to go pick up her furniture because of bad checks.

"Yeah, I remember," said Aubrey smiling. "My brother was sick and Mama told you to call me."

"I'm glad we met. Why did you return to Georgia, especially this part of the state?"

"Only because Mama was so sick," Aubrey reluctantly said. "Fate works out doesn't it, Frank? I wouldn't give anything for the life I have with you and Leacy."

"Why, thanks for the compliment. Are you sorry we didn't get to make sandwiches, Aubrey?"

"I think it's safer to make them in your kitchen than this damn place, Frank."

"I agree," said Frank. "When December rolled around, I was finally getting my bearings straight. As I had done for a long time, I wrote all of those people end-of-the-year cards and letters. A teacher taught me that. At the end of the year write all of those that you must thank for what they did for you during the year, and all those that hurt you. So, I did it in my usual matter. I wrote Anastasia and Samantha and Helen, and a final letter to Doris J. In that letter I told her how much she meant to me in the beginning and how cruel she had become to me recently. I told her I hoped when she was an old woman and at death's door she would recall all the cruelty and pain she inflicted on a man that loved her. I sealed all those letters and, as my tradition goes, dated them all December 27th.

"One Saturday afternoon, Doris' mother came in the store with one of Doris' aunts. In a typical Ms. Jeanette fashion with her head held high, Jeanette zoomed into the store and headed for the back. Eve, Steve and I were laughing at the front desk and telling stories. Ms. Jeanette, boy, was she a good-looking facade with no depth.

"Doris always told me the things Ms. Jeanette did for the church. I had such contempt for this high and mighty church worker. What a monster I thought. What did you do to Doris when she was growing up? Did you never pick her up or hug her? Doris was taught, no doubt, by this witch, as a young girl to hide her feelings. Men only want one thing from you. Never show your love or affection. Ms. Jeanette, as I looked at her, was so cold, so calculating. A block of ice, cool on the surface, but dripped and ran an ugly stream to the side for no one to see.

"When she left the store, still without a word, she looked back at me as though I was a low class fabric not suitable for her fine daughter. I guess it takes a monster to have a monster. I had an outside sale going on that day and a few of Doris crude family members were outside milling around the assortment of tools, etc. 'If I can help y'all with anything, just let me know.'

'We will,' said one of Doris' cousins. I knew who the acne-scarred guy was. 'We will,' said one of Doris' cousins. I knew who the acne-scarred guy was.

'You're Doris' cousin?' I asked.

'That's me,' he snapped back.

'Well, she must be kin to everyone in town.'

'We got a lot of people. You got to watch out for your family. If someone tries to hurt one of my family members, I guess I would have to beat his ass!' He looked up defiantly, his face contorted. I said laughing, 'That's a good policy.'

"Doris and April had become big friends. They'd started a town civic group to undo Chamber of Commerce projects. I'd look out the window and see them in Doris' car, laughing. On Wednesday I'd see Doris go on her usual journey to Macon. Merchants in town had planned 'Eatonton at Night' to bring folks to town for holiday shopping and good eats in front of the stores. I was to tell Christmas stories out front of my store every Thursday. All the merchants in town, at my request, mounted gold stars on poles to display as a sign we are on tour. Eatonton was becoming so festive.

Frank pulls out his black diary and looks at a date, Dec. 1, '94, notes from law firm secretary.

"On Wednesday, around noon, I saw Doris' car head toward Macon.

V

In a richly paneled office with overstuffed furniture, Doris walked in. "Is Keith in?"

"Let me see, Doris. There was a man asking about you a while back. Said he was writing a book about you. I didn't know you had become so famous."

Doris frowned. "You were going to see if Keith was in his office?"

He said, "Come on back." Doris entered Keith Barrow's office and closed the door, turning the lock.

"Hello, Keith. Can we be private for a while?"

"Sure, Doris. What's on your mind?"

Miss Jo burst out laughing. "Frankie got embarrassed and turned red as a beet when Patricia Stone kissed him."

"Miss Jo, you have two fine looking boys." Carrie puts her hands on her hips.

"I have a problem in Eatonton." Doris looked straight at Keith. "There is a man, named Frank Moss, who is writing a book. He is going to tell about us, Keith." Keith looked at his paper strewn desk, confused.

"He came by here asking questions about you," Keith said, frowning, looking up.

"We have to do something, Keith. Frank is a driven man. He usually gets what he wants,' Doris said.

"What kind of reputation does he have in town?"

"Impeccable, Keith. People love him. They want him to run for mayor of Eatonton." Doris got up and went behind Keith's chair, leaning over in his face, lightly kissing his cheek. "Help me, Keith," whispered Doris.

"I know someone who's a real bastard. He is a real fabricator, used to work for Sheriff LaSurre. His name is Bixby, G.B.I."

"I don't want Frank hurt, Keith."

"I'll pass it on," said Keith.

"Is this afternoon still good for our rendezvous?" asked Doris.

"Yeah," Keith reluctantly said.

"Meet you at the Inn."

**vi**

*Journal Entry Dec. 2, 1994*

*"Late one evening, I was ready to close the store. I saw Doris and a strange man with a ballcap on, sitting at the traffic light in Doris' car. Doris kept pointing with her hands to my building. Like, this is where he lives. I thought perhaps she had found a new victim for her spider's web."*

**vii**

As the reflection of the Christmas lights shown on the car's windshield and the glass windows of the stores, Doris and April sat in Doris' car.

I was in front of my store on the step, telling Christmas stories to a group of children and their parents, "And that's how Santa Claus and Baby Jesus came to know each other. Y'all have a very Merry Christmas." An echo of clapping hands and caroling down the street was heard.

# PART THREE

"Frank I am going to see an old girlfriend be back later."

"Aubrey Harrison don't you kill LaSurre, I'll be damned if I see you go to the electric chair. Remember you have a boy that loves you." Aubrey walked away without a word.

Frank pulls out his Diary.

"On December 7th, Pearl Harbor Day, I had supper with two of my dearest friends, Tom and Kathy Coleman. Tom told stories with me at the Tour of Confederate Ghosts."

"We laughed and ate wonderful jumbalaja Kathy prepared. What a great evening! The drive home was filled with holiday thoughts. I thought about tomorrow. Leacy and I were to spend the entire day together. I had missed Leacy so much—just to hug her and kiss her, what a gush of feelings. When I entered the city limits of Eatonton, I drove slowly past Doris' house. I did that as if I was checking on her—just to see if she was all right. Thinking about what I had found out, she was having an affair with Keith Barrow, a married man. Doris' mystery for me was solved. Why she hated me so much.

"The next morning I awoke refreshed and ready to start the day. Exercising as usual, I thought about all the special details for my day with Leacy. O.K. I have the wine, two glasses. Oh, I have got to get a flower. About 9:00 a.m. I went to Pat's Florist to get a single fugi mum.

'Pat, you know these fugi mums always bring me good luck.'

'Are you sure you don't want paper around this?' said Pat.

'No, just one of those little water things on the end is all I need.' I planned also to put flowers in the church for the anniversary of our baby's death.

'Are we set for the flowers in the church on Sunday?'

'Yes, Frank.'

'Susan Green called about color. She wanted to coordinate the flowers with the Christmas decorations,' Frank replied. 'I told Susan it was fine as long as I had some pretty flowers. Pat, wasn't last Thursday a great success for the merchant open house?' asked Frank.

'Sure was, Frank.'

'It did a lot of good for my business,' said Frank.

Pat said, 'Frank, you sure have done a lot to improve this town.'

'Thank you Pat.'

"A little before 10:00 a.m., Bobby Dure, the plumber, was checking on the heater, and Fred Anderson was working on some wiring for upstairs. I got a phone call from a man asking what the store hours were.

'Normally I am open Monday thru Saturday, 10 a.m. to 5:30 p.m., but I will be closed today. I will be glad to set an appointment up.'

'That's all right,' said the caller. Somehow, I felt uneasy about the call.

"A few minutes after 10 a.m., my descent into Hell began. Entering the front door of the store was Ralph Riley, Chief of Police of Eatonton, Earl Coons, the City cop and a fat ass cop that I recognized from the Sheriff's office and a little S.O.B. that I have grown to hate with a passion, Hugh Bixby, G.B.I. All I could think of was delaying the devil his due.

'Bobby, before you go,' said Frank.

Bobby said, 'Looks like you didn't pay your traffic ticket, Frank.'

'Bobby, give me a price on the plumbing.'

Bixby interrupts and says, 'Mr. Moss.'

'Let me finish with this man, then I will be with you. Bobby, I need a price on a hand sink here.'

'About $500-$600.'

'Thanks, I will be in touch.' Bobby eases out of the door in amazement. 'Now, how can I help you?'

"Bixby looks right at me and says, 'Mr. Moss, you are under arrest for stalking Doris J. Anthony. Here is the search warrant for these premises. ' Bixby's face, how could I ever forget that bastard's face? He looked like Joseph Goebbels—one of Hitler's henchman. A medium height man with cold brown eyes. Bixby had a hatred of all mankind. He was a smug, lying bastard, who just followed orders. He had a cheap blue suit on, his trademark, and a small pin on his lapel. He had this matter of fact attitude about him, real pompous and cocky. He had teeth that looked filed down and false. A small protruding belly that looked like it was starting to lap over his cheap discount store belt. Bixby was about Doris' age. I wondered how many innocent souls went to their death because of Bixby. He had an aura of evil around him. I could see the face of Bixby at the foot of Jesus' cross. Bixby's what you would imagine the elixir of death to look like. 'You have the right to remain silent. Do you know your rights? The blood left from my face, and I became cold.

"I stared at that bastard's face wondering with all of my prayers how had this evil crept into my life. I said, 'I loved Doris Anthony.'

'Sit down in the God dammed chair, Moss!' Bixby yelled.

'This is my building. How dare you!' I said.

Bixby looked me in the eye with his dead eyes and said, 'Not any more, Moss. This is my building. Now sit down in the G.D. chair.' Bixby pulled back his coat and put his hand on his gun to show me he meant what he said. I knew I had the pistol I bought from Beth Roberts in my desk drawer, but I was too afraid to make a play for the gun. I knew then and there, if I had made a play for the gun, Bixby would have shot me in the head. So I sat silent. It was if a force said sit there and take it, keep your mouth shut.

"As I sat in the chair, I saw Chief Ralph Riley, a fat buffoon of a cop, going through all of my files and papers. I looked at that fat bastard. Belly lapping over his belt several times, the low life, what a joke. The only job the idiot could get was this cop job in Eatonton. I thought about the drug strip down from my store. At the Kiwanis Club meeting I asked the guest speaker, Riley, 'Why don't you clean up the drug deals on Jones Street?' Then I thought, that's probably Riley's retirement fund. Riley's eyelids half covered his eyes so all you saw were slits like a snake. The cop known as Coons was there. Coons was an old man that used to walk with me on occasion, and his daughter worked at the drug store with Millie Hawkins.

"Riley picked up a joke book someone had given me during a play, and started to read it. Matter of fact, he read it through all of the raid. Riley was grinning and chuckling, his fat jowls jiggled with each page. They went through everything, as I sat there refusing to speak. All I wanted to do was capture the faces of those bastards.

'He's got a gun in the desk drawer. It's an old one,' shouted Rick Mays, another fat ass cop from the Sheriff's department. 'Looks like a .32, no bullets.' Then Mays put my gun back in the drawer.

'Ok. Moss, you've been writing a book. Where is it?' Bixby shouted.

'I said, and I say to you again, I demand to call my attorney! I have rights under the Constitution of the United States of America.' It was as if I was talking to the wind.

"Further papers were gathered, and Bixby sat at another table and recorded all that he stole. The Germans were excellent record keepers too.

'Where did this come from, Moss?' Bixby snapped back.

'I refuse to answer any questions until I have legal counsel.'

'I told you, Moss, you are not calling anyone. Now sit down in that damn chair.' Riley got my keys and locked the front door. I thought of what my mother used to tell me, that the policeman is your friend. He will help you in time of need. How wrong you were, Mom. The cop is made to frame you and fabricate evidence against you and harm you. I wondered if my fate would be the same under Bixby's stick.

"Calls came in on the answering machine. 'Frank, your fax is in.' Praying Leacy wouldn't show up, a call came through. 'Hey, Frank, it's Leacy. Justin is sick and I'm going to have to cancel today. Maybe we can do something tonight, if he's better. Call me and let me know. Just don't give up on me.' I thought, just don't give up on me, Leacy.

'Where did you get this?' The questions continued to break my silence, but I was determined they were not going to break me, this Barney Fife of a police force. Bixby opened the letter I had written to Anastasia and the final letter to Doris. Group photos of the Chamber meetings and Kiwanis Club functions were seized. Anything that had an image of Doris on it or any reference in writing that spoke of Doris was seized. Another cop banged on the door and said, 'I have got another letter he sent Martha Anthony.' The letter was one I had sent her requesting more information for my book.

"Bixby opened bills and business correspondence, and I sat there and said to myself... 'this is America?' They ripped my store apart throwing antiques on the floor.

'Your house, that's upstairs, right, Moss? Give us the key,' Bixby demanded.

I said, 'Do you have a search warrant?' and Bixby produced a search warrant, but no house number for my home.

'This does not include my home,' I said. Bixby didn't like the challenge.

'We will fix that!' Then off he goes down the street to get still another paper.

"Guess who signed my search warrant? Joyce Stevenson, the magistrate in town. She was big buddies with Doris and Stevenson knew me .. sat next to me in Church! Fifteen minutes later, the S.O.B. Bixby came back, and shoved a paper in my face. 'Happy now, Moss?'

"Upstairs, the entourage went. They ransacked my bedroom, pouring Christmas presents on the floor from shopping bags. Riley touched each item. Mays went through copies of old Playboy magazines, naturally examining each page for clues. Bixby raised the backs of oil paintings and looked behind each one. I doubted if the uneducated Bixby even knew what an oil painting was. He stuck his hand under my mattress and said, 'Ever been in the military, Moss? Never seen a bed made so neat.' I said nothing.

"'Oh, we need to examine your billfold,' said Bixby, and he made me stand. He removed it with the precision of a pick pocket. He took business cards with Doris' law firm name on them. Cards that I had given out trying to help her build her practice. 'You a member of the Law Enforcement Association?' Bixby looked up with one of his stupid grins. I said nothing.

"Going through my chest of drawers, Bixby began reading legal pads that were the manuscript for my book.

'This must be your book...is this all of it, Moss?' I said nothing. 'You know, I have been in three books so far,' as Bixby leans back with great confidence as if he thought he could lighten me up.

Again I said, 'I demand to call my attorney.' Bixby knew at this point his little trick didn't work. I think Bixby was trying hard to trick me with his smooth little ways, but, you see, I wasn't the poor white he and his cronies were used to baiting. This made Bixby uneasy and jumpy. Notes from Daddy's funeral were seized, but not the final work.

"Bixby read through the gift of adversity book Samantha had given me. Thank God Samantha taught me to write everything in code...a good Jewish trick, I thought, to fool the enemy. Bixby didn't take to that. Riley stood near my bed and pulled out another drawer and exclaimed like he was the hero of the day. 'Look, look, he has another picture of Doris.' Then he held up a large 15 x 16 photo of a woman. I couldn't stay quiet any longer with such stupidity in my home. 'That's a picture of Scarlet O'Hara from 'Gone with the Wind'.' Riley quickly put the photo down, as all the rest of the henchmen looked on, laughing at the stupid fat fool. 'Well,' Riley says, 'it looked like her...' Throughout the upstairs search, Coons, the cop who used to walk with me, gazed on with his arms crossed. Coons and Riley, after roaming the vast expanse of my home said, 'Nothing back there but old papers and furniture. He's fixing the place up. Guess Frank's not going to be fixing anymore.' Riley laughed and his jello belly jiggled. These men were like vultures flying overhead, ever now and then swooping down to the ground for a kill.

"They took photo after photo of everything. Magazines that Doris had given me that still had her address label on the back. 'It's a federal offense to steal someone's mail, Moss,' Bixby said as if to scare me. I sat quietly on my sofa wishing to smash all of their evil skulls. The clicking of the camera and rustle of papers were the only sounds heard, and my mantle clock ticking.

"'I think we have enough,' Bixby said, 'Let's go downstairs. Moss, since you refuse to talk to us, we are going to take you to the Sheriff's Department and arrest you for stalking Doris J. Anthony with the intent to do bodily harm to her.'

I told Bixby, 'I'm no criminal unless it's criminal to love Doris J. Anthony. I have no criminal record.'

'You do now, Moss,' Bixby gloated.

'Again, I ask to call my attorney,' I said.

'Again, Mr. Moss, I say no!' as Bixby pushes me on the shoulder. 'Take him to the Sheriff's department and book him,' Bixby orders. In a stupid fashion, Riley asks whose car is he going to ride in? 'If he rides with me,' Bixby says, 'I'm going to handcuff him.'

"Riley looks at me and says, 'Lock up the store, Frank.' He reached for his handcuffs. 'What do you think I am going to do, Ralph, run down the street?' Riley laughed, 'Guess not. Earl, take Frank with you.' It was, I guess after 1:00 p.m., and Coons put me in the back of the cop car unhandcuffed. The smell of mildewed carpet and cigarettes filled the air of the car. I looked back as Coons made the illegal left turn in front of my store.

"I glanced back and saw the name of my store on the sign shingle. 'Uncle Remus' Attic,' and I saw John Pinkston standing on the sidewalk looking puzzled. Sitting silently, I wondered if I would ever see my family again or be able to call my attorney. Or would I land up in the bottom of some well or on a piece of LaSurre land? Thoughts of what Mars Strickland had said, 'Doris is trying to set you up,' thoughts of the August letter, 'I can be ruthless!' What attorney to call. I thought - who do I know I can trust. Phil Fougerty. He is probably the best in town, and he is from Atlanta.

"The drive was short and we pulled into the LaSurre Sheriff's temple. Coons spoke into a speaker near one of the garage entrances and slowly the garage door came up. When I had picked up men to work for the town, I went through the same procedure. I thought about how LaSurre cheated the men, especially black men, out of a minimum wage to fill his pockets. Some of those men would never work off their trumped up D.U.I. charge. Slave labor. That's what it amounted to. Slaves to work the roads of Putnam County and LaSurre properties. Why am I here? Why, God, is this happening to me?

"Coons pulled into the garage and the metal garage doors slowly came down like the last curtain on the final performance. Through the iron clad doors we entered the booking room. A buzzing sound was heard, and the smell was like the hospital where Lynn's and my baby died. When the iron doors slowly shut, it was if a grave vault was being closed. 'Empty your pockets, Mr. Moss,' said Goff, one of the cops there. Coons went into the fingerprint room and fingerprinted me like I was a drug dealer on the strip. I was so scared, but I showed no fear to them. I was not belligerent to any of them. 'By the way, Frank, did you ever see your arrest warrant,' asked Coons. 'No,' I replied. I read it briefly before Coons snatched it up as to taunt me. It said I was being arrested with the charge of stalking Doris J. Anthony with the intent to do bodily harm to her. Thinking as I read the trumped up charges, I thought, what a joke. Coons directed me to stand in front of the camera, then told me to sit and wait in the next room.

"Everything was real quiet. I was the only one in the room. All I heard was the vault door opening and closing. The cops had taken my watch, so I had no clue as to what time it was. The cop named Goff came over to me and said, 'We have a few more medical questions for you.' Then he asked if I was allergic to anything. '

No, I am in perfect health,' I said.

'By the way, what have they got you here for?'

'They claim stalking a woman in town,' I said.

'Hell, that ain't nothing, boy. You see, my ex-wife, I went over to her house one night with a baseball bat. I was going to put some hurt on that woman. Hell, they charged me with stalking, but I was out in 24 hours.' Goff reared back and said, 'Glad the cops came when they did. No telling what I might have done.' As I looked into Goff's weatherbeaten red face, I thought, 'My God, and this man is employed by the Sheriff's Department?' Goff said, 'Mr. Moss, I am going to put you back here in the holding cell, till we figure what to do with you. We have got some real rough ones coming in. You'll be safer there.' My throat closed up at the thought of what lay behind the last vault door.

"Goff put me in a cell that was no larger than a broom closet. Very utilitarian in function. A bunk bed with a plastic-covered mattress, a stainless steel toilet, and sink were the only fixtures in the cell. The walls were painted a bright pink paint over porous cement block walls. I sat on the bed with my hands folded like a child in grade school. I prayed to God to get me out of this hell.

"All of a sudden I heard all of these sirens going off. It was like an air-raid drill in school. The sound deafened to my ears. The vibrations pierced my skull and head like a knife had been thrust through my head. I prayed, 'God, don't let me die in this pit of hell. Please, God, hear me.' I didn't know what was going on. It was as you would imagine the end of the world coming. The screech of the sirens got louder and louder for what seemed eternity. I thought how perfect for Bixby to come murder me resisting arrest. Then the steel door of my cage opened, and a prisoner was brought in. He had an orange uniform on. As soon as he entered, he looked back at Goff, and Goff slammed the door shut. I didn't know at this point if this were to be my assassin.

"The unnamed prisoner cupped his hands and looked out the tiny porthole of a window on the door. He kept his hands inside his pants as if he was playing with his genitals. The sirens got louder and louder, and I didn't know how much more I could endure. The sirens didn't seem to bother this prisoner, probably a hardened criminal. The prisoner then turned for the first time and looked at me. 'They set the jail on fire,' he said. I thought, please don't let me die like this.

"All I could think of was smoke filling the tiny cell and myself and the prisoner climbing on top of each other. Then LaSurre would dump my body down some well.

"When the wail of the sirens receded, the unnamed prisoner sat down on the lower bunk with me, his hands still inside his pants.

'What you in here for?' '

'They claim I was stalking a woman.'

The prisoner said, 'They got me for burning and tearing up churches.' I looked at the prisoner and didn't say a word. He looked like he was probably 19 or 20 years old, and he spoke with an almost cajun accent or Southern Louisiana drawl. He was thin and had dark eyes and sandy colored hair. He was very street wise, but not a punk. Somehow he reminded me of a young gangster from the 20's.

"I heard all of this scuffing in the hallway, and yelling, 'I am going to beat your ass if you don't get in here!' 'G.D., let me out!' It was as if someone, or some animal, was screaming. The echoes bounced against the masonry walls and pierced my skull. A huge door was heard closing and I heard another prisoner banging on the cell door. 'Let me out!' The prisoner in my cell said, 'Those dudes are crazy. They got a 99-year sentence. We all escaped the other day.' Then I looked at this kid's face and I remembered, he's one of the ones I saw on T.V. 'LaSurre said nobody could escape from his jail. Proved his ass wrong!' gloated the kid. LaSurre probably set the escape up, so he could hunt them down for sport and kill them. Perfect alibi. 'They escaped and we shot them.' I could hear the pig. All I could think of is how a good education could have helped this kid. Why is he here?

"Thinking about my own mortality, I wondered if LaSurre would frame me. I thought he was my friend. His words echoed in my mind. 'Frank, if I hear anything negative, I will squash it.' Maybe I was the negative, and LaSurre was going to squash me like a bug on the floor. I could hear LaSurre saying, 'I know Jeanette J., Doris' mother.' I thought about what Doris said of LaSurre. 'He thinks women are only good for one thing.' If the mighty LaSurre really knew what people thought of him, he would screw anything that had a hole. I remembered his grimy appearance and tattooed arms, a cross between a Marine and a grease mechanic. I thought about all the newspaper articles done on LaSurre. How he was drunk with a female cop, and they wrecked the cop car. I had rights! I deserved a call to an attorney. I thought about how that night I was to tell Christmas stories in front of my store. I thought about Leacy. A thousand things ran through my head. Time was meaningless. I had no clue if it were tomorrow or just an hour had passed.

"It seemed forever. Then the door opened and Goff said, 'Come with me.' A fear and great anxiousness raced in my brain. Upon entering the hallway, my God, all around me on the floor was urine and spoiled food and burned mattresses. Goff opened the steel door to the ante-room where I once was and said, 'Sit here,' and he pointed to a plastic chair. It seemed only a few minutes and Goff came back and sat down by me. 'Moss, here are your things.' In a little plastic bag was my wallet and keys. 'We took your cash. There is a check in the bag for what you had.' Sure, I thought. You probably stole most of it, like when Bixby raided my cash register this morning. When you are about to enter hell, your few personal belongings are put in a small plastic bag. When you die, it's a full body plastic bag.

'Does this mean I can go? Has someone bailed me out?' Goff sat there with no emotion on his face.

"Then another brown shirted black cop came up from the back room. 'Mr. Moss, are you ready?'

'Yes, where are you taking me? Are you going to take me home?'

'I am taking you to Central State Hospital for an evaluation.' I couldn't speak. My God, I thought, that's the hospital for the insane!

My jaw quivering, 'I demand to call an attorney.'

'Later, Mr. Moss. Now don't give me any problems.' The blood rushed from my face, and I sat there cold and still. See, cops in the nineties don't kill and maim you. They just plead you're crazy, and if you are not after a few days in the hell of the insane, their point was correct.

"'God, do you hear me?' I kept saying over and over.

'I am not crazy. What will they do to me?'

'I handcuff all prisoners, it's my personal policy,' the cop said. For the first time in my life I was handcuffed with the jaws of steel tightly around my wrists. Under the metal detector I passed as if through a gateway to hell. The main steel door clicked, and I was in the garage area again. The cop put me in the back of the car, and we drove off.

"Familiar fields, which I drove past many times to see Anastasia, passed on my window side. Everything was so brown and lifeless. I saw a billboard advertising my store, 'Antiques and Good Junk.' I thought about Doris, how in a million years could you devise a plan such as this one? What I have done is open Doris' Pandora's box. All the men that ever rejected her, all those that didn't love her I was to blame. I am a decent human being, I kept saying to myself over and over. My mind raced again with thoughts of the perfect day I had planned with Leacy. How this could be a turning point in our lives. I thought about the flower I had bought her, laying on my desk as the vultures swarmed and picked at my belongings. What would people in town think about me? Would my business ever be the same?

"The sun started to go down, and I thought of the many folks that would gather at my store and see no lights tonight, only my truck sitting abandoned in the parking lot. 'Is Frank dead?' I could hear the voices. My friend, Lynnette, was to come hear my stories, what would she think? All the unfinished business of the day. 'Why didn't Frank call me back?' I could hear Leacy say. 'He always calls. Where is Frank?..."

I spoke not a word to the cop until I saw a convenience store and said, 'May we stop here and let me try and call an attorney? Look, I will cause you no problems. I am a business man, not a criminal,' I said.

'All right,' said the cop.

'Hey, could you take these handcuffs off so I can call?'

The cop gave me the stare down and said, 'Don't you even think about running off.' I nodded and said O.K.

"'Hello, may I speak with Mars Strickland?'

'I am sorry. Mars is at a bank meeting.'

'Please, it is an emergency. Can you call him? This is Frank Moss. Is his wife, Kay, there?'

'No, she is gone.'

'Please, I have to talk to him.'

The secretary said, 'I told you I have got to go home. Look, Frank, Mars won't get the message until the morning.'

'Please tell him to call the Sheriff's department in the morning. I need help,' I pleaded as the cop looked on. 'I don't have the time to...' Then the secretary hung the up phone. It was if she was briefed on what to say, as if Strickland was part of the set up. He was the County Attorney. God, this man and his wife are supposed to be my friends.

"'We have to go, Frank,' the cop said.

'Just let me try one more attorney.' It was so late in the evening and with all of the Christmas Festivities in town, it would be near impossible to reach anyone. I called Phil Fougerty's office and home and left messages. The cop put the handcuffs back on and put me back in the car. I felt so abandoned, so defeated. Doris had a perfect plan and it was working beautifully because she was a lawyer and she knew the law.

"All day long these bastard cops have denied me access to a phone. As we pulled into the Central State Hospital facility, I could not begin to imagine what lay behind those doors. Keep calm, collected. You are tough, Frank! I said that over and over in my mind. The cop pulled up in front of a large multi-storied brick building and we entered the glass doors. Hospitals, I thought. I hate the smell of them. They all smell of the same pine cleaner and alcohol. Daddy died in a hospital, so did my baby. Anyone I knew that went into a hospital never came out.

"We entered a hallway, and it reeked of antiseptic and floor polish. Plastic chairs were lined up against the wall and the cop told me to sit. 'You are going to see the doctor,' as the cop said patronizingly, like to a child. I felt I was in a waiting room with my mother when I was 10 years old. Again, as I had all day, I waited and waited. I noticed a clock on the wall. It was nearing 8:00 p.m. and I had not eaten all day. I was not hungry, though. My stomach was tight. My God, I thought, where has the day gone? 'Mr. Moss, Dr. Burns will see you now.'

"Dr. Burns was a man in his late '50's. Bald-headed with thick glasses, he looked overworked and aggravated.

'Any physical problems, Mr. Moss? Moss, that is your name, isn't it?' he said sharply.

'Yes, and I am in perfect health. I had a complete physical in May of 1994, and yes, Moss, is my last name.'

Immediately Burns strapped a blood pressure wrap around my arm. 'Uh, high blood pressure.'

'I have never had high blood pressure...but in light of today's events...,' I said as Burns scribbled down on a chart. He had to get real close to the paper to see.

'I am going to prescribe a high blood pressure medicine for you and some Valium for you to sleep.' Burns never looked up from his chart.

'I have never taken any pills in my life, and I am not starting now,' I fired back at Burns.

"Burns looked up from his writing and said, 'Oh, you are a bi-polar personality' and wrote on his chart. 'Do you hear voices, Mr. Moss?'

'No,' I said.

'Do you see illusions, Mr. Moss?'

'No. Look, Dr. Burns, I have been asking for an attorney all day. My constitutional rights have been violated all day long. No, I don't go around pretending to be a rich man. No, I don't have illusions of grandeur. I am a creative person, I write, I act, I am a storyteller as a hobby. I have entertained thousands of people and children with my talents.'

'Mr. Moss, it is obvious to me that you have a bi-polar personality dysfunction, and you are very suspicious of me because you won't let me give you any Valium or a sedative to sleep. Let me tell you, if we determine you need medication, we will give it to you, because I am the doctor. If in any way you become belligerent to anyone in this facility, I will recommend medication if we have to hold you down and force medication.'

"I thought, Shit! I should only have said yes or no. Damn, why did I tell him I was creative. Damn!

'Mr. Moss, I have before me a signed order from a judge to put you on a suicide watch. From here, Mr. Moss, we are going to take you to the Binion Building for observation. Let me warn you there are a lot of psychotic people there.' I said to myself, it never ends. God, why is this happening to me? 'Go sit in the hall, Mr. Moss.' About an hour later, 'There is a call for you, Mr. Moss.'

"My heart almost leaped from my chest. Maybe someone is coming for me, someone has posted bail for me. 'Frank, this is Phil.'

'Thank God. Phil, where are you? Get me out of here!'

'Frank, I am in Colorado. I won't be home until Tuesday.'

'But, Phil, this is Thursday. You just don't know what this place is like. They are going to send me to some place called the Binion Building. Phil, there are psychotics there! You have got to fly home or call someone. Just get me out of here! How can Doris do this to me?'

"'Frank, calm down,' Phil said. 'Frank, by law they can keep you for observation for 72 hours. Remember the state cutbacks, 72 hours for the state means they work only three days. So we won't know anything until... at least Wednesday. The state's work days are Mondays and Wednesdays. Frank, cooperate with these people. Keep your mouth shut. Don't go into anything with them.'

'But, Phil, how can Doris do this?'

'Apparently Bixby from the G.B.I. is involved. Doris is a lawyer and she knows the law. Frank, I will be back Tuesday. You can make it until then.'

"How can I survive until Tuesday? I thought in the U.S.A. all citizens had rights. You had a right to a bond hearing. Hell, a scum bag drug dealer had more rights than I had been dealt this day. 'Mr. Moss, it is time to go.'

**ii**

*Journal Entry Dec. 9*

"Down the same hallways illuminated by florescent fixtures we walked. The black security guard put me in the back CSH car, and we drove to what they called the Binion Building. It sat up on a rise, a lifeless brick structure with no windows and razor wire strung all along the top of the building. Later, I would learn this was where all the extremely violent people were housed. The rapists, murderers, and truly insane from all over the state.

'Just keep to yourself,' said the security guard. 'You will be out of here in no time. It seems you don't belong here. You don't seem crazy to me.' I kept silent for fear this was another trap.

Then I said, 'Well, thanks, at least someone thinks I am not crazy.'

'A lot of these folk like to start fights, just come up and hit you for no apparent reason. Just keep to yourself, and cooperate. You will be fine.'

"We entered the front lobby of the Binion building. It was an unattractive small room with institution lime green walls. It reminded me of elementary school in the '60's. Seated at the reception desk was an older man with slicked-back hair. Overweight, he could hardly get up from his chair. He looked like he could have been a former patient. 'Process him.'

" I was taken into the adjoining room where two black guards frisked me and told me to hand over my personal items in the plastic bag. The guards were not menacing in any way, but one knows that a live frog won't jump out of a pot when the heat is turned up slowly. The guards were dressed in casual clothes and were generally friendly. They warned me again of the unprovoked attacks and to cooperate with the guards for fear of forced medication. 'Keep to yourself, and you will be fine.' 'Let's see what you have in your wallet. Oh, look here, Joe, this man is an American Express man, a big shot, he didn't leave home without it.' Both guards laughed; I was not amused in any way. 'Look at these credit cards. What do you do for a living?'

"'I owned a business until this morning.'

'Joe, we got our first business man.' After being humiliated by the black guards, one of the guards was writing on an inventory list the description of my personal effects. 'Now, how do you spell American Express? We need to lock these cards up, Joe.' Then the guards took me upstairs into another room. They told me to strip, and my clothes and I were searched. 'White men do have big ones, Joe.' I was further embarrassed. 'Ok, put your clothes back on, Mr. Moss. I will show you the day room, Mr. Moss, that's where all the patients stay.'

"I entered the day room and all about me were men. Most looked to be 19 or 20 years old. A few older men were there, but not many. I quickly chose a seat and followed the advice of my mentors of the day. One man kept pacing the floor, back and forth. He must have walked back and forth a thousand times that night. His head was facing the ground, and he mumbled to himself. The T.V. was blaring out some nonsense sitcom show. More guards were at a plywood counter desk. Everything in the room looked like it was out of the '60's, a testament to the great state of Georgia mental health care system.

"Trying to place the setting in more pleasant surroundings, I imagined the day room to be the rec. room at UGA, the student center where students were laughing and playing pool. Then I looked up and saw a man with a shaved head. His entire head was covered in stitches. Mark Newberry, as I began to learn their names from roll call. Newberry's was a face from the 7th grade, but for sure he was 19 or 20. Newberry looked like the kind of kid that always got beat up in elementary school. Not because he was a bully; rather he just appeared like he asked for it. I tried to keep my eye contact to a minimum for fear of an attack.

"Across the room I saw a man that looked to be my age. Later I learned his name was Brooks. Brooks looked like T.V. joker Thomas Powell. But Brooks was far from being a joke. I felt so sorry for him. He shook all over like someone going into a seizure. From my lay opinion, Brooks needed to be hospitalized in a regular hospital. Sliding as he walked, he was bent over in excruciating pain.

"It was nearing 10:00 p.m. I looked at my watch and thought it had been a long day. I thanked God Daddy didn't live to see me in a place like this. Looking around the day room, men were slouched over tables and sofas and chairs. It was as though they had been slaughtered; perhaps they had been. 'Bed time, gentlemen,' the guards yelled. I was assigned to a room near the front of the hall. Guards were posted out front of my open room. I guess so they could see if I would try to kill myself or them. The room looked like my dorm room in college. There were two beds on either side of me. My roommates were quite notorious, I later learned. One man that slept next to me killed his girlfriend and baby. The other bed was occupied by a man in a straight jacket. This man moaned and groaned all night. 'It's hurting, it's hurting.' Then sobbing, he would drift off to sleep.

"I thought, laying there on my pillowless bed, Doris, do you know what you have done to me? Sure, I can hear you hide the facts and say, 'Oh, Frank, it wasn't me. It was Bixby, it was the State of Georgia that arrested you and sent you to the state insane asylum.' The mattress on the bed was probably one-inch thick and you could feel the springs under it. They allowed a single sheet for cover. With the sheet pulled over my mouth for fear the guards would see me talking to myself, 'Oh God, please deliver me from this hell.' I kept all of my clothes on in hopes that during the night someone might rescue me.

"As I lay flat on my back with my eyes open, the man in the opposite bed began talking to me.

'Have you seen any ghosts?'

'No,' I said.

'They are here in this room...the shadows, do you see them?'

'No,' I repeated.

The man rambled on, 'How long you been here?'

'Just got here,' I said. 'Oh, I have been here four weeks.' God, I thought, a week here, but not four. Please don't let me suffer that long. The man finally drifted off to sleep.

"The entire sleeping quarters were divided with partition walls that did not go to the ceiling. So, all through the night, I heard screams of 'help me, help me,' followed by sobbing. I heard moans and groans all night. If you ever wanted to know what hell is, like I have been there. Jail is one thing, but this?

"Outside in the hall were my the guards. All night I heard the echo of their laughter and jokes. The mumble of their voices filled the echo's of the hall. That first night I began to hate those bastards.

"These guards laughed and carried on all night. All they talked about was when they were getting paid. A deep voice came from the bed next to me. The man in the straight jacket, 'I can't sleep. This thing is hurting me. My shoulder hurts.' Then the man sat straight up in his bed and wiggled himself to the floor. Stumbling, he made his way to the hall.

'I got to go pee,' he said to the guards.

'Go to bed, Newberry. You can pee in the morning.'

'But I got to go,' he said in a childlike whimper.

'Go to bed!' the guard said, as he grabbed Newberry and slung him back on the bed. I thought, what barbarism. A straight jacket, is that the archaic device mental health people use? Surely it would be kinder to the human race to handcuff an unruly person to the bed. That first night never ended. It must have been the longest night of my life. I kept glancing at my watch all night. Time seemed to move in seconds. The room was semi-dark.

*Journal Entry Dec. 10*

"When daylight came, the guards were still sitting in the hall. 'Everybody up!' they shouted. You were allowed at this time to go to the rest room. Splashing the cool water from the sink, I looked at myself in the stainless steel mirror, just to see if I was still here. I made it day one, and now for day two. The whole scene seemed like a dream. Like some sort of movie and I was cast in this part. The rest room was crowded with shirtless men, their tattoos and other battle scars visible. Trying to ease myself, I again thought of my old dorm room and community rest room in college.

"We were all herded like cattle into the day room. Remember, I had not taken a shower nor shaved nor eaten in a long time. In the day room, like musical chairs, I quickly chose a chair and sat down. About 6:45 a call came from one of the guard. 'Pill call!' Just like mice all the men lined up in single file. It was just like elementary school, just the pupils were older. Everyone marched down the hall to a little open window where the pills were dispensed. 'Next, next.' Then it was my turn.

'My name is Frank Moss. I am not on any medication.'

'Mr. Moss, Dr. Burns has prescribed this high blood pressure pill for you.'

'I am not on medication,' I said again.

'All right, Mr. Moss. The doctor will see you later.' I felt good. I had won a small victory. Walking away, I hoped I hadn't provoked the nurse into any reprisal.

"Back in the day room, I quickly chose a seat again and waited for the next instructions. The dry heat from the furnace blew on me, and I wanted so badly to have a drink of cool water, but I would not ask anything of these people. The windows of the day room had so many bars and mesh wire on them. Only a flicker of an outside street light could be seen. I was so afraid. All the men were back from pill call, and I began to study them, looking up from my out of date magazine periodically. I felt so sorry for these men. Due to poor education, or whatever, they freely took the pills forced on them, not knowing why, not knowing their rights. Even if they are killers, they have rights under the Constitution. 'Don't take the pills,' I wanted so desperately to say. After all, how many people take the same medication, the same time.

" About thirty minutes later, 'Breakfast call.' All lined up again, some pushing and shoving started. I stayed back and waited for a safe position. I felt like a rat as we were marched through a maze of corridors. Down the stairs we went to the cafeteria. The sickly smell of cleaners mixed with oven-baked toast nauseated my hungry stomach. One by one all the men lined up at the stainless steel counter. I grabbed a tray quickly and looked for an empty table where I could sit. The food was hog slop. I had fed dogs and cats better than what was on my plate. Eating what I could quickly, I looked up and observed all of the guards had clipboards and were constantly writing. None of them ate the slop. I noticed they were studying everyone in the room as one would a rat in an experiment. I thought sitting there of a beautiful butterfly in a glass jar with the lid on right. Never would I cage any creature ever again. "Second row." We all grabbed the plastic plate of slop and took it to the dropoff window. On my way up several grabbed at any uneaten portions and I said nothing. 'Line up.' Then we all were prodded down another hall and into a vending machine snack room.

"There, lining the walls, was every conceivable vending machine. Quickly the men raced over and freely emptied their pocket for the state. Their stomachs were so bloated, clearly from junk food and poor nutrition. I sat in a chair and observed. Well, I had no money. The guards took everything I had, but I wouldn't give the state of Georgia the satisfaction of one nickel of my money. A man came up with a fat belly. '

Got any money?'

'No.'

'I got some, if you want some,' as his deranged eyes looked at me.

'No. No, thanks, I am fine,' I said and he walked away. Later I heard him over talking to another man of how he killed some family member with a shot gun.

"From there, we went down another maze and a steel door opened and a cool December breeze hit my face. It was so cold and all I had on was a short sleeve shirt, no coat. Bixby wouldn't let me take a coat with me when he arrested me. I had perfected my being invisible. I chose the first available plastic chair as far away from the others as possible. As I looked up, the sun was blurred by a gray overcast sky. Looking up, towering masonry walls soared. They must have been 200 feet high. It was a walled courtyard. To my horror, laced around the tops of the walls, were bands and bands of razor wire. My God, I am a prisoner! Fear crept in on me again. I wanted to cry out loud but I didn't. I just sat there. What other horrors does Doris have in store for me? I am so scared. What if they convict me, and I have to spend years in a place like this? I am innocent! I wanted to scream out at the top of my lungs, but I kept my mouth shut as I observed the guards writing on their clip boards.

"The other men paced the courtyard as they smoked cigarettes. The smoke choked me as I tried to breath cool air. It was so cold. I sat there, shivering, in the plastic chair. It seemed for hours. All I did was look up at the sky and the razor wire. I could see Doris tangled in the wire. Her blood dripping below on all these poor men. Her black hair and beautiful skin shredded by the sharpness of the razors. 'Line up.' Thank God we can go where it is warm, I said to myself. Same passageways, same stairs, same corridors we walked. When we arrived back at the day room, we all were searched. When my system was done, I went for the first chair. I chose a chair near the guard counter; if an attack broke out, my chances for survival would be better.

"Observing the room, a man named Bunch paced the floor back and forth. Most of the men slouched on tables, or under them, on sofas, chairs. The monotony, the boredom was almost unbearable. The guards always had the T.V. blaring as loud as it would go on some stupid show. Sometimes they had it on a music video show, blaring, beating drums. If I could hear one classical piece, one selection from Mozart or Wagner. In my mind I heard it. There were only a few out-of-date magazines to read, and I read every one of them cover to cover at least 100 times.

"Brooks, the man that was shaking uncontrollably last night, seemed to be getting worse. I wanted so much to help him, but I was afraid of what the guard would do to me. Write something on their stupid chart, and I would never go home. Thus I did nothing. The only way to keep sane, I thought, like a P.O.W., was to repeat your name. 'My name is Frank F. Moss, Jr. I was born on May 19th, 1957. My social security number is 520-78-4523.' Over and over I said that. They can take away my dignity, humiliate me, but they can't take my creative mind. They can say I am crazy, but they never can take my intelligence or imagination away.

"The nurses kept checking my blood pressure, slapping that damn wrap around my arm several times a day. 'Seems normal. Did they tell you that you had high blood pressure?' 'That's what Dr. Burns said. I told him I never had high blood pressure.'

"'Locker call,' another guard shouted. 'Lunch call.' The same routine. The guard would drug the men, feed them slop and herd them to the vending machines, just like cattle. Never once did I see anyone work with these men, counsel with them. Sure, maybe once a week they got to see a psychiatrist. Other than that, they sat and mindlessly watched T.V. or slept. Why didn't the State just exterminate them. It would have been far more humane. 'Rec room,' the call went out. Down some more corridors we entered a large rec room with a pool room and a ping pong table. Several men chose teams and started playing. Pretty soon a fight broke out near one of the pool tables, and a man got hit with a pool cue. Guards quickly raced over and squelched the unrest.

"Sitting in a chair, I heard the echoes of the men, like the sounds of children on a playground. I repeated again with closed eyes, 'My name is Frank F. Moss, Jr. I was born in Tampa, Florida on May 19, 1957. My social security number is 520-78-4523.' I recalled stories that I told children of B'Rabbit and B'Fox, and the ghost stories I told at a tour of Confederate Ghosts. The faces, the clapping of the audience, I could hear them. I thought about my brothers and I could see each feature of their faces. Daddy's, Mom's voice. I could hear them telling me to cut the grass or clean my room. I could smell my Granddaddy's sweat from working in the garden or his Old Spice after shave. He was a builder and I could, in my mind, smell the wood on his hands when we would build things together in the work shop. I could see us fishing and the feel of the fish when we pulled it up on the line., My Popo was a 32 degree Mason, and I could hear his words of wisdom. 'Frank, your word is your bond. Never give up trying.' Then I would be snapped back into realty by opening my eyes and seeing a man rocking back and forth on the floor. A man crying for his mother, 'help me, help me.' I would hear the true sounds of the hell Doris Anthony had put me in.

"The only escape I had from this hell was my time tunnel of imagination. Back into the tunnel I would think myself. I could see Leacy standing on the White Cliffs of Dover, her long blond hair blowing in the wind. I could see her face only from a distance. 'Line up!' the call went out. As I walked down the hall, I thought this hall looked like a submarine with its low ceilings and glass tube lights. The ceiling was so low I thought my head would touch it. I sat down again, my back and kidneys hurt so bad from all of the sitting. I thought I was going to snap, and, I thought, this is only day two. The day lasted forever. I must have looked at my watch 1,000 times.

"Overhearing some of the other men talk, I learned I could ask for a phone call. 'Hello, is Phil there? Hi, Jo, have you talked to Phil?'

'He's not back in town yet, Frank, but as soon as he gets in, he will be in touch.' 'Jo, you just have to get me out of here.'

'I know, Frank, just have patience.' Quickly, I hung up the phone and looking around like a shoplifter, I dialed another number. This was a no-no, but I did it anyway.

'Anastasia, this is Frank.'

'Where the hell are you?' Anastasia asked.

'Listen, Anastasia, I don't have much time to talk. Doris had me arrested on stalking charges.'

'Tell me...'

'I can't now; just call Phil Fougerty and see what you can do.'

'Frank, where are you, are you in jail?...'

I paused and said, 'They have put me in CSH.'

'Oh, my God!' Anastasia exclaimed.

'Keep calm. Don't say anything, Frank Moss. Keep that damn big mouth of yours shut. I will call Dr. Joe Duff, Bonnie's husband. You know him, he used to work there. Maybe he can help you.'

'Love you, Anastasia.'

'Love you, Frank,' Anastasia said.

'All right,' as a guard approached, 'you have been on the phone long enough! Number of who you called.' I lied and told them only Phil's number. As I looked at that guard's face, my hatred grew and grew.

"Supper call, pill call. I became so sick of their voices. Everything about them I hated. Their music, their smell, everything. The day grew into evening, and I was so glad. 'Shower call.' My first shower in two days. It was dorm style showers. The men's bodies were for the most part covered with tatoos. Naked, we each waited turns for a shower. I asked the guard if I could take out my contacts like the night before. 'Put them in this medicine cup.'

'Yes, m'amm.'

"Ten o'clock was mandatory bed time. I lay there with the same clothes I had had on since my arrest. A pair of blue jeans and a Ralph Lauren shirt. Ironically, the shirt was a red, white and blue shirt. A patriotic shirt for a country supposedly with equal rights for all. I prayed again to God with the sheet pulled over my face. All night the guard laughed and carried on like they were at a party. Their voices mixed with screams from patients all night.

*Journal Entry Dec. 11*

"Maybe I slept two hours. The lights went on for day three. 6.00 a.m. 'Pill call.' I went to one of the guards at the counter after all the men had left for pill call.

'I took my contacts out last night, may I put them in?'

'Contacts? I don't know anything about any contacts,' replied the guard in a stupid tone. 'Let me go see.' Then she got her fat ass up and was gone only a few minutes. 'Can't find them. Mr. James can't find Moss's contacts.'

'All right, when the men get back from pill call, search everyone!' My heart stopped as fear of attack grew increasingly. My silent anonymity was uncloaked. I wondered if this was a trick by the guard to see if I would get mad so they can write in their charts.

"I sat motionless in a chair when the decree went out. 'Search everyone!' Odds were, I thought, the idiot guard threw them away. 'What the hell are they looking for?' one man said angrily. 'Somebody's contacts.' Another said, 'What asshole wears contacts?' I looked straight ahead and said nothing. 'We can't find them,' one of the guards exclaimed. I thought, how stupid, you jeopardize my life for your stupid mistake.

"Things settled down after Breakfast Call. I was glad in a way I could see only blurry images. Having no contacts made the pain of seeing things clearly less raw. I went into my imaginary world again. I thought about Popo and my two brothers and about all the notes Doris had left me of 'let's go exercise walking.' I thought about how I was going to sue the hell out of Bixby and Doris, and get my just revenge. Why, every author in America would be outraged at the seizure of my book. I thought of Leacy on the White Cliffs and her last words to me, 'Just don't give up on me.' I saw Anastasia Baby's face and how mad she must be because of what the small town bastards had done to her friend Frank. I could see Samantha's face and the watercolor of the boat. I could hear Samantha's words, 'Through your strength of writing, you will find your peace and love.'

"In the walled courtyard, I would look up and see the cold grey sky outlined with razor wire, and I could see Doris toasting glasses with her friends at Christmas parties and laughing, pretending she had won a great victory. Still, I saw her blood drip down on me.

*Journal Entry Dec. 13*

"Sunday came, day four, and I thought of the flowers I had put in the church for Lynn's and my baby that had died. I could think in my imagination that Susan Green had picked out a beautiful arrangement to coordinate with the church's cantata arrangements. I remember kissing little baby Peter on his cold head and saying goodbye to him as he faded away to be with Jesus. I wished I could have seen the flowers and hear James' voice proclaim how beautiful the flowers are. 'To the glory of Frank Moss's baby that had died.'

"Of all that Doris took away from me that Sunday, to be in my church honoring my baby. She took away a precious moment in my life. God have mercy on her wretched soul. The thought of flowers were on my mind all day. If I could just touch the petals of a flower and put it up to my nose and smell its fragrance, I would sign away all that I owned just to see a flower in the desert. If I could just walk in the grass again barefooted and feel the cool green bristles against the souls of my feet. I looked out through the iron bars and saw grass. It was brown, and I said brown grass would be fine.

"Late Sunday evening, word came I had a visitor. It was Dr. Joe Duff. Anastasia, thank God, got through to someone. Joe was a clinical psychiatrist and his wife Bonnie wrote books. Bonnie is the one who introduced me to Anastasia.

'Joe, thank God!' as I shook his hand firmly. 'You are the first person I have seen in four days.'

We chatted and Joe said, 'Frank, what do you need? Can I get you anything?'

'Joe, I've had the same clothes on for four days. A clean change of clothes would be great. I think Eve has a key to the store. She can let you in to get what I need. Oh, Joe, any books to read would be great,' as my eyes beamed. 'My attorney is Phil Fougerty. If you could jot down these contact names, have Phil call them. Maybe my friends can help.' So, I gave Joe a list of names. 'Joe, I want you to know as a friend I am innocent, and I am not crazy! It's all so trumped up, Joe. Every constitutional right I thought I had has been denied me! I loved Doris Anthony. Why and how can she do this?'

Joe looked up from the table, 'Frank, let me tell you how to survive this place. I used to work here, you know. Keep to yourself. Don't talk to anyone, as badly as you want any conversation. Don't speak to anyone, with the exception if one of the patients asks you a direct question. Don't ignore them. Frank, you don't realize you are in the Binion building, the top psychotic criminals in the state are housed here. They sleep in the cot next to you. Listen,' as Joe's eyes got more intense, 'Frank, cooperate with the doctors here. I can't see how they can hold you here. I know you are not crazy, Frank. Frank, just keep that creative mouth shut, just look at it this way, look at all of the great character studies you will have for your book. Bonnie will want some for sure.'

'Yeah, the book.' I looked at the table.

"Late that night, the guard called my name and in a brown paper sack were two new pants, two new shirts, three packages of cigarettes to trade as Joe told me, new underwear and three good books. The guard said, 'Looks like you got a friend.'

'Yes, I do,' as I thought about Joe's kindness.

*Journal Entry Dec. 14*

Monday morning brought hope - five days of captivity. I repeated once again my name and social security number.

"One of the guards came over to me and introduced himself as my case worker. A tall slender black man named Charles Jordan. He was soft spoken and had meticulous manners about him. I looked at him as a new type of guard, kind of another cop there to extract information from me. I know it sounded crazy to view this whole horrible experience as the Third Reich, but that's what kept me sane. Jordan promised to see me later in the afternoon. I was overjoyed, but later I came to learn Jordan lied like the rest of the guard. That's the way they would operate. Tell you day after day you will be leaving here soon. Get your hopes up just to dash them the next hour or day to see how you would react, so they could write some medical term on your chart to make them look knowledgeable. Nurses continued to check my blood pressure. 'It seems normal, Mr. Moss,' and I would look at them and think how stupid.

"A new call rang out, 'Doctor Call.' We all lined up and marched in a single file line down the hall to a half window door.

'Mr. Moss, how do you feel today?'

'Fine with the exception of my contacts being thrown away.' The personnel looked startled as if a perfect record had been spoiled.

'I will see you later this afternoon.'

'Sure,' I said to myself, another S.O.B. lie.

"Later that Monday afternoon, Dr. Benson, another doctor, was to see me. Dr. Benson's assistant motioned, 'Come with me.' I was led down a long corridor painted a light blue. As I entered a small closet type room, a guard stepped in front of me. Dr. Benson said, 'That's policy.' Dr. Benson was a middle-aged light skinned black woman. A cheap plastic fan attached to her desk blew air on her fat face. She introduced herself as 'Dr. Benson.' I sat quietly in the chair in front of her metal desk. Mentally I was preparing for the interrogation.

'Mr. Moss, do you hear voices?'

'No.'

'Mr. Moss, do you see people whom no one else can see?'

'No.'

'Do you know why you are here?'

'For a pretrial evaluation to see if I am competent to stand trial.'

'Now, Mr. Moss, why don't you tell me what happened.'

'I had rather not discuss my case until I have conferred with legal counsel. Every due process of law has been denied me and my constitutional rights have been denied.'

'Mr. Moss, you know anything you tell me can be subpoenaed and used in court?'

'Yes, I am aware of that.'

"As we spoke, Dr. Benson spoke into a tape recorder turning it on and off at will, thus probably editing as she desired. She analyzed my personal appearance. 'White male in reasonably good health. His eyes are twitching.'

'Let me remind you, your personnel threw away my contacts and it is hard for me to see!' I firmly stated.

'Tell me about your family history, mother, father, etc. Tell me about this woman that they claim you stalked.'

"'Doris J. Anthony. I loved her,' I said boldly.

'Mr. Moss, we will be evaluating you over the next couple of days. By the way, what type of business are you in?'

'Antiques,' I said.

'I have two occupied in Japan statues I wish for you to look at. Perhaps when this matter's cleared up I can drop by your store.'

'I am a certified antique appraiser. I charge $50.00 for an appraisal, but your appraisal will be gratis. Just get me out of this place.'

Dr. Benson said, 'It shouldn't be much longer.' Thinking to myself, if I'm so damn crazy, how the hell does that bitch think I can appraise anything, much less know what occupied in Japan is.

"The balance of the day was spent with a book Joe had brought me. I held the book as close to my face as possible so I could read the print. My head ached trying to squint and read the fine print. The books Joe brought me were wonderful. One was *Good News for Modern Man*, A Collection of Short Stores, and my favorite was by Dietric Bonhoffer, the German theologian who was put in a concentration camp during the war. Dietric became my friend in this hell hole of a place called CSH. Although the Nazis murdered his kind soul in the end, his words fifty years later enabled me to make it one more day.

**iv**

"Periodically, I would look up to rest my eyes and gaze around the room. Bunch would pace the polished floor back and forth. Now he was joined by Newberry, the kid with all of the stitches. Same scene, men under tables crying for their mothers, the T.V. blaring out some music video. The guard sat at the counter and laughed and carried on about Christmas dinner and collard greens or some nonsense. My hatred grew for these bastards. I could smell them where I was seated, their stench turned my stomach. Constantly they wrote on clip boards as if they all were writing epic novels.

"Poor Brooks, he was still shaking on the sofa. I really thought he was going to die. The guard paid no attention to him. The only exception was to say amidst their laughing, 'Brooks, you still alive?' I looked around the room in disgust and thought, This is America? With life, liberty, and the pursuit of happiness? Hell, I would have had more rights in Iraq.

"I thought about this land of freedom called America. Land of justice, yeah, for people like Doris. What a farce. I thought about that bastard's face, Bixby. That S.O.B. from hell. God, I hated his guts! Maybe a shot gun blast to his ugly face, perhaps during a drug raid. I could visualize the S.O.B. out there with all of his G.B.I. friends, busting in a door, and Bixby the first to be greeted with a blast. The G.B.I., hell, why don't they call it what it really is, 'The Gestapo Bureau of Investigation.' I imagined Bixby before God with his smug voice saying, 'God, I did nothing wrong. Frank brought it all on himself.' I could see Bixby falling into the caverns of hell. With his small arms outstretched trying to grab on of the jagged rocks as he descended into the pit. Through Bixby's own ambition, how many were sent to the grave? How many innocent have suffered at his hands? How he had bragged on the three books he supposedly was in. The only book Bixby appeared in was the Book of the Dead, bound for hell.

"Focusing on more pleasant thoughts, I could see Leacy on that cliff by the sea. This time it was Ireland. We were holding hands, expounding on all we had been through, and there we were, a happy ending. I was so free, so happy holding her in my arms. The green grass beneath our feet and the blue sky, crystal clear. I could feel her hair in my fingers.

"'Supper call.' My thoughts broke. Down the blue hall we all went just like rats. I ate what I could of the hog slop. Christmas plastic tablecloths were on the tables. I thought how last year I was entertained at one of the wealthiest family homes in Eatonton. A long mahogany table with a linen tablecloth and sterling silver. I remember how Doris wasn't invited. 'First row! Second row! Line up. Moss, carry the milk.' 'Yes, sir,' I said. Maybe this is a brownie point, carrying the milk. I took the crate of milk up the stairs. I didn't feel strong because the heaviest thing I had lifted in a week was a fork. The guards took the rest of the men to the vending machines. 'If you don't have any money, then we will go!' echoed the guard's voice down the hallway.

"I was summoned to go to the courtyard with the other men. It was a cold damp air that touched your face. Still, I had no coat and I did not complain. I was becoming so sick and tired of the same routine. So tired of not being able to see.

"Through one of the second story windows where the women were held, I heard excruciating cries, 'God..God..help me.'The woman went on and on. As if someone was begging for her life. The sounds of her crying bounced off the walls of the courtyard. None of the other men seemed to care. You see I did care because I was sane.

"'Line up.' We marched to the rec. room. Pool and a ping pong match started. Again, I sat in a chair and read a book. Some of the men toppled over plastic chairs and crawled under them. One black man wrapped his arms around his legs and rocked back and forth moaning and groaning. Another man kept talking to an invisible spirit, and would start yelling at the top of his lungs and cussing the tormenting mentor of his mind. I tell you, it was hard to concentrate on my book.

"Another boy, named Hornbuckle, sat quietly in a chair next to me. Hornbuckle was tall and thin and had a pair of eyes that were close together. His eyebrows went up in a devilish point. I heard Hornbuckle would come up and hit you in the face for no apparent reason. That's where Newberry got all of his stitches. Most of the faces around the room were so childlike, yet the monsters that inhabited them were real and played for keeps. Their cries for help were, for the most part, child-like. I saw Michael Smith, one of the men, help Brooks down the hall. He helped Brooks get his medicine and carried his tray for him at chow time.

"Brooks' legs gave out on him in the hall one day, and Brooks fell to the floor with great force. Hell, you think just one of those fat ass guards would have come to see about Brooks. It was Mike Smith who helped Brooks up. I kept saying to myself, 'Why, God, must I see all of this human suffering?' That night, I prayed, and I did not lose my faith.

*Journal Entry Dec. 15*

"Tuesday morning, I awoke with a sense of hope because this is the day Phil is back in town. The same routine started. But after 'Break-fast call,' I was told I had a visitor. Thank God!

"The guard led me down to the vending machine room and there was my attorney. 'Phil, thank God you're here!' Phil was about 50 years old, with a suntanned face and dark eyes. He looked Italian with his patch of black hair on a balding head. Phil spoke very fast like a New Yorker.

'Come, let's sit.' I started immediately.

'Phil, you've got to get me out of here,' I said frantically.

'You are a pretty popular guy in my office, Frank. We have been getting calls from all over the U.S.'

'Phil...'

Phil put his hands up and said, 'Frank, now listen, these people have got to do an evaluation on you to see if you are competent to stand trial.'

'That's a bunch of shit, Phil.'

"Phil raised his hands again and looked straight in my eyes. 'Frank, anything we do to spring the system will look just like that. Just cooperate with them.'

'How much longer, Phil? You don't realize, these people....the doctors lie about seeing you...hell, Phil, be honest, how long can they continue on this charade?' Phil looked at me without blinking an eye, 'Frank, they can keep you for 45 days.' My heart stopped when I heard that. My life is over, I thought. Survive this place for 45 days?

"'Frank, don't worry. You won't be in here that long. You aren't crazy. Doris is the crazy one.'

'When can we discuss the case, Phil?'

'Frank, one thing at a time, just keep your mouth shut and cooperate.' Phil looks around the room. 'You know, Frank, this is a hell of a place to get into. I didn't think I would ever find you. Then when I told them I was your attorney. That's probably going to cost you extra.'

I looked at Phil sarcastically and said, 'I don't care, Phil. Just get me out of this pit of hell! Call my brother, Mike. Let him know. He will arrange for your retainer.' I thought as I said retainer, that's all you bastard lawyers care about. How much bigger a house or car you can buy. Shit, you don't care about your clients, just the bottom line, how much money can you pump out of them.

"When Phil left the table, my spirits were low. I thought how a scum bag drug dealer or child molester had more rights that what I had. When I returned to the day room, I was searched again. As I sat down and looked around at all of the faces in the room, I wondered how I could survive 45 days in this hell hole. A few minutes later they told me I had another visitor.

"It was my friend and minister, James Weldon. James hugged me with his big bear-like body, and we were both so proud to see each other. With his big blue eyes and deep voice in a soft tone, he looked at me and said, 'Frank, you all right?'

'Contrary to popular belief, I am not going to kill myself.' We both chuckled.

'I know that, Frank. You're the sanest man I know. You're a storyteller.' I told James of the injustices that had been done to me since December 8th, and I asked him to help a man called Brooks.

'He needs to be hospitalized. He is in bad shape.'

"'I called Doris, I wanted to know if she was all right, and I told her you were my church member and my friend and I will stand at your side.' I told James what a true friend he was, with so many that sat in that church on pews next to me, and some that were among the first to slit my throat. It was so refreshing to know James Weldon hadn't abandoned me. 'James, were the flowers beautiful in memory for my baby?'

James said, 'They were the prettiest I have ever seen.'

"'James,' I said, 'You have preached a lot of sermons on evil. Let me tell you when you see that little smile on Doris' face, that beautiful face, just know that behind that facade is a woman of total evil. Evil cloaked in beauty.' James didn't say a word; he already knew about Doris Anthony.

"We talked for a long time until a guard said it was time to go. More blood pressure checks, more locker calls and hog slop food filled the day like clock work. Jordan interrogated me some more. 'Do you hear voices, Mr. Moss? Why are you here? Do you have illusions?' Constantly testing me to see if my answers varied.

"Late in the evening another visitor call came for me. It was my brother, Mike, and his wife, Becky. Becky hugged me and Mike did, too. Mike's looked worried and concerned.

'We would have been here sooner, but we didn't know what was going on.'

'I'm sorry, I have been trying to call an attorney for days.'

'What can we do?' Mike asked.

'I need some things. First, I need glasses, the stupid idiots threw away my contacts three days ago.' I rambled on about other things. 'If you could get with Phil on the retainer. The key to my safety deposit box is in the desk drawer in the store. Eve or Fred Anderson has got a key. Deposits have to be made for the store.'

'Don't worry, we'll take care of it,' Mike said. 'We just want to get you out of this psycho place. What happened?' Mike asked. I shared with him everything. 'They said you were going to kill yourself. That's bullshit!'

'Mike, they stole all of my notes for Daddy's eulogy, and my manuscript for my book.'

'Daddy's funeral?' Mike looked surprised and said, 'There was over 100 people that heard the eulogy that you wrote. They all loved it!'

'I know, I know. I guess you can't write anything in this damn country any more with fear of the cops raiding your home.'

"Becky held my arm and patted it and said, 'It's okay.' Over and over Mike kept saying, 'If we only knew. We called your friend Helen at the B&B, and she gave us sketchy details that you were going to kill yourself and Doris.' That traitor, Helen McCannon.

"When Mike and Becky left, I thought my brother really loved me. No matter if I was the oldest, and no matter how bad the circumstances. I could always call Mike, and he would be there for me. With Mom and Daddy both gone, all I have is my two brothers. I felt I cheated him, by not calling him first. He had to find out my fate through two-faced Helen McCannon. I guess I was so embarrassed Bixby had sent me to the state crazy house.

"When I walked up those stairs to be searched again, I felt sad, never again will I not call my brother first. The guards ran their hands all over me again, and I was free to sit down again.

"Later that night, the guard called my name, and I came to the counter. Mike and Becky had gone to my house and store and gotten me some clothes and much needed glasses. Later, Mike told me they wanted to hand deliver the items to me but because curfew was in one minute, they refused to let them see me. God, to be able to see clearly again. But see what? The degradation of men? I will never forget that night as long as I live. One of the black men was stretched on the sofa next to me and, looking up at the ceiling, he said, 'You know what Christmas is, mister? It's looking up at that big black sky and seeing all of those big stars. That's Christmas, mister.' His words were so beautiful. A poet could not have put it any better. I thought about a painting I once saw of a black starry night with all these poor pathetic souls looking up. It was done by a holocaust survivor. The words of that man on that sofa were true words and the hope of Christmas. Unknowingly, that black man gave me hope to face one more day in hell.

*Journal Entry Dec. 16*

"Wednesday, December 14th, my seventh day of captivity, was Doris' 44th birthday. I awoke to the same florescence lights shining in my eyes. It's 6:00 a.m. and time to face another day in the pit of hell. Same routine. 'Breakfast call, pill call, locker call.' While sitting in the day room, I noticed that one of the men was all beaten up and hopping on one foot. Later I learned this man was lying in his bed last night and another man, the one in my room next to me that saw the ghosts, was the perpetrator. Apparently, he got up during the night and jumped on this man, bent his leg back so far, it snapped, and beat him about the face. Soon after we got back from 'Breakfast Call,' these two guys were at it again. One punched the other in the face, and they both fell on the floor, taking bloody swings at each other. The man with the broken leg yelled as the guy bent it back further. The guard ran over to break it up only after sufficient blood had been spilled, a state policy, I am sure. I sat in my chair petrified. I must have read the same paragraph in my book 20 times. My emotional state was wearing thin.

"With the constant lookout for potential attackers and the on-going interrogation, I just did not know if I would make it. I'm sure Doris would have liked my demise for her birthday present, but I was determined to live. When am I going to get out of this place? Phil, can't you do anything? Perhaps the most frightening part of that day was lunch. I was sitting at the lunch table, all alone, as was my custom, and I looked down at this hamburger. I had put mustard and ketchup on the hamburger, but I looked down and I saw a bite had been taken out. Did I take the first bite or did someone else take a bite? I was so frightened I was losing touch with reality. I pushed the disgusting hamburger out of my sight. Immediately I began to say my name, social security number, date of birth. I said it over and over and I said, 'God, let me make it.'

"That afternoon brought three visitors. James, my preacher, came first.

'Frank, how are you?'

'I'm fine, James. It's tough, though.'

'Frank, you look so thin.' 'The food is hog slop, James. I am sure your dogs and cats eat far better than me.' I shared with James the hamburger story and how it scared me. I told him about the morning fight also.

'James, if I don't get out of here... will you work to clear my name, and tell all you know about the wickedness of Doris Anthony?'

'Quit talking that way, Frank. I'm the one that would have bashed in a head, not you, Frank. You are a survivor.' James prayed with me and told me of the many people in the church that were praying for me and loved me. 'There are a lot of good people in Eatonton who care about you, Frank.'

'It's good to have friends, James.' James said another little closing prayer and hugged me. 'Have courage, Frank.'

"Phil came next. 'Frank, how are you?' 'As well as can be expected.' 'I want to tell you there's been no newspaper articles or anything on your case.'

'I am glad to hear that,' I said. 'Now, Phil, when are you going to get me out of here?'

'They should have your evaluation completed in the next couple of days. I spoke with Dr. Benson, and she wonders why you were sent here to begin with. Frank, it's the system; you have to play along with them.' '

Sure, Phil, and when you leave here you get to sleep next to your wife in safety and not worry about getting your head bashed in during the night or your leg broken!'

'Here's what they have on you. This Bixby is a real piece of work. He set a surveillance camera up in the trees and has film of you walking past Doris' house and business. Frank, the worst case is this stolen mail thing.'

'What?' I said.

'Bixby claims you stole her mail. He has magazines with Doris' address label on them.'

'Damn, Phil, Doris left those magazines at my store when she would bring me lunch.'

Phil continued, 'Also Doris claimed you stole pictures of her from her Aunt Martha Anthony's house.'

'What the hell,' I said. 'I helped the old bitch carry groceries into her house. She gave me a tour of the house. I never stole anything in my life! Why do they claim I need to be here?'

Phil looked up. 'They say they have a suicide letter, and you were going to kill yourself and Doris Anthony.'

'That's bullshit! I wrote the eulogy for my father's funeral. Bixby has dishonored the dead, damn his soul!'

"'What's our defense, Phil?'

'We will discuss that later. Here, Frank, I need you to sign this retainer form for $2,500. Thank you. Our main objective is to get you out of here as soon as possible. Now when the evaluation is complete, there will be a bond hearing. I am going to recommend you live with your brother Mike in Atlanta.'

'That's great, Phil, but how about my business?'

Phil looked up and said, 'It's probably gone, Frank.' When Phil left, I felt like I didn't know anymore than when he arrived. It sounded to me like Phil was just a spokesperson for the prosecution. He had to live in Eatonton with his wife and children. He wasn't going anywhere, but, Frank Moss, hell, he said it, Frank Moss's home and business was history.

"Later that evening, Mike and Becky came. They drove two and a half hours to come here.

'Mike, I just hope I picked the right lawyer.'

'Well, he seems sharp, like a New York lawyer, but you know, Frank, he doesn't want to shit where he eats,' Mike said.

'That's what I am worried about.'

'We told Phil that you can come live with us, Becky says. The girls miss Uncle Fry.' Mike said, 'Anything else we can do?'

'Yes, there are a few things. In my safety deposit box is the original letter that Doris sent me, along with some other evidence that can help us. Get that and take it home with you.'

'Sure, we will,' Mike said.

*Journal Entry Dec. 17*

"December 17th in the day room was filled with Bunch pacing the floor again, and one man uncontrollably rocking back and forth. Some new old man, probably in his '70s, was brought in and he was going on and on about how he was locked up because he killed his own hogs. 'She put me in here for killing my own G.D. hogs. All she wanted was my money.' Over and over I had to listen to this old man. He was a broken record. Then there was Tommy, a frog sounding black man. He kept swinging back and forth when he walked, like some sort of dance.

"I saw, like most days in that hell pit, a lot of sad things. Michael Smith entered the room in a straight jacket. He refused to take medication. He was the one that helped Brooks. You never knew when you looked up who would be in a straight jacket. I just prayed the guard would leave me alone. It seemed to be a sport with them as to who would be the next straight jacket candidate. Brooks, who lay on the sofa day after day, was finally strapped in a wheel chair, handcuffed and rolled away. That's the last I saw of him.

"I remembered Brooks in the same shower with me and he was shaking so bad. He turned to me and said, 'Partner, could you help me dry off?' and I blotted his shoulders with the thin towel. I felt so sorry for Brooks. I couldn't do anything to help him. Just pray for him. How cruel, I thought, to handcuff a man who couldn't even put food in his mouth or walk. Talk was I was going to be transferred to a quieter place. I guess the guards didn't figure me to be a security risk any more. I didn't take much hope in being transferred. They had lied so much before. I remembered what a Jewish man told me once, 'The Germans hurt us in degrees, little humiliating degrees, so when the gas chambers came, we felt nothing. This was the humane way.' After breakfast and the vending machines, we went outside to the courtyard. There, I chose a chair and looked up at the morning sky. A long-winged bird flew overhead. Then as the bird passed over, I saw the ribbon of the razor wire. I heard a woman screaming through an upstairs window. She shrieked and shrieked . I hope Doris screams one day like that when she enters the Gates of Hell. I wished that woman to be Doris. How would you like a straight jacket on, Doris J. Anthony?

"Before I was transferred to another section, I gave a pack of cigarettes to Michael Smith and said, 'Thanks for helping Brooks.' He never said a word. In 2 North building, the men seemed a little quieter, a little more subdued. One of the men I recognized was from the Binion Building. He looked just like Robert Duvall. As always, I chose a chair near the front and sat down.

"Immediately, Charles Jordan, my case worker, came over to me and said, 'The forensic team will see you later today.'

'Great.' Like I really believed him. Truly amazing, I did see the 'Forensic Team.' The name sounded to me like I had murdered someone.

"The forensic team all sat around a circle. When I entered the room, I greeted all of them by a handshake and introduction. Always on guard, I mentally prepared myself for the attack. As I scanned the room, I saw one doctor twitching his shoulders, several obese men and a couple of nurses that I had seen with clip boards in the cafeteria.

'Mr. Moss, why are you here?'

'For a pretrial evaluation, sir.'

'How have you been treated, Mr. Moss?'

'Fine sir, with the exception of the staff throwing away my contacts.'

"Everyone in the room started writing notes. They could smell a lawsuit coming. 'Can you tell us about your case, why you were arrested?'

'I was in love with a woman named Doris Anthony. For a brief time, I saw an arrest warrant. They claim I was stalking her with the intent to do bodily harm to her, and, ladies and gentleman, this is false.'

'Can you tell us what led up to the arrest?'

'No, I have not conferred with legal counsel. My due process and constitutional rights have been violated since December 8th.'

"They assaulted me with questions. I answered 'Yes' or 'No' and referred back to my constitutional rights issue.

'Mr. Moss, we can't understand why you are here.'

Notes

"Over the next couple of days, Jordan would schedule meetings with me, then cancel because the state says he must work on certain days or hours. Dr. Gibson, the head man at Central State Hospital, with his expensive suits on, would waltz into the day room as a commander would view his troops and tell me words like, 'It won't be much longer, Mr. Moss. I will do what I can to get you out.' Perhaps Gibson also could smell lawsuit coming his way, and possibly he, after his superiors at the state found out, knew it would be an end to his Armani suit buying days. Of course, every chance I would get I mentioned to Gibson I was friends with Dr. Joe Duff.

"Let me not forget the tests I was given in this grand hotel. 'Frank, do you play with dolls? Have you or do you now wet the bed? Do you hear voices? Do you see things other people don't see? Are you preoccupied with sex?' On one test, I had to look at a series of flash cards and tell Jordan what was missing from the picture. I got so sick and tired of trying to prove my innocence. My hatred toward Jordan and Gibson grew.

" I remember one night sitting in the day room and two of the nurses were talking at the guard station. All the other men were either asleep or taking showers. One of the nurses looked over at me, 'You don't say much, do you?'

I glanced up from my book. 'I am just trying to cooperate with you people.'

'What did you do before you came here?' They asked the question like they already knew the answer.

'I used to own the antique store in Eatonton.'

'Oh, I know you...you're the man who owned the Uncle Remus Attic.'

'Yes, that's the place,' I said.

'Are you going back and run it when you leave here?' the nurse asked.

'I'm probably going to sell the business.'

'Well, you will have to give me a good deal on some of those pretty antiques.' I didn't say a word, but I would burn the place to the ground before I would sell her anything.

"Later in the evening, I saw a man named Perry, a black man, go into a seizure. He dropped to the floor and started shaking and gurgling as if he were on fire. The fat ass nurses just sat on their asses and said, 'Perry, you all right?' Then, with the force of lifting a building, the nurses heaved themselves up and shuffled over to check on Perry. Again, I could do nothing to help.

*Journal Entry Dec. 18*

"On the day of December 18th, I had been a captive for 11 days. I wondered if I would see Christmas with my family. The guards had strung up some blue aluminum garland on the walls. It looked more like a mardigras festival than a Christmas celebration. A cheap artificial tree was installed by the guards void of any decoration for fear one of the patients might eat an ornament or make a weapon out of one and kill themselves or someone else. Christmas, I thought, as I looked around the room, with men drugged out of their minds. Bandages on several of the men's wrists, apparent suicide attempts. Then those with no bandages, you could see the deep unhealed scar of the last razor cut.

"I heard 'pill call' every three hours, more than the last place I was. I learned through conversation next to my chair one man was a Vietnam Vet. His name was Jim. Jim sat next to me and told me how he cussed out a Gwinnett County cop during a November argument in a neighbor's yard. Jim said he pulled an ink pen from his pocket and the cop thought it was a gun, and because of earlier treatment of Vietnam they sent him to CSH. Here you had some punk cop, and I know the Gwinnett type, I used to live there, some tin badge cop, that was a baby when Jim went to Vietnam, persecute a veteran, its disgusting.

"The 11th day passed, and the 12th day brought forth a face of evil I hadn't seen in 12 days. One of the guards came into the day room and said, 'Someone is here to see you.' I was so elated thinking Phil was in the hall and had come to get me out of this hell.

"As I entered the hall it was that bastard Bixby and another G.B.I. black cop. Bixby had on the same cheap suit with a lapel pin that looked like a Nazi party pin. He grinned and nodded his head as he delighted in my appearance and surroundings. He looked me in the eye and said, 'Mr. Moss, we are here for a sample of your blood. Here's the Court Order signed by Hines Carroll.' He waved the paper in my face as he was taunting me.

'I demand to call my attorney.'

'Moss, you're not calling anyone. Here's a court order.'

"I looked that S.O.B. right in the eye that day. His eyes were flat, dead, like the eyes of a corpse. For the first time in my life, I wanted to kill another human being. I looked over at the black G.B.I. and thought, how could you stand near this oppressive bastard? If you only knew how many of your people had suffered under Bixby's hand.

I turned and looked at the nurse and said, 'You are my witness. Bixby refused to let me call an attorney.' Two of the nurses looked at me with compassion in their eyes. Then they looked at Bixby.

"The nurses signed their names as witnesses to Bixby's barbaric act. Bixby looked at the ground like he had won a first round match. The nurse drew my blood, and Bixby grabbed the test tube and strutted down the hall with his henchman. As I looked at the back of that bastard, I thought, God is going to draw a lot more blood from you, Bixby, than you carry in that flask.

"When I went back to the day room to sit, I was boiling mad. Then fear overtook me. What does Bixby plan now...rape charges against me? Doris is capable of anything, I thought. What if I have to spend 45 days in this hell hole? The evil air that Bixby breathed blew on me in the form of fear, but I was not going to let Bixby beat me with his evil. I remembered what I read one time about General Patton's Chaplain; he once said, 'Courage is fear that said its prayers.'

"During the day we were informed that a well-meaning church group was to have a party for us in the cafeteria. That evening, with my holiday spirits at an all-time low, we all marched single file to the Christmas party. An old upright piano was in the room and a big fat man was playing Christmas tunes on a piano that probably hadn't been tuned in 50 years. When we were all assembled and seated, the fat man rose from the piano bench and said, 'We are from the Milledgeville Methodist Church, and we have brought you some Christmas cheer. We are going to sing Christmas carols and have punch and cookies.' Song books were passed out, and they looked like collector's items, probably from the '60's. We sang Silent Night with a host of out of tune voices. It Came Upon A Midnight Clear, I looked around the room and wondered if Christmas ever came to hell. All of these poor tragic men. The church folks, when I looked up at the piano, were singing their hearts out. Why were they here? Are they doing it out of a church tradition as one would pass the collection plate, or are they doing this from the goodness of their hearts? I thought of the many times Lynn and I had taken food or gifts to the poor at Christmas. Now I am on the receiving end.

"Kelly, a man that was sitting at my table, looked up from his plate of store-bought cookies and said, 'Christmas. It don't mean a damn thing to me.' I could almost look into this man's soul and feel his pain. Probably Kelly had horrible Christmases at home or maybe no Christmas at all.

With bravery I looked at him and said, 'Christmas is hope. It is the only thing that will get you out of this hell.'

Kelly snapped back 'What have I got to hope for? When I leave here I go back to prison.'

'You have got to hope,' were my final words to him. Kelly looked at me and said nothing, but through my fear I think he got the message.

"As we all drank our punch and ate our hard cookies, I thought here in this room amidst these killers and rapists and God knows what else, was Christmas for me. For so many years, Christmas was such a struggle financially and emotionally for me. So many of the people I loved died at Christmas, and now this hell near Christmas that Doris had given me. So much has been taken from me, but you know, Frank Moss has hope. Just like I saw on that stained glass window the first time in Eatonton. Faith, Hope, Love. My faith has given me hope, and through the hope, I trust love will come my way. I look at Christmas in a different light now.

"When we departed the cafeteria, we were handed a brown paper sack filled with apples, oranges and candy. I left that cafeteria with a great peace in light of the evil that Bixby had started my morning off with.

*Journal Entry Dec. 20*

"On December 20th, my 13th day of captivity, I awoke to the same routine as I had for almost two weeks. Florescent lights shone in my eyes. I got up and made my bed to the guard's specifications. I slept as I had for almost two weeks, maybe three hours a night. The guards carried on all night in the hall, laughing and telling jokes. In the bathroom, I brushed my teeth in front of the stainless steel mirror and shaved with a plastic razor that was numbered and handed to me by one of the guards. 'Shave call' was after you had peed with 20 other men, some definitely not morning people. The calls went out, 'Breakfast Call, Locker Call, Mail Call, Pill Call.' Eat the hog slop and sit in a chair for hours on hours. That was my job. The smells of CSH was getting to me. The microwaved sandwiches, popcorn, in the vending machine room made my stomach turn. The smell of the floor polish, and pine cleaner filled my nostrils and I would rub my eyes as I would read the same books over and over.

"My back hurt so much from the lack of exercise. My hair had not seen shampoo in two weeks. I had not held a bar of soap in two weeks, rather when I showered, soap was dispensed in a box like a service station wash room. I had not eaten a fresh salad in two weeks, and my insides were thick with hog slop as if I had swallowed wallpaper paste. I wanted to smell Leacy, to hold her in my arms and feel her soft flesh against my hairy chest. Just the simple things, the things everyone takes for granted, that's all I ask for at Christmas.

"While day dreaming, Dr. Gibson approached me and said, 'Frank, we are going to try and release you this afternoon.' Sure, I thought, as I looked back down at my book. After lunch I was called to the pay phone in the hall.

'Frank, this is Phil. Great news, they have set a bond hearing for 4:00 this afternoon. The sheriff will send a man to pick you up.'

'Phil, that's great! I won't have to stay in LaSurre's jail, will I?'

'If everything works out, you will be going home with Mike and Becky.'

'Thank God the nightmare is almost over!'

'Moss, come on, we are going to the courtyard.'

'Yes, sir.' Maybe I won't have to say 'yes sir' to those bastards much longer.

"Out in the courtyard, it was warm, and the sun shone brightly. A strange wisp of clouds painted the blue December sky. As my eyes drifted downward, I saw the razor wire shinning in the sun. The masonry walls seemed to close in as the shadows mixed with the echoes of the men's voices. I saw a little weed sprouting up from the crack in the asphalt. It was so beautiful. Like one of James' sermons. The men were playing basketball, and the sound of their tennis shoe souls screeched when they made a stop. With their shirts off, tattoos of skulls and strange demons decorated their bodies. Cigarettes were behind the ears of some.

"Nervously, I kept looking at my watch every few minutes. It was almost 3:00 p.m. Almost time to go. Let's see, they had better come on, because it takes 30 minutes or more to get to Eatonton from here. I wonder if they lied to me. Closing my eyes and the warm sun touched my face, I dreamed as I had done for 13 days to escape this hell. I could see Leacy waiting for me. Feeling my arm around her and the first touch of our lips. I could see Anastasia's lips as she sipped from a glass of red wine. Toasting, I heard her voice 'You beat them, Frank.' Then fear crept in on my happy thoughts of what the bond hearing would be like in a crooked town, filled with a crooked sheriff and judge, and that fabricator Bixby. What if Phil doesn't get me free on bond? LaSurre will have another chance to kill me. When I opened my eyes, I saw the razor wire, and I saw Doris laughing at me. What if she sends me to prison? Then, I remembered the words from my dear friend Samantha after she read the August letter. 'Frank, imagine in your mind a black hole in space, throw Doris in that hole and watch her get sucked away to oblivion.' I tried it, then I thought, why did Doris hate me so much? James once told me, 'Frank, there are some things in this life you don't want to know why.' Maybe that's what happened. I opened the wrong door on Doris' wretched life, and she threw all the snakes she could on me.

"It was nearly 3:45 and the sound of the bouncing of the basketball was like my heart beating. It was too late to make the 4:00 hearing, so I tried to comfort myself as best I could. Looking down like I was beaten, one of the guards summoned me to get up. I thought about Deitric Bonhoffer when he was giving his last sermon a few days before the war ended, the Nazis came for him and murdered him. I climbed the two flights of stairs. 'Moss, ...go get your stuff.'

'Yes, sir.' I went down the hall into my room. Jim, the Vietnam Vet, was arranging some clothes on his bed. Reaching under my bed I quickly put all of my belongings in the garbage bag. The brown paper sack with the fruit and candy, the church folks had given me had been untouched. I walked over to Jim. 'Jim, give this to Kelly...tell him just don't give up hope.'

"Walking down the hall back to the day room, I felt tired. I remembered what Mr. Donny, my old Eatonton Sunday School teacher, said, 'To have a great victory, you must have a great fight.' For 13 days I fought for my life. As I sat down on a bench in the day room, I thought it was like I am the last train out. I was all alone in the room with the exception of one of the guards talking to his girlfriend on the phone. It was nearing 4:00 and the guard called me up front for check out. They were arguing over what happened to my belt.

'Keep it,' I said. 'Just get me out of here.' The phone rang.

'They are here. Come with me, Mr. Moss.' With plastic garbage bag in tow, I headed down the hall and stairs to an uncertain future.

"We came to a door I recognized, and I saw the lime green walls of the main entrance. A brown-shirted Putnam County cop was sitting in a chair. 'Sit.' The cop pointed to a chair. Then, he handcuffed me so tight my hands were white and felt cold. He chained my legs like a dog. I could hardly walk and he said, 'Carry the bag,' pointing to my bag of clothes. The handcuffs were so tight I could not feel the bag I was carrying. 'Put the bag in the trunk.' Then the cop lit a cigarette. 'Get in!' Looking out the window I saw my first tree in two weeks, and the brown grass so close, I could see every blade. The windows in the cop car were rolled up, and the smoke from the cop's cigarette filled my nostrils and lungs. I thought I was going to suffocate. The cop radioed, 'We are en route.' As I sat on the seat, I stared out the window, desperately wanting to get a glimpse of every passing thing. Even a junk car or trash pile was a joy to see.

"As we drove past the farms and open fields, I thought about all of those tragic men left behind: about Brooks, if he made it, if he still was alive; about Kelly, and Michael Smith and David Hornbuckle. I remember one day Hornbuckle came up and patted me on the shoulder and said to a nurse, 'I want to be just like him.' Then I remembered the screams at night, the fights, the ones I saw, the ones I didn't see.

"We passed my yellow billboard which said 'Uncle Remus' Attic, Antiques and Good Junk,' and what would be left of my business. When we pulled into the parking lot of the Sheriff's department, I saw Doris' car. It was parked as far away from the front entrance as possible, although many parking spaces were available. Just like her to distance herself and claim she had nothing to do with the tragic tale of Frank Moss. The cop drove in the prisoner unloading area, and the garage door closed, shutting out the last light of day.

"Entering the same door I did 13 days ago, I was told to sit in a chair. A few minutes later the cop came up and took the handcuffs and chains off me. Thank God, my family doesn't have to see me chained like a dog. Phil came and sat next to me. 'Frank, we are going to have a bond hearing, and if everything works out, you will be able to go home with Mike and Becky. Now listen to me, Frank. I know you would like to kill a few of those bastards in that room, but for God's sake, keep your opinions and comments to yourself, all right?' I nodded my head in agreement. 'Bixby will probably say a lot of lies about you, and Doris will be in the room. Just sit calmly and let me handle this.' A cop came toward me, 'let's go,' and we walked into the courtroom.

"I did not look around the room to see who was there. All I knew was that my brother Mike and Becky were at my side. Then I focused on who was there. Across the table sat that bastard, Bixby, and next to him was some young guy with a balding head. Phil sat on my other side. At the end of the table was the Judge. Finally I get to see what Hines Carroll's S.O.B. face looks like.

"Carroll was an old man, probably in his '60s. He had dyed black hair and an red alcoholic face. He spoke with a slow southern drawl. I stared at him right in the eye. So this is the bastard that signed the papers to send me to hell. Carroll was a scary looking man. His eyes were black and cold. He probably has delighted, over the years, sending innocent people to their deaths. Phil once told me Carroll was big into history, how his people fought for the cause and so forth. Hell, Carroll's Civil War hero great grandfather sold out to the enemy for a few pieces of silver. At the opposite end of the table was Sheriff LaSurre. He had a sweater on and a soiled white shirt with the remains of all the food he had consumed all day.

"Tucked away in a neat little corner of the room was the queen herself, Doris J. Anthony. Distancing herself from the whole affair. Doris looked like she had aged since I saw her last. Her hair was flat and straight and not pulled back in her traditional barrette. She made no eye contact with me at all; I was invisible to her. At her side were all of her supporters; and one woman, April Preston. It was strange that none of my supporters, like Anastasia and my many other friends, were not allowed in this closed hearing. Jerry Knight, the newspaper man, sat in the back of the room. Carroll spoke.

'The next case before us is stalking. Mr. Bixby, take the stand. Mr. Bixby, did Mr. Moss stalk Miss Anthony?'

'Yes, in his place of business, we found photos, and he wrote letters to Miss Anthony. We felt Mr. Moss was suicidal, and in one of his letters he wrote he wanted to lie in the coffin next to Miss Anthony.' It was all I could do to keep myself from bashing that lying bastard's head in. I looked Bixby dead in the eye, not moving a muscle. He continued, 'Mr. Moss went to Miss Anthony's old place of employment and pretended to be a lawyer.'

'Do you wish to call a witness, Mr. Bixby?'

'Yes,' Bixby said. 'I call Miss Doris J. Anthony to the stand.'

'Miss Anthony, come forth. How has this affected you, Miss Anthony?' asked the Judge.

'I had to go home sick.' I thought about the time Doris said, 'Sometimes I can be an actress.'

"Doris squinted and twitched in the chair. Never once did she look at me. Hide, Doris, hide. That's your style, I said to myself.

'Any more questions for the witness, Mr. Fougerty?'

'No, your honor.' Phil looked down at his papers.

'Anything further, Mr. Bixby?'

'Yes, your honor. Mr. Moss apparently has a history of stalking women. I have another witness here...' Phil looked up.

'Your Honor, that has nothing to do with the bond hearing today. My client has not been officially charged. Let the state save this witness for the trial.'

'You have a point, Mr. Fougerty.' Bixby looked disgusted.

"I glanced over at April Preston and thought, what a bitch! The nights I helped you on your business, your crying about how Dan beat you. Doris and April whispered back and forth to one another like two school girls. With hands covering their faces, they would occasionally look over my way as if planning their next performance on stage.

"'Mr. Moss, you have a bond set today at $25,000. You are hereby banished from Putnam County. The only way you can enter this county is with your brother. The Eatonton City Police must be notified 24 hours before you plan to come. Your business must be completed by sundown. You are not in any way to contact Miss Anthony or any of her family or friends. Sheriff LaSurre's office must also be notified. Mr. Moss, let me remind you, if you are found in this county, you will be arrested immediately. There will be no other bond. Do you understand me?'

'Yes, Sir,' I said.

"Mike signed over his house to make bond, and I was free to leave this Nazi, Germany, place they call Eatonton. Doris and April quickly exited through a back door. When Mike, Becky and I left the Sheriff's office, I saw Doris, April and Bixby all huddled together. I am sure they were planning their next move. They looked like a bunch of vultures.

"Mike drove up to the front of my store, and I saw my truck parked. It had been in the same spot for two weeks. When I opened the door to my store, the air inside was cold and damp like a tomb. Everywhere, I felt Bixby's presence. The contents of my desk and files were everywhere. The bastards during the raid didn't care. The lone flower I had bought for Leacy had wilted, and lay on the desk, dead. My Christmas tree was in the window along with the gold star I had made for all the Christmas merchants. Upstairs, I gathered Mom's sterling silver and other valuables, like Samantha's boat picture. Bixby had ripped up my bed, and I could smell his evil stench in my home along with that greasy pig Riley.

"Mike insisted on Becky driving the station wagon and his driving my truck. Sitting on the passenger side, I rolled down the window and felt, for the first time in two weeks, fresh air blowing on my face. When we passed Doris' house, a huge commercial security light hung from the trees. It looked like a guard light from a prison. Maybe Doris was afraid of the darkness of her life. A Christmas wreath and garland hung from the porch railings. If Doris was so distraught, how did she find time to decorate with holiday cheer?

"Mike and I talked about the future on the way to Atlanta. As I looked at his kid-like face, I realized he's not only a good father, but the greatest brother one could have. I felt so grateful to have Mike as a brother.

'Good news on Daddy's truck. I think Ford Motor Credit is going to rescind the sale...so we can pay Daddy's funeral expenses off.'

'That's great, Mike.'

'Did you make Aunt Ruth and Sue's Christmas supper? Did you cover for me-why I wasn't there?'

'I told them an extreme emergency came up and you couldn't make it.'

'I guess I have a lot of explaining to do.'

'Frank, nobody in the family knows anything about your deal, so don't think you have to answer a bunch of questions.'

Thanks, Mike, that's good to know.'

"That night, we all went to a Mexican restaurant. It was so strange standing there waiting for a table. Men and women were at the bar laughing. I hadn't heard laughter in so long. Waitresses were buzzing up and down the aisles with drinks. The echoes of the customers were different than the cries for help. When a meal was served I could hear, 'Supper call.' I wondered what these people would say if I told them what my day had been like. We settled down to a table and for the first time in two weeks I had a real meal. The salsa, the chips, I tasted each flavor, every morsel I delighted in.

"That night at Mike and Becky's, I took a long hot bubble bath, and washed the filth of Eatonton off my body. I went straight to bed, and I got down on my knees and thanked God to be free from hell. The night was filled with nightmares from the hell I had gone through. I still have them. For the first time since December 8th, I slept in my brother's house on a real bed, not a dog pallet.

**iii**

*Bixby called for about a week to Doris' office with no returned phone calls. One Friday, Bixby dropped into Doris' law office unannounced. The door to Doris' office was locked, and Bixby knocked on the door. "Just a minute." Doris opened the door slowly and not very wide. Doris' hair was pinned back with a barrette and she had on a black Victorian dress with a high collar. Doris had a startled look on her face. "Why....Hugh...What are you doing here?" Doris said, looking all around.*

*"I want to talk, Doris." Bixby pushed the door open.*

*"I...just don't have the time. Hugh, maybe next week or a couple of weeks, when I am caught up." Bixby slammed the door shut and shoved Doris against a filing cabinet.*

*"I am sick and G.D. tired of your put-offs. I have done everything you wanted me to do. Frank Moss is out of your life forever, he's will be banished from Georgia, and your little secrets, thanks to my new mo-*

*tion to Judge Carroll is safe. Everything that has your name on it has been censored. Moss's book will never see the press. I had it all covered up, Doris" as Bixby moved closer to Doris' face "...including your lesbian adventures and your affair with Barrow."*

*Doris' eyes got blacker with rage. "How dare you come into my office." Bixby forced himself on Doris, groping for a kiss. He fondled her bound up breasts. Doris slapped Bixby, then Bixby, with a powerful slap, knocked Doris to the floor. Doris' mouth bled, and she looked up with tears and rage in her voice. "You will pay for that." Bixby got down on the floor, looking at the wounded animal.*

*"I want you for myself. Moss can't have you, Barrow is never going to marry you, you think he's going to give up his house on Country Club row in a divorce settlement? You are nothing but a bitch, Anthony. Maybe it's true what Moss wrote about you. We are two of a kind, Anthony, we are ruthless.... I will have you." Bixby stormed out of the room.*

*Patrice came into Doris' office as Doris was getting up off the floor., "Doris, what happened?"*

*"Oh, I did a stupid thing. I fell and hit my mouth against the desk." Wiping the blood off her mouth and straightening her hair with her hands, she felt the red mark from Bixby's hand on her face.*

*"Doris, are you sure?" Patrice asked again. "I heard all this shouting..." Patrice continued to stammer around.*

*"I am fine, Patrice," said Doris as she regained her composure. "Now, if you will excuse me, I must get back to work. I have all of these closings to do."*

*"Sure, Doris." Patrice exited the office and closed the door.*

*"Hello, Keith, this is Doris. I have got to talk to you." Doris looked out her window. Bixby was sitting in his unmarked G.B.I. car staring as Doris lowered the shade. "Keith," as Doris sobs, "Bixby just stormed in here and slapped me. I want you to do something, do something to him."*

*"Doris, this has gone far enough. One of Frank Moss's friends sent my wife an anonymous letter saying we are having an affair."*

*"What?" Doris said. "Keith, listen, I want you to fix Bixby like you did Frank. Frank has already sent tons of letters to everybody from the Governor to the U.S. Justice Department to investigate Bixby. It*

*will be easy to set Bixby up and tie him to the Lasurre corruption ring. The F.B.I. is already snooping around, and they are going to tie Bixby to LaSurre sooner or later. Why don't you push a little with your contacts?" Doris' eyes were wide open in a hypnotic state.*

*"Doris, we have got to end this. Moss was a decent guy. He has a lot of friends. Good people, Doris, from the church."*

*"I did it for us, Keith, so we could be together."*

*"Doris,"...Keith stammered.*

*"Keith, fix Bixby. We have got to get rid of him. Bixby thinks he loves me," Doris laughed.*

*"Okay. Doris, but this is the last time." Doris sat down in her chair and remembered her meeting with Hugh Bixby.*

*There was a restaurant on the lake. Seated at a table with a lake view, Doris and Bixby sat talking over a glass of wine. "Every time I drink wine, I think of the time Frank was over at my house, and he said he didn't drink beer. I told him to mix it with wine. That's how I got to like beer at all those legal parties." Doris and Bixby laughed.*

*"Moss really loved you, Doris."*

*"Oh, Frank, was a nothing." As the waitress came over to take another drink order, Doris looked up from her glass of wine in a seductive manner. In a sexy voice Doris said, "I will have a little more," as she moistened her lips and looked up and down at the slim busty waitress. "She's cute," Doris said. "So, Hugh, tell me, what's going to happen to poor old Frank?"*

*"We have got him in Central State Hospital."*

*"What?" Doris almost dropped her wine glass.*

*"Frank's been there for almost 13 days. If he's not crazy by now, then he never will be. They have got him in the Binion building. That's where all the psychotic killers are taken."*

*Doris took Bixby's hand and patted it. "Now, Hugh.... I didn't want Frank hurt."*

*"On December 21st, we are going to have a bond hearing. The judge is going to order a $25,000 bond. Somehow I doubt Moss will be able to come up with that, and I have asked for Moss to be banished from the county and Eatonton. They will put so many restrictions on him, he will go bankrupt.*

*Doris looked up. "I know Alice Meeks, the Planters Bank's attor-*

*ney. She is going to help me by calling all of Frank's loans due."*

*"Doris, I need you to be at the hearing, and we need another witness."*

*"Oh, I think we can get April Preston. She is so afraid Frank has written about her wife beater husband, she will help I am sure. How are we going to explain all of Frank's writings?" Doris asked.*

*"We can always twist Frank's words. He's crazy, remember," Bixby laughed. He smiled. Under the table rubbed his hand on Doris' leg and moved up her dress. Doris quickly removed Bixby's intruding hand.*

*"Hugh, somebody might see." Bixby withdrew his attempts and looked disgusted.*

*A few days later, Doris called Keith Barrow in Macon. "Keith, I was wondering if I could see you. Frank is up to his old tricks. He has sent the Georgia Bar Association a letter trying to call a disbarment hearing on me...Keith."*

*"Doris, it's over. Jill and I have worked out our differences. I don't want you calling anymore." Doris stared as if in a trance and hung up the phone.*

*Journal Entry Dec. 21*

"I was up early December 21st and ready to get my business life going. I called all of those people that prayed for me and helped me through it all.

'Hello, Joe, thank you for bringing me the new clothes. I'd have the same clothes on, if it weren't for you. If I could only repay you.'

'Frank, don't worry. I am glad I was there to help.'

'Hello, James, thanks so much for all of your prayers.'

'As long as you are okay, Frank.'

'Hello, Clyde Smith. Clyde, I just want to thank you for all of your prayers, and I want you to know everything is stable in my business, and I see no problem with continuing with Planters Bank.' After that call to banker Smith, I really began to know who my friends in Eatonton really were.

'Hello, Helen? This is Frank.'

'Thank God, Frank. Are you all right?'

'Yes, Helen. I'm fine. I'm safe at Mike's house in Atlanta. I wanted to thank you for all of your prayers and concerns for me.'

'Oh Frank, Brian and I love you. I can't begin to imagine what you have been through.'

'For 13 days I was in the pit of hell, thanks to the legal mind of Doris J. Anthony.'

'Now Frank, Doris has been through a lot also. She is a nice person, like you.' When I heard those words from my supposed friend, Helen McCannon, I began to doubt her as a friend. Words that Anastasia told me long ago, 'Frank, Helen is out for Helen. She is a sharp business woman, watch her, Frank.' How true, a prediction from Anastasia Hudgins came true.

"'Frank, you know how depressed you had been over your Daddy dying. Remember you said one time there just was no reason for living.' That's the very words Helen told me on her thoughts when her son died. I felt Helen was baiting me for answers and the words of my dear departed mother were ringing, 'Frank, never trust a Yankee!'

'Frank, I heard there was concern that you might have been suicidal. You were so thin, Frank, and you let your hair grow long. No matter what the circumstances, Frank, I still love you.'

'Thanks, Helen. We will be in touch.'

'Oh, before you go, Frank, what are you going to do about the store? I heard you were going to have a Going Out of Business sale?'

"I hung up that damn phone and felt I had turned three shades of red. Doris is a nice person, hell, I guess Hitler was a nice man. He loved dogs and children. Nothing to live for...you, you lying Yankee. Then I remembered how Sheriff LaSurre wanted to put a night club next to Helen's B&B. Helen raised holy hell with the zoning people. I really shouldn't hate Helen, hell, LaSurre probably forced her hand to get rid of me. Helen would do anything to save her B&B, even if it meant an antique man from Atlanta would have to be sacrificed.

"It was a few weeks later, when I was trying to get my furniture out of the store, that I found out the real reason. When I was in Greensboro, I told Helen I would meet her for lunch. Helen had called and left a bunch of messages at Mike's house. I would call and give vague information on Phil's progress.

'Oh Frank, it's so great to see you.' Helen hugged my neck.

'I have missed you, too, Helen,' I said.

'Frank, let me tell you, I saw Doris the other day. I didn't recognize her...it looked like she had lost 25 lbs.'

'Maybe she has cancer of the soul,' I said.

'Frank,' Helen smiled, 'you're such a card.'

'Helen, I want to be very blunt with you, as my mother always said, a phone is never too far away. There are several times I could have called you, but I didn't. I think someone has gotten to you...did Bixby come see you?'

Helen looked around the room and paused and said, 'Frank, Bixby and Chief Riley came to my house a few days after you were arrested. Bixby told me you were going to kill yourself and kill Doris.' Helen turned her head back and forth as if she fought tears in her eyes. She held my hand, 'Frank, you had been through so much. I knew that Doris had broken your heart. Oh, Frank, Bixby was so smooth. I had never dealt with cops before. They were so convincing. They said they even found a suicide note. Riley said in the back room of your house were B&B checks. Riley claimed you stole them.'

'Well, what did you tell them, Helen?' Helen looked down at the table.

'I told them we had stored things in your empty rooms. That you let us store for free because we were friends. Frank, Bixby asked me if you and I were having an affair, and I told him no, that we were just friends.'

'Well, I guess Bixby must've figured I was in every woman's bed in Eatonton. Helen, don't you know who one of Doris' clients is? It's Jan Ramsey. Jan would like to put you out of business so her B&B could be the only one in town. So, isn't Doris a nice person with a sweet smile? You still think Doris is a nice person, Helen?'

'No, Frank, that was a poor choice of words on my part.'

'Let me set the record straight on two bastards known as Bixby and Riley. The supposed suicide note was notes that I used in the preparation for Daddy's eulogy. You know, you have been in my home before, I keep a legal pad by my bed if I wake up in the middle of the night and have an idea. You read the final finished product! I have never wanted to kill myself. Ever! Sure, Doris broke my heart, but I wasn't going to kill her. How about April Preston? I told you how Dan beat her. You know the flake that girl is.'

'I am sorry, Frank. I wouldn't have done anything to hurt you.'

'I forgive you, Helen, but the next time you see that fat bastard, Riley, tell him never to come on your property again without a warrant!'

'Frank, I can't do that, I have to live here in Eatonton.'

"The next morning I received a phone call from my friend Bill in Florida. Bill had consigned a good deal of expensive antique furniture to me.

'Frank, I have got a problem.'

'What's that, Bill?'

'The last check you sent me from Planters bank was returned.'

'What! Bill, there's no way, there is over $4,000 in that account. The check should be good. Let me call my friend, Clyde Smith, at the bank and see what is going on. Hello, Clyde, this is Frank. A furniture consignor in Florida just called, and he said a check has been returned to him. Surely this must be a mistake. Can you check on it for me?'

'There's no reason to check. In light of today's newspaper article saying that you are banned from the county, the bank has called in all of your outstanding loans.'

'Clyde, what are you saying? I have had a perfect banking record with Planters Bank. I have run over $15,000 through that checking, never a bounced check. I have never missed one payment on my mortgage, Clyde. I thought we were friends.'

In a sharp voice, Smith said, 'There are friends and there is business. Make arrangements to pay the debt!' Smith convicted me from an Eatonton newspaper article.

"The article was written by one who I thought was a friend, Jerry Knight. But why should I think otherwise? The paper is owned by Doris' relatives. And the Planters Bank's attorney was none other than Alice Meeks, Doris' big friend. She knew me. I never could stand the cocky bitch. Clyde Smith, what a little bastard. He was a short little man with thick glasses, and he had this pip squeak voice. He looked like a military cadet with his neatly combed black hair. All he was, was a puppet for the man that owned the bank. My brother, Kevin, made the remark one time that Smith looked like the kind of kid that always got beat up in school."

"Sunday was Christmas, and it was the best Christmas I ever had, because I was free. Looking at the Christmas tree, I could hear Kelly's voice at the Christmas party. 'There is hope.' At night I went outside and looked at the Christmas stars for that black man at CSH. Christmas passed and later in the week. We called the local police, as well as the sheriff's office. It was like I was a serial killer coming to town. Fear permeated the air, and Mike and I loaded the truck quickly. We hadn't been able to load everything the last time because of time. Several well wishers came by to see me, but I did not have time to chat. Time was of the essence. Cop cars swarmed in front of my store as if to frighten me. Millie Hawkins came up from the drug store and hugged me.

'Frank, you have done so much for this town. Not all the people here are bad.'

"Mike and I packed the truck with as much merchandise as possible. When we pulled out of town, Coons sat in his patrol car along with a couple other sheriff cars and followed us to the city limits. I thought of the many times I just couldn't wait to get back to Eatonton. Now, I hated the place with a passion. The next couple of visits to Eatonton were filled with increased harassment as I tried desperately to honor my commitments by getting sold furniture to its owners. Leacy had over $1,000 worth of furniture I needed to get to her. I remember her saying, 'Frank, just don't worry about the stuff. It's too dangerous for you to be in that town.'

"My brother Kevin went with me a few days after New Year's. Up the street walked Smith from a restaurant foreclosure. He motioned for Coons, the cop, to come with him. Kevin and I were loading furniture from my home.

'Frank, that's bank property. Coons, take note. You are my witness. He is loading bank merchandise.' His voice was screeching, as it got louder.

'This is my family furniture, Smith. My grandfather made this bed. This is not your damn bank property!' Coons told Smith, they have been loading furniture from the store.

'Frank, you are to cease loading from the store until we take inventory!'

'I am going to get sold items to customers, Smith, because, unlike you, my word is my bond!' I was nearing the front of the truck, and I was about to jump down on Coons and Smith and beat the shit out of both of them. Kevin grabbed my arm.

'Frank, it's not worth it. They are bastards. Let's load up and get out of this hell place.'

"Kevin and I went on Sunday in hopes that we would not be harassed. Dream on, if you think otherwise, in a town where cops have nothing better to do than harass the down trodden. I hired Larry Williams, to help me that day. We were loading out the back dock like a bunch of thieves when it started again. Coons rolled up in his cop car.

'Hey, Boy, what you putting in that truck? That's bank merchandise.' Coons went on, Larry saying nothing, just doing his job. 'Hey, boy, hear me talking to you?' I came out at that time.

What do you want?'

'Does Clyde know about this, Frank?'

'I don't give a damn what Smith knows. We are loading consigned goods that belong to a man in Florida. Do you want to see the inventory list?' I jumped down from the loading dock and headed towards Coons' cop car. I could see him put his hand on his gun. What a bounty and promotion that would be for Coons to kill the town stalker! I looked at him. 'Earl, I thought we were friends. We used to walk together, remember?' Coons looked down ashamed. 'Why do you want to torment me more? Does it give you pleasure to keep stomping me in the ground?'

'I have got to go and get Smith,' and off he went.

Larry said, 'Mr. Frank, I don't want no trouble with any white cop.'

'You won't have any trouble, Larry. Just load the truck as fast as you can...let's get out of here.'

"We all were in the front of the store and here comes the high and mighty banker Smith. He was all dressed up ready to go to Church and Sunday school and pray. Smith, a real walking witness program. Get all dressed up, and before you go to church, drop by and slit a man's throat.

'Frank, I told you not to load anything else. Do you want more police trouble, because I sure can send them your way?'

'You hypocrite, you with your Sunday clothes on. Have a good day at church, we are leaving!'

"About another week passed, and I got with Phil to clear passage with Larry to go back to Eatonton for the final load. My brothers would not let me go for fear I might retaliate against the bastards. Larry was armed with legal papers and phone numbers, and he was instructed to call me at any hint of a problem. Later in the afternoon, I get a call. I could hear Larry shaking on the phone as he spoke.

'....Mr. Frank....'

'Larry, is that you? What's wrong?'

'Mr. Frank, we haven't got your furniture...these white cops came up, Mr. Frank, as soon as we put the key in the door. It was like they had set a trap for us. They said you boys come with us, meaning me and Melvin. Mr. Frank, they took us to the police station and checked out our truck all over, and harassed us, Mr. Frank.'

'Larry, did you show them the papers from the lawyer?'

'They said, we don't care what papers you have, boy. You aren't taking one stick of furniture out of that building.'

'Then, Mr. Frank, they said, Nigger, get out of this town and don't you come back! They followed us all the way to the town limits, Mr. Frank. Mr. Frank, them folks are crazy!' Thirty days later Larry was dead of a heart attack.

*Journal Entry Feb. 1*

"In February, I went bankrupt. The bankruptcy attorney knew of a Jewish man in Greensboro who said he could help me get my remaining store fixtures out.

'Frank, don't worry. It's just like they did us in Germany. Harass, harass. I will help you at no cost. I think you would be a good Jew, Frank Moss.' Mike Zuckerman sent his men free of charge to get the last of my store things. When they got there, the locks had all been changed. I wasn't even 30 days late on my mortgage payment when I got foreclosure papers from Alice Meeks. Doris had finally broken my back every way she could.

"I was really getting fed up with Phil's Mickey Mouse lawyer tricks. Living at brother Kevin's house, I was getting ready to leave for my morning errands. I felt uncomfortable that day for some reason. Looking out the front window, I saw an unmarked car pull over to the side of the driveway. Kevin's house sat far back from the road with only a couple of houses on either side. It was strange to see a car there. I became afraid, what is this, is this a cop car, and is it starting all over again? My heart started to pound. My mind started working on a plan.

They would never chain me like a dog again. I would run, if they shoot me down, so be it! What to do, where to go? The car sat there for 30 minutes or longer. I called my answering service.

'There is a white car out front of Kevin's house. Please, if anything happens, you will know.'

**I called Phil. 'Phil, I don't want to seem paranoid, but there is a** suspicious looking car outside Kevin's house. Is anything going on I don't know about?'

"Phil started laughing. 'Frank, calm down. The cops from Eatonton aren't there.' I hung up the phone and felt stupid. I got brave and drove down the drive. I rolled my window down and said, 'Can I Pass?'

'Sure,' the cop said. Ever since December 8, 1994, I have hated anything with a tin badge on it.

"My last meeting with Phil was when I fired him. We met at the Murphy Inn in Roswell.

'Frank, I say we go in and plead guilty to stalking.'

'Hell, no, Phil. I am not guilty of anything!'

'Okay, Frank. Bixby's got a lot of evidence on you. He has this surveillance camera tape of you walking past Doris' house, and Frank, this book telling of Doris' sexual adventures, and April Preston. Bixby deposed her last week. Preston is claiming that you stalked her. Frank, you can really pick the women to get involved with. First, a 44-year old immature kid, then an insecure flight attendant. Bixby is romanticly interested in Doris. Fat chance he's got, Doris is just using Bixby, and he's too stupid to know it.'

'Phil, how about this blood sample that Bixby took?'

'Frank, don't worry. It costs too much to run a DNA test. I will tell you I have seen less work done on a murder case in Putnam County than this case. Bixby is out to crucify you.' With that last statement, I sent him a kind letter and promptly fired his legal ass.

"I hired John Straton next, through a recommendation from a friend. Straton got off to a good start filing all kinds of motions. Then Straton stopped talking to me. Boy, let me tell you when a lawyer gets that retainer, he's like a car salesman. Forget the customer service. From that point, I had to deal with a cocky legal secretary.

"My friend, Peter, in Arizona called, and we made plans for me to visit. I cleared everything through Straton and the cops. When my plane left the ground, I could see Doris and Bixby, and all the bastards on the ground shaking their fists at me and saying, 'How dare you leave!'The trip did my soul good. My lifelong friend from Atlanta, Peter, and I hiked the desert canyons and rugged terrain of Sedona, Arizona. For the first time in a long time, I felt free.

'Frank, when the time is right, Lisa and I want you to come live with us for a while,' Peter said.

'Peter, I can't do that. Why, y'all are building a house, and you have a new baby coming.'

Peter looked at me and said, 'Frank, what would you do for me as a friend?' '

'Anything, Peter. I would lend you money or give it to you. Give you a place to....Okay, I think I get the point.' When my plane landed back at the Atlanta airport, the fear of Doris Anthony was once more.

Notes

"The months clicked off, waiting, waiting. Every time I went to the mailbox, I dreaded to see what new horror awaited me. When the doorbell rang, I went to the back of the house for fear it might be a 'tin badge' to take me away. I didn't just sit on the sofa and watch T.V. I did every kind of job you could think of. Cleaning houses and offices, cutting grass, raking leaves, trying to sell a few antiques I had stashed away for a rainy day. I did it all just to make a little money. I paid Straton the last money from my IRA. With the comfort of friends and prayers, some how I got through. Like a piece of used furniture, folks couldn't bear the thoughts of putting me on the street, and I was too good to be thrown away, so from attic to basement I went. I floated between my brother Mike's house, Kevin's house to my Aunt Betty's and Lynn's aunts. Now Lynn's aunts' house, isn't that a good hiding place? Hide out at your ex-wifes aunts' house. I knew all these folks loved me, but I felt I was becoming a burden.

"I would stay a couple of weeks at one house, then the cycle would start all over again. I longed to have my things around me again. Photos of friends and my paintings and my furniture and my own bed. My possessions were scattered from one house to the next. All the things from Eatonton had been just thrown haphazardly in a box, like a refugee trying to flee a hostile country.

*Journal Entry April 1*

"The first of April brought not only azaleas blooming, but a new job. I had been planning to sell restaurants antique metal signs, the junk they put on the walls. I presented the concept to a competitor of mine, Al Brown. Brown was a handsome looking fat man. He looked Greek in a way, and he had these incredible blue eyes. What a temper that man had, and I knew of his reputation as a ruthless businessman. So, one Saturday morning, Brown and I shook hands on a $30,000 a year salaried job for old Frank Moss.

"With that job came another good turn of events. My cousin told me of a guy that needed a roommate, and he had an empty condo. The roommate would stay at the condo maybe once a week when he was in Atlanta. God, everything was coming together. I was back in the antique business, and I was going to get my own place again. Like the two good brothers they are, Mike and Kevin went all over town gathering my things up and helped me move.

"Anastasia came up, and like she had done with the store, she took all of my boxed belongings and made that condo a home for me. It was so good to see all of my things once again. Amazingly, nothing had broken during the chaotic moves.

"Things were coming together until May, and I went to the mailbox. I received a letter telling me to report to the Eatonton Sheriff's department for an arraignment. I called Straton repeatedly, but none of my calls were returned. Dealing exclusively through Straton's secretary, I was able to get Straton's phone number in St. Simons, Georgia, where he had a house.

'What do you want, Frank? How dare you bother me at my home! Just show up May 3rd!' I hung up the phone and thought what a lawyer asshole! If Straton only knew how scared I was, hell, he didn't care. May 3rd was the hearing date, my younger brother Kevin's birthday. The morning sunshine brought rays of a return to Eatonton. I dressed in one of my good suits and off Mike and I went. These trips going to Eatonton with Mike was putting a strain on his business. It had been four months since I had been in Eatonton the time Kevin and I were there, and I almost punched out Smith from the bank. I recalled his short little body and thick glasses and squeaky voice, 'how dare you take...' Passing by my store, I noticed the Christmas tree was still in the window along with the gold star I had made for the merchant open house. The building looked dead and lifeless, as did the town. The flower pots that I had gotten for the town had dead flowers in them, and several other businesses around the square had closed.

"When we pulled into the Sheriff's parking lot, a lot of old memories came flooding back. I saw Doris park her car and start walking toward our car. She pranced, shaking her hips back and forth as a school girl would do walking down the hall. She had on an unflattering light blue dress, probably from one of those mail order catalogs I was supposed to have stolen. Her hair blew as she walked and shined like silk when the sun hit it. Doris had a harsh look on her face, and she looked like she had lost weight. At that moment, I wanted to grab the steering wheel from Mike and floor the car and run that bitch down, but I sat still. I am sure she saw Mike and me in the car, but she quickly turned and ran over, like to greet a long-lost friend and shook the hand of Don Meek, Alice, the Bank's lawyer's husband. Doris laughed with Don in a fake sort of way. Don kept patting his cheap toupee, and Doris squinted in the sunlight. I guess light on darkness hurts. Both vanished as Mike and I got out of the car. James Weldon greeted me in his usual way, hugging me.

'How are you, brother?'

'I'm fine, James. Ready to go to Hell with me?'

'We can face anything, Frank,' James said.

"Inside the lobby there were a lot of lawyers mingling about. Echoes of cases were heard, and then my eyes focused in on one person in particular. Bixby. Bixby was talking to another cop and, trying to be a big shot, he kept raising his eye brows like, I know. He had on his trademark, another cheap suit.

'James, see that man over there talking,' I pointed to Bixby.

'Yeah, Frank, I see him,' James said.

'That's Bixby, the G.B.I. man that's caused me so many problems.' James nodded his head. 'You know, James, it's not many people can boast they bought a first class ticket to Hell.'

'Oh, there is passage for one more front seat that is saved for Doris.' James looked at me and he knew their fate.

"A lot of the lawyers in town that knew me came up and shook my hand and wished me well. Even Phil came over and said hello. I thought, standing there by James, this man had risked his job standing there by me. I was so proud to call James my friend. Still, I saw nothing of my compact attorney, Straton. Jack Sawyer, a lawyer I knew, briefed us on which room to go in. In a packed room we all assembled.

"Doris was sitting in a chair with her back towards me. I looked at the back of her head and thought, why? Judge Carroll was seated at the end of a long conference table. He was like a crumb of food all slouched over with the lawyer flies buzzing all around him. Around the room were black men with orange uniforms on, and I looked at their faces and said to myself, 'What chance do you have in this kangaroo court?' A photocopied sheet filtered through the room, and Doris studied it with the intensity of a jeweler. I looked over at Bixby; he turned and gave me this smirky grin like, I got you. Smiling, he looked at the floor, and I thought you will burn in Hell for what you did to me.

'Mr. Straton, how does your client plead?' Carroll asked.

'Not guilty, your honor.'

'So noted.' With all of the stress and wondering what was going to happen, the whole procedure took a few minutes and James, Mike and I exited the door.

'They are supposed to give me the discovery materials today. I will be in touch,' Straton said in a hurried fashion.

'John, I want you to meet my brother Mike and my minister, James Weldon.'

'Hello.' Straton scurried off down the hall.

"Late in May, as a matter of fact, my birthday, Brown fired me at the antique store. People warned me that Brown would fire you at the drop of a hat.

'This just isn't going to work out, Frank,' he angrily said.

'Give me another chance,' I asked.

'No more chances, Frank!' Brown shouted and went into one of his blood bursting vessel tirades. Brown had sent another employee to buy merchandise for the restaurant package deal. The kid didn't know what he was buying, so I was stuck with all of this high-priced junk to try and sell. Brown had promised week after week to fund me a checking account and get me a warehouse, but as all the competitors in the business had told me, Brown is a two-faced liar. I thought as I looked at him storm out of the store that day, if you only could know of my pain, what I had been through. After all, a man like Brown that had the best of everything, how could he ever feel the pain of another human being?

"With the advent of losing my job, came the prospect of packing all of my belongings up again and once again sleeping in a borrowed bed.

Anastasia said, 'Frank, at least you got to enjoy your things for a little while. Now you have everything organized, you can pack everything up for your new home, and wherever that is, just get me a bottle of wine and I will decorate for you.' Lynn's aunts lent me their garage and I was once again all boxed up.

"I got some more Mickey Mouse jobs, working at a flea market, doing garage sales, even got a job selling linens at a department store. My nights and days were filled with what would come in the mail next or what Doris would do to me. I had lost hope in Straton. He had become another Phil Fougerty. Penniless, I had no more money for anything.

"My cousin invited me to a party that summer. There I met a host of professional people. I was talking to a man that used to be an attorney. He was retired and I ask him if he knew Straton.

'Yeah, I know Straton. We went to law school together. He's a real prick,' laughed his former classmate. Mingling through the crowd, I shook hands with a man named Jim Forrest. Jim was in his fifties and had a hard look on his face. I asked him what he did for a living and he said, 'I work for the G.B.I.' I could smell the manure on my hand after shaking his. I looked at him through his thick glasses and felt hatred. I thought I could use my hate creatively.

'Do you know anyone in the Milledgeville office?' I asked.

'Yeah, a few.'

'Do you know a man named Bixby?'

'Yeah, I know Bixby. He used to work for Sheriff LaSurre. Funny thing, a couple of years ago, the G.B.I. staged a raid on some gambling machines in Putnam County. Turns out they were LaSurre's machines.'

'What ever became of the raid?' I asked.

'Don't know. It was all hushed up.' Laughing, Jim said, 'You know how small town Georgia politics work.'

'How well I knew."

"I had written Leacy a lot of letters and called when I could. Early in February I had talked to her, and she told me she was involved with someone else. How in the world things ever worked out in my life, God only knows."

# PART FOUR

*Journal Entry Aug. 5*

"It was nearing the year's anniversary of Doris' letter. How much had passed since that August 28th letter. Doris had destroyed so much of my life. As she said in her letter to me, 'I can be ruthless,' thinking, as I would ride in my truck, 'How much more cruelty must I endure from this beast that I once loved?' Every day that I would check my post office box, a new disaster would be disguised in a letter from Putnam County.

Around August 10th, I received a copy of a letter saying 'Your trial to be held August 28th at 9:00 at the Putnam County Courthouse.' A pit of sickness came to my stomach that morning as I made it from the floor of the post office to my truck. Sitting there motionless, I looked up at the faces of people coming out of the facility. None of the nameless faces knew my pain, what I have been through, as I looked through the windshield. Panic and fear overtook me. That damn nothing of a lawyer I got, Straton, hadn't talked to me in weeks. Hell, I didn't know what was going on. I heard his voice, 'Frank, I am still trying to negotiate a deal with the D.A. He really does not want the political heat.' The whole thing had polarized the town.

"Driving back to Ruth and Sue's, I kept thinking, 'What can I do?' The waiting, the anticipation of what is to come, that's the worse torture. You can torture a man to death by just making him wait. Wait for the unknown. The aunts could see the pain in my face. They both were so wonderful to me. Sue would always have some rambling story that seemed to last forever. 'Aunt Sue, maybe I will write a story about that someday,' I said, then she would reply, 'Now, Frank, save me some material for my book,' we would laugh.

"The nights were always the worst. I dreaded the night because of the anticipation of what the morning would bring. My nights were like a series of mini plays. In one scene I could see myself in an orange prison uniform lying on a one-inch cot looking up at the paint peeling on the ceiling. Every so often I would hear a guard say, 'Get up, Moss, God damnit, get up.' Lying there with my eyes closed, but hearing every sound, I would be comatose, and the guard would begin to swing his nightstick and beat me about the face. Blood ran into my eyes, but I felt no pain. I had it in my mind that if I were sentenced to jail, I would lie there on a cot and eat nothing. Just waste away, they couldn't make me eat. Through fasting I could drain away. Hearing news reports, 'Frank Moss was found today in a Putnam County jail cell beaten beyond recognition. Inmates say Moss refused to eat in defiance of his book being seized. Sheriff LaSurre denies any wrong doing.' Crazy thoughts would race through my mind like that. I was so scared, but who could I tell these things to? Hell, who could I trust? The great and almighty tin badge could use a dream against me. Claim I am crazy again. It went on some nights I could see me gunned down. The faces from Central State Hospital, oh, every time I looked in the mirror to shave I saw them. Brooks, and David Hornbuckel and Sandy, 'Help me, Frank, help me.'

"In nightmares I would see the face of a dark-haired woman with fire all around her, throwing furniture and me into a great pit.

"The beast, as I began to call Doris, was everywhere. On the road each Chrysler Le Baron convertible I saw, I looked to see if it was her. Driving everyday, I had a vision of Doris' car flipping over and over, blood running down the windshield like rain drops. I could see her pinned under the car, gasping and hopefully remembering all the inhumanities she caused, not only me, but others. Her accident was as clear as we sit here. A Don Hudson Lumber trailer coming straight at her, head-on collision. Fitting end for the company that was made from blood money. The cold-blooded killer that Doris' grandfather set free.

"Some nights I would see Doris in a different light. The old Doris, the quick-witted Doris that I fell in love with.

"Every day leading up to the August 28th trial struggling with 'What to do,' I thought and thought till my brain hurt. Monday usually was my off day from Mark's flea world, and I would try to go on some sort of adventure. Thinking, lying in bed, I thought a trip to the cyclorama in Atlanta would be fun."

"The Cyclorama is the largest painting in the world; it's painted in a circle. It depicts the battle of Atlanta from the Civil War."

" That Monday, I sat in the audience of the cyclorama and thought, look at all of this bravery and courage for a cause for which the enemy had overwhelming resources. Look at all of the blood spilt on the ground. I thought of the great battle ahead for me. Regardless of resources, I must fight to the end. My great, great grandfather lost his life in that war because he believed in a cause, a cause greater than himself. At the giftshop I dropped in and bought a post card of R.E. Lee. What a man of courage, and always a gentleman. I'm going to form my battle plans after him.

"Leaving the cyclorama that day gave me hope that I could fight one more battle against Doris. That night I went to bed and had a dream of a Confederate General on a horse. He looked and had the presence of R.E. Lee, but I didn't know. All I knew he was of great courage and fortitude. His sword was drawn, and I heard the words, 'Have courage, Frank, have courage.'

"The next morning I had a few last details to wrap up with Mark, then the war would start. I repeatedly called Straton, my attorney, to get a last minute update, but to no avail. His secretary would shun me. I sent faxes. 'I want to know the status of my case.' Still nothing.

"Anastasia called and wanted me to come help her with some paint stripping at her home. I would do anything in the world for Anastasia, but I dreaded the drive to Milledgeville. Judge Carroll had made it so difficult to travel. I couldn't go through the royal Putnam County, so I had to go a round about way, about another hour, thru Macon, to get there. Anastasia's home was too close to Central State Hospital and Eatonton for my comfort. I consented to go. First, I got my 'battle plans ready.'

"As far as resources stood, the only money I had was in my pocket, less than $100.00. The three resources I knew I had were: number one, my friends, both in Eatonton and Atlanta; number two, my belief in God; and number three, I knew that, through past experience, Frank Moss knew how to get a story to the media.

"I sent Straton one last fax. 'Got to know the status, if no response by 12:00 noon, going to the media.' No response. That Wednesday morning, I got on the phone and burned up the lines talking. I called every news source I could think of. Radio, TV, newspaper, I covered them all. I contacted every church in Eatonton, the Baptist, Presbyterian, Methodist, all to pray for me for strength and guidance on Monday the 21st. I called all my friends and asked who could be there for me Monday, and if you can't, pray for me.

"I was on top of the world again. The response was the same.

'This is unbelievable.'

'Yes, this is a true story, and it happened to me.' I called all the newspapers in the surrounding Eatonton area. My grandfather always taught me that to get a snake out of its hole, you have to pour gas and light a match. The one thing I knew about Doris J. Anthony, and a lot of the scumbags in Eatonton, they hate to have to come out of their hole."

"I didn't know if the media would take the bait, but it was out there. Two newspapermen, one from the Milledgeville paper, and one from the Madison, wanted to interview me. That was great because I could see them and then go work at Anastasia's house.

"I pounded all of the government people I could, also. A fax to the Governor, Attorney General of Georgia, U.S. Justice Department, DEA, all of them. Possible corruption in Putnam County. Anything I could do to body slam that bastard, Bixby, I did. Hell, I bet I spent $50.00 on faxes that day.

"That afternoon I saw the two newspapermen and told my story. While passing through Madison, I stopped at my favorite little church to pray. That day when I entered the sanctuary, I felt God there. I prayed for strength and guidance.

"With shocked faces, the newspapermen jotted notes of the bizarre tale.

'May we copy some of these documents?'

'Sure, copy all you want.' I took with me my entire box of evidence. Both newspapermen laughed when I showed them the picture of Vivian Leigh that the stupid Chief Riley mistook for a stolen picture of Doris.

"When I reached Anastasia's home, I was wound up like a coil. Driving down the long gravel drive to Anastasia's house, I thought of the many great parties I attended there. Anastasia's Greek Revival home sat perched on the rise. I saw Anastasia with her long, brown hair feed her babies, as she called them. Chickens, dogs, cats, everything you can think of.

"Anastasia hugged me, and we greeted each other.

'I missed you.'

'Me, too,' said Anastasia.

'Frank, I want you to make yourself at home. James has got to take me to drop the car off in Macon, so we will be home in a couple of hours.'

'Okay, Anastasia, baby. I'm going to try to call my damn lawyer again.'

"I used to feel so comfortable at Anastasia's home. The huge magnolias, the old porch. Anastasia used to say that angels came to Windward Hill around 3:30 every afternoon. I sure hoped they were here today. I needed every one of them. Inside the pine paneled kitchen, bric a brac was arranged on the tops of counter and cabinets. Little vignettes of the past.

"Finding the phone, I called Straton's office. 'Debra, is John there?'

'No, he will be in later,' she replied.

'Look, I have got to talk to him about what is going to happen on Monday.'

'John wants me to send you a fax. What's your fax number?'

'I will have to go to town. Wait, there's a fax machine here.' Looking on James' paper strewn desk, 'It's 706-555-5858. Have John call me as soon as he gets in.'

The paper slowly came through the machine. 'Frank, don't understand your latest correspondence. Thought we were trying to work a deal with the D.A. Have not been retained to represent you in a trial.'

'You haven't been retained? What the hell is the damn $2,500 I gave you, bastard lawyer! Damnit! I have got to get my mind off this shit!'

"Outside, I scraped the paint from one of the doors. I was thinking of every solution; my friends, the media contacts I made. What else? What haven't I done? An hour or so passed. I'm going to try Straton again.

'Hello, Debra, did John come back?'

'Yes, he wants to talk to you.' It's about time, I thought to myself.

'Frank, I presented your idea that if they drop all charges against you, you will move to Arizona, but I still have no response.'

"'John, what the hell is this fax you sent? You aren't paid to represent me in a trial? You are not going to become another Phil Fougerty, are you?'

'I told you, Frank, a trial is costly, and I don't have the money to fund a six day or more trial. Our best option is to plead guilty to the stalking charge and see if they would drop the theft charge. We can plead an Alfred plea.'

'A what?'

'An Alfred plea is that you are not saying you are guilty or innocent, you don't have the funds for a trial. Look, Frank, I know you are innocent. This stalking charge is hogwash.'

'I am innocent, John. I loved Doris Anthony, I did not stalk her. I just hope years from now when you write or tell about your legal experiences, you remember Frank Moss, a man who lost everything because he loved a beast. An innocent man, but because he didn't have money, he had no defense. It's the end of the justice system in America. Do we still show up Monday, the 21st?' I asked.

'Yes, Frank, Monday at 9:00.'

"When I hung up, my face must have been blood red. I went out the back door of the house. I was furious! Walking at a rapid pace, I went into the pasture in the backyard and looked up at the sky and yelled, 'Is there no justice, God? I have prayed and prayed till my knees hurt, yet you let Bixby and Doris walk Free?!! Is there no justice?!!' I yelled again at the sky. Dropping my head, tears ran down my cheeks. 'Have you left me, too?' I walked the entire length of the pasture that hot, humid August day. It was about 3:00; the time angels are supposed to come to Windward Hill. I guess I disappointed the angels, too. Maybe the spirit of Anastasia's daddy was disappointed. Composing myself, I scraped paint again and worried about what Monday would bring.

"Late that evening after supper, Anastasia and James were in the kitchen fighting over money. 'Who do you think has helped us out?' said Anastasia.

'Other people, hell!'

'My mother, is that all she is, other people? Oh, James, just go over and kiss her and tell her she's beautiful.'

'I am not kissing that bitch,' James said pompously. 'Frank knows more about me than you ever will,' said Anastasia. James left the room and there was silence.

'Anastasia, I hope I haven't caused any problems by being here?'

'No, Frank, James is just an asshole. I love you being here with me.' Anastasia came over and sat at the breakfast table.

'Anastasia, I tell you I am so afraid. I'm innocent.' Anastasia put her small hand on mine and patted it softly.

'I know you are afraid, Frank, but have courage. You have come this far, just a little more pain and it's over.' With her big brown eyes, Anastasia looked me in the eye and said, 'Look, Frank Moss, I want you to put on the best looking suit you own, and I want you to go into that courtroom on Monday and be a class act. Like you are. Show those country bumpkins the gentleman you are. If you have to plead guilty, do it! Tell them, hell yeah, I am a handsome horny man, and I stalked the hell out of Doris Anthony. I wanted to fuck the hell out of her. Then leave that cesspool of a town called Eatonton and go to Arizona and finish your book, file your civil lawsuit, and be happy again. Frank, you have to grow in order to learn patience. With patience, it will all work out, and Doris and all those small town thinking bastards will pay.'

'Let them see you on talk shows and book signings and let them remember how they ran a brilliant writer off just to protect some nothing of a human Doris Anthony. I will never forget how you helped me, Frank, with all of my problems with James. I will always love you for that and, hey, we had some great times.'

"With her smile and strong eyes, I thought, never have I had a greater sermon from a greater friend. I loved Anastasia so much that night at Windward Hill. Although she didn't know at the time, she gave me the strength I had prayed so much for. The night brought restless turns and the image of the Confederate General on the horse with sword drawn.

"Friday morning, I left Windward Hill for Atlanta. 'Anastasia, I'll see you Monday. Love you.'

'Love you, too. Keep that chin up.'

'I will.' As I drove down the long gravel drive, I saw Anastasia waving from the porch. Looking back, I knew within my heart I would never pass this way again.

"Back in Atlanta, I sent more faxes, shoring up my position. Saturday, I stayed on the phone almost all day. 'If you can't come on Monday, just pray for strength and guidance.' I repeated that sentence over and over.

"That weekend that led up to Monday the 21st was like a farewell. When my daddy was so sick, I took him on a farewell journey to see everyone a last time. I prayed this was not going to be my fate. Sunday was a torturous day. I was bound up like a thousand rubberbands. The aunts talked idle conversation and finally I said I had a couple of places to go. Really, I needed a quiet church to pray.

"I drove to downtown Atlanta to the High Museum of Art. Maybe art would take my mind off Monday. Studying each piece of art, I looked for the works depicting the struggle of man. Striving, trying to make it. Flashes of color in the canvas hit my eye, swords, blood, but you fight on was the theme. Walking down the entrance ramp, I thought I saw someone from Eatonton. I brushed if off as coincidence, and walked on.

"Next to the High Museum was a Presbyterian church. I had met Doris' preacher, Bill, and his wife there for a choral concert one time. I really liked that church. With its tall gothic spires and wonderful stained glass, it felt warm and cozy. Entering the church, I found in the corridor a dark chapel, lit only by a beautiful stained glass window. The smell of old wood and cloth permeated the air.

"I sat in a pew toward the front and bowed my head. 'Oh, God, please don't let me die. I am dealing with such evil. Don't let me die.' A tear rolled down my face. I cried so much that weekend, I didn't know if I had any more tears to shed. I went on, 'God, give me a career path; what am I supposed to do with my life? With all this adversity, how can I make good come from this? Forgive me, Jesus, for loving the beast known as Doris Anthony.'

"Slowly, I raised my head, and, through the brilliant colors of blue, yellow and red of the stained glass window, I saw a man with a quill pen writing. 'Is that what you want me to do?' I said. I looked at that image a long time that day, and I heard a small voice, 'Tell your story, Frank.' I rose slowly from the pew and walked softly because I was in the presence of God.

"When I lay my head on the pillow Sunday night, I thought, I have done all I can do. I did a good job, and I drifted off to sleep. I saw the same Confederate General on the horse with drawn sword, and the words, 'Have courage, Frank, have courage.'"

*Journal Entry Aug. 21*

"Monday, I dressed in my finest suit, and we all piled into the car, like going to the drive-in movies, for a trip to Nazi, Germany. My brother, Mike, and my aunt Betty, Teresa, my cousin, and Lynn's two aunts all went. That Monday it was raining cats and dogs, a real frog strangler. Silently, I sat crammed up in the backseat of the car. Thoughts flashed in my mind, as I looked out the rain soaked window. Remembering how they chained my wrists and legs like a dog. The choking smell of cigarettes and no fresh air. I thought about the rolling pastures, when the cops took me to Central State Hospital that sunny cool December day. The rest of the gang were chattering about all sorts of things.

Every once in a while, someone would say, 'Don't you think so, Frank?'

'Yes,' I would quietly say.

"The rain had almost stopped when we reached the Putnam County line. I was so tense. On the road, I saw a sign that said, 'Helen's House B & B, 5 miles ahead.' I thought how Helen had betrayed me, and was on the witness list for the State. Further down, I saw a Welcome to Eatonton sign. As we entered Eatonton city limits, we passed by my old store. My merchandize was in the window, haphazardly arranged. For sure, it was not the work of Anastasia.

"The Christmas tree had been taken from the window. I guess the bank deemed that not appropriate. The top windows where I lived were blank and lifeless. Void of any curtains, the entire building sat there like a great ship docked forever, its captain gone, no passengers, no crew; a dead ship, a Titanic building.

"Mike pulled around the courthouse and parked unknowingly near Doris' law office. We all got out of the car and walked up the sidewalk toward the newly renovated courthouse. I was surprised that with all the media calls I made, there were no newspapermen there. Even the two men who promised me they would be there were nowhere to be seen. I suppose I expected a fanfare of TV cameras and microphones shoved in my face, just like in the movies, but, after all, this is real life.

"I was not afraid, as you might think. I held my head up high and if it was to be, I was prepared for anything Doris and Bixby dished out. These are the same sidewalks I used to walk. God, I loved this town so much. My fellow car passengers surrounded me as if they were my bodyguards. On the portico was my friend, Sam Dunn. He drove two hours to be here.

"I remember him saying, 'Frank, I can't represent you as an attorney due to conflict of interest, although I am one, but I can be there as your friend.' I shook Sam's hand and thanked him for being there for me. Entering the courthouse, a smell of new sheetrock and paint filled the air. The old marble floor had been roughly cleaned. Typical of Eatonton, a good facade of paint and clean, but rotten decaying wood was underneath, for none to see.

"We all climbed the steps to the main courtroom. An old black man with a thousand pencils protruding from his pocket sat in a metal fold-up chair. Next to him an older woman who used to trade with me in my store. We all went through the metal detector and passed. Opening the door to the courtroom was like going on stage. Huge tacky florescent lights hung from a glossy white painted metal ceiling. Everything seemed painted glossy white, a lily white, but on the ledge of the window sill crawled a cockroach. Where there is one roach, there are a thousand. All the theater type seats were upholstered in a burgundy fabric. It seemed Eatonton was trying to create a mock church in its courtroom, but a true believer in God could see right through the facade.

"Looking around the room in my peanut gallery, as Anastasia called it, were my friends Anastasia, Jeff Hancock, my college friend, Tom Coleman, my story-telling friend, Lynnette, my then girlfriend and her wonderful friend Mygra. Slowly trickling in were my Eatonton friends Millie, from the drug store, Eve, who kept my store, Florence Harell, a wonderful church friend, Dixie the cookie story lady, Russ and Chris from Kiwanis and church, and, of course, the man who risked his job, my friend and minister, Rev. James Weldon.

"James gave me a big bear hug when he came in, for all to see. Even Doris saw as she slipped in through the back door, so no one would see her. I hugged all of them and thanked them for being there.

James was sitting next to me, and I said, 'You know, James, when you go to heaven, you will have a lot of friends with you; just look around at my peanut gallery. And when you go to hell, you go all by yourself; look at Doris over there, all by herself. The ruthless tyrant of Eatonton, who has more family and friends than one could count. Wonder where they all are this Monday morning? This would be a great sermon, what you see here today.'

'Frank, maybe in another town. I think folks here would figure out who I was talking about,' James chuckled.

"About that time, one of the side doors opened, and I saw that bastard Bixby. 'There's that bastard G.B.I. man who has caused me so many problems. Look at him with that cheap brown sports coat on.'

Then Anastasia looked straight at me, snapped her fingers, and said, 'Can it, Moss.'"

"God, I feared the wrath of Anastasia a lot more than the Judge. Bixby has this gaping sort of walk, strutting around like he was so important. I'll swear that bastard could buy the cheapest clothes. You would think that, with all the LaSurre payoff money, he could afford to buy a decent suit, but when you have no class, what's the good of money.

"Each time he passed by my row of seats, he gave me a smirky smile like he did at the May 3rd hearing. I hope you burn in hell, you bastard. More of the players entered the stage. Rick Mays, the fat-assed bald-headed LaSurre man who ripped up my store was there. Standing beside the Judge's bench was Sheriff Billy LaSurre, one of the crookedest men alive. It was strange. He was only there for a short time and then left.

"Looking around, Doris moved from the back of the courtroom to the front where all could see her. She had on one of the tackiest outfits I have ever seen. A black loose-fitting skirt that looked like a cheap polyester. Her top was black and white stripped. The entire ensemble probably came in a box from one of those cheap mail order places; the magazines that she would bring to the store and show me. 'Frank, buy me this,' she would say. Later she framed me with those damned magazines. Doris' hair was pulled back in a barrette, and it looked uncombed.

"Several lawyers gathered near her in the front and they talked back and forth with one another. I was getting concerned that I had not seen my lawyer anywhere. A few minutes later, Straton pranced in and worked his way to the front of the courtroom. Judge Carroll called a roll of the attorneys present and their clients. As my name was called, I felt I had swallowed a rock. It had begun.

"The courtroom was still barren of spectators except for my peanut gallery. Judge Carroll announced, 'Any jurors here will be dismissed. Attorneys wishing to speak to the D.A. come forward.' Straton approached the bench along with several others I had known from town. Then Straton and some others disappeared into a back room. My fate, I thought, was to be determined in a back room.

"Doris got up and walked across the room to talk to Bixby. With their hands covering their mouths, they whispered words. Then Bixby and Doris got up and left the room. Fidgeting, I moved from seat to seat, visiting with my friends. Time seemed to last forever that day. All the players of this play would filter in and out of the lily-white courtroom. Bixby would walk up and down the aisles like he owned the place. I never missed the chance, when he passed my seat, to look him square in the eye. With that stupid little smile of his, I thought how fortunate I was to be able to look evil right in the eye and not be afraid.

"Up at the front of the courtroom, Rick Mays held his head as if he were sick. When he rubbed his bald head, I hoped maybe he would throw up on the new carpet.

"I sat down next to Tom Coleman, my story-telling friend from Louisiana. 'Tom, thanks so much for coming to be here with me.'

'Frank, you would do the same for me, I'm sure.'

'You're right about that,' I said.

'Frank, there is something scary about this place. It's so lily-white. The buildings in town look like a Norman Rockwell setting; but there is something wrong here. I feel evil here, Frank. I am glad you don't live here anymore.'

'Me, too, Tom.'

'I guess you will get another Cajun ghost story out of this place.'

"Straton walked down the aisle and signaled for me to come with him. 'Let's talk outside, Frank,' Straton said. Walking down the stairs and outside, Straton propped himself up on one of the entrance pillars and began. 'Frank, why the hell did you go to the media?'

'Hell, John, you would never talk to me. What did you want me to do? Come here and get slaughtered?'

'Frank,' as Straton rubbed his forehead, 'Bixby is in the back room raving mad, cussing you to everything known to man. He is pushing for jail time. I just don't know,' Straton said, as he looked at the ground.

'Did you present the plan of me moving to Arizona and them dropping the charges?'

'Yes, but Bixby...'

'To hell with Bixby! And that's where he is going.' John lit a cigarette and looked across the street.

"'See that building, John? That was my building, everything I worked for. All my life is across that street. Doris Anthony took it all. I hope you remember Eatonton. There's no justice. Do the best you can,' was my final reply.

'O.K.' as Straton looked up at me in a no win smile. Straton and I were on the first riser of the steps and rounding the corner was Bixby and Doris walking at the same pace with their heads toward the ground. All I saw was their backs.

Straton looked at me, and I said, 'Guess they are looking for a motel room.'

Straton said, 'Come on, Frank.' Looking back one more time I saw the last glimpse of Bixby and Doris walking side by side down a marble floor. I could see an image of two steel doors opening and flames shooting forth, possibly the gates of hell.

"There were more hours of waiting. Still the same repetitive scenario. Straton appeared from a back door and motioned for me to come with him. Down the same flight of stairs and outside we went again.

Straton began, 'Here's the deal. We plead guilty to the stalking charge, and they will drop the theft charge. A 12-month suspended sentence, no supervised probation, and you are banished from the State of Georgia for 12 months. You can only fly into the Fulton County airport to see your family. You still have a lot of friends in Eatonton, Frank. Attorney Duke Cody is back there with Bixby cussing, telling the judge and everyone what you did for the town. What a good citizen you are.'

'Duke was my friend,' I said.

Straton paused and said, 'I thought you would like this. Bixby wants to sue you for everything you got. I told him you don't have anything.' We both chuckled. 'Take the deal and do the best you can.'

'Did we cause ole Bixby some problems?'

'You sure did, Frank.'

'Good, maybe that will put that bastard one step closer to hell.'

"That day I raised my head and looked forward. I had stared the devil right in the eye and I had courage. Perhaps my eyes told my story, although no word was spoken.

"Another hour passed and I heard my case called. Judge Carroll announced. 'The State of Georgia vs Frank F. Moss, Jr.' Straton and I approached the bench. Doris was sitting on the front row, and I looked straight at her. She kept her eyes forward, as she had done the entire time since that August. She couldn't bear the thought of meeting my eyes. Doris twitched and squirmed in her seat. Her face tightened up, and she squinted as she always did. She needed glasses, but she was too vain to buy any.

"I met Judge Carroll's eyes. This was the man who signed so many documents against me. This was the man who knew nothing about me and cared nothing except the fabricated lies of Bixby. Carroll signed the paper that sent me to Central State Hospital for the insane. He signed Bixby's request for a blood sample. Paper after paper. I stared Carroll right in his eyes. He had no eyes. If a man has no eyes, he has no soul. His eyes looked like two round black patches sewed on a white background.

"Staring down at him, as I stood tall, he looked like he had no legs. A mere puppet of a man. Thinking about the image of the Confederate General on his horse, I thought how Carroll's great grandfather sold his troops out to the Yankees.

'Mr. Moss, speak clearly. This is being recorded. How do you plead to the stalking charge.'

'Guilty.' I caught a glimpse of Doris; she squirmed.

'The theft charges are dropped, 12 months suspended sentence, 12 month unsupervised probation, $200.00 fine. Mr. Moss, you are not to have any contact with Doris J. Anthony, and you are banished from the State of Georgia for 12 months with the exception of flying into the Fulton County airport to see your family.'

I heard, 'Oh no,' from my friends and family. Straton spoke up and said, 'I want the record to show we are pleading under the Alfred Plea, your honor.'

'So noted.'

'Also, your honor, we request all items seized during the raid, since nothing, is contraband, be returned to Mr. Moss.'

'Get with Bixby to return these things. If that does not work, file a motion.'

'Thank you, your honor.'

"As I walked away from the bench, I turned and looked straight at Doris. There was no way she couldn't see me. Did you win, I thought? Did you win, you beast, that I once loved and prayed to God not to take away from me? She sat there straight in the chair with perfect posture and pose, both arms on the rests, looking like a Queen. She was totally insensitive to what she had done. Cold, she stared out into space like she had sent a thousand to their deaths before, with the same feeling of no remorse. Doris looked straight ahead. She looked like a little kid that had broken something and hid the evidence...no remorse, just a blank stare on her face. I turned and sat on the row a few seats from her. In a few minutes, she got up and went across the room to sit with her compadre, Bixby. What a pair of beasts. They deserve each other.

"As I waited for the Probation officer, all my friends came up to the front of the courtroom. Later, l learned that my Jewish friend, Mygra said, as Bixby walked by, 'He sure has a cheap coat on.' Bixby strode up and down the aisle. 'Wonder who we are going to get to play him in the movie?'

Bixby looked at Mygra and said, 'Look, lady, if you have anything to say, say it out loud, don't whisper.'

'I never whisper,' Mygra retorted. Then out loud Mygra said, 'I hope his little pecker falls off.'

Anastasia turned and said, 'He hasn't got one.'

'Bet he's sleeping with her,' Mygra said. Lynnette later told me that when she was trying to find a rest room, two of the bailiffs were talking.

One of the bailiffs, an old black man said, 'Don't know why this ever come to trial. They liked each other, you know. Then she sued him. What a shame. Two folks, one loved, one hated.'

A woman bailiff said, 'He was the one that owned the store across the street. He did a lot for the town. He was a real asset to Eatonton. What's that woman ever done for this town, but cause trouble? They sure didn't do him right.'

"Standing at the front of the courtroom I felt like I was in a receiving line after a great performance. All of them told me how sorry they were about what had happened.

Millie Hawkins said, 'Frank, with what you did for the town. It's not just a sad day for you, but rather a sad day for Eatonton as well.'

I hugged Millie. 'Thank you.' Eve came up and I hugged her. 'Eve, I am going to miss you.' A lump came in my throat and tears were coming in Eve's eyes.

'You have been so good to me, Frank. You're the best man I ever worked for. I am going to miss you.'

'Me too, Miss Eve, thanks for everything.' We hugged each other again because I knew in my heart that would be the last time I would see this wonderful lady again.

"It wasn't long before the probation officer came up to me and said, 'Let's talk back here.' The probation officer looked like a high school girl. She could easily be on the cover of Eatonton's premier trailer park magazine. Bleached blond hair with a country accent, probably she was a reformed hooker. 'All your paper work seems to be in order. My name is Marci Bell. Mr. Moss, you need to go to the Sheriff's office to pay the fine. I can't collect no money.'

'Are we done?' I asked.

'Yes,' Marci replied. I got up from the chair and walked back into a farewell of friends and family.

'Well, where are you taking us to eat, Frank? Let's blow this popsicle stand,' Anastasia said out loud.

'Anywhere but this cesspool of a town.'

Anastasia grabbed my arm and said, 'It's over Frank. You were a perfect gentleman, except when I had to scold you for calling Bixby a bastard. Frank, you are Doris Anthony's worst nightmare. Let the ruthless bitch cover this up. Every lawyer in this place knows who she is.'

'Let's go to Madison.'

'Madison, it is!'

"As we filed out of that courtroom that Monday, I felt I was victorious over evil. I was free to go after eight months of worrying, I was free to go to Arizona to start a new life. Doris and Bixby could have each other, and they deserve each other. Doris would live the rest of her life remembering what she did to me. For me, I would live with the scars for the rest of my life.

"Outside the courthouse, my family and friends surrounded me once again as if to protect me. We all got into the car and pulled away. We passed Doris standing on the front porch of her law office. She was talking to her cousin, Joanne Anthony, who owned the local newspaper. I looked back through the window, and that's the last time I ever saw Doris. She seemed cocky, but scared, as she stood there in a hunched position. I thought how she would have to live in this cesspool of a town, and put on her fake little front of 'Hello, how are you. My name is Doris J. Anthony.' While her back would be turned, idle gossip would tell the story of how she destroyed the man from Atlanta. Maybe, that's what destroyed her idle gossip. Doris was such a beautiful facade, maybe the gossip started a crack that she couldn't patch. Like the dye she put on her hair to cover the gray; it's just a matter of time before people learned her true color.

"A funny thing happened as we saw Doris on the porch. My cousin Teresa, my shy cousin Teresa, leaned back and waved at Doris. Doris quickly hid behind a column. A little Moss humor never hurt anyone.

"Leaving Eatonton that day, all the buildings clicked off one by one. All the sidewalks rolled by, as we drove past. I never thought or wanted to walk this evil ground again."

*End of Journal Aug. 21*

**ii**

Wilman had told Aubrey when J.C. LaSurre's nurse would go out for errands. 'Just like clockwork man, she's gone for four hours in the afternoon. Kill J.C. in the afternoon.'

Aubrey slipped around back of J.C.'s house. The brown grass seemed to crunch when his shoes carefully marked each step. A pair of French doors were open off the patio and Aubrey heard demented cries.

'I told you, you damn nothing of a nigger, put that sack over there...Mama is that you...looking for Billi...BILLY, BILLY,.....He's in the barn fucking some girl... Daddy old man Forgerty is dead....'

J.C. rambled on and on like a crazy man. Aubrey slipped in the door and saw J.C. for the first time since he was 10 years old. The room had a rotten cancerous smell about. Rotting flesh. The smell of a heat salve and vaporizer perfumed the rotten air. J.C. sat in a wheelchair. Strains of white hair attached to his head like a mangie dog. He was grey in color and both of his legs were amputated. A drule of slobber ran down one corner of his mouth onto his shirt. Food spots and crumbs sprinkled his clothes. Raising his arms high in the air he would yell out an awesome groan, then with a slur, 'I'll kill you nigger. I am the richest man in Putnam County, I am God in these parts.' Two plastic tubes ran up into J.C.'s nostrils and an oxygen tank was on the back of his wheelchair. A urine bag filled to capacity hung from one side of the wheelchair. The nightstand was littered with every conceivable pill and ointment. Family photos and newspaper articles were framed in 10¢ store frames and lined the walls like wallpaper.

J.C.'s skin had lesions all over and he looked like he was a termite eaten piece of wood. Aubrey snuck up behind J.C.'s wheelchair and put an arm hold around his neck.

'Remember me, you S.O.B.,' Aubrey whispered in J.C.'s ear.

Aubrey's grip was getting tighter and J.C. started to choke. J.C. coughed up flem and it spued onto Aubrey's face, J.C. smiled, 'You can't kill me nigger, just because you owe me money.'

'I don't owe you any money you bastard! How do you want to die you S.O.B.?'

J.C. reached down and flung his urine bag at the side Aubreys's head. J.C. laughed. Then Aubrey hit J.C. in the face so hard it broke his false teeth and shattered his glasses. Blood poured from J.C.'s mouth and nose. Some glass had gotten into his eye.

'Kill me nigger, and do me a favor,' Aubrey reached inside his coat pocket and pulled the revolver. Pressing as hard as he could Aubrey drove the barrel into the side of J.C.'s temple like driving a nail home. J.C. slobbered blood.

'I don't know who you are, you black S.O.B.'

'Your brother Billy raped my mama in Hugh Parks store and you S.O.B., you cut my balls off.'

'Billy fucked a lot of nigger women. I don't know who the hell you are. Just kill me nigger and get me out of this hell hole of pain.'

Aubrey pulled back and put the revolver back in his coat pocket. He studied J.C., that S.O.B., for a few minutes in disgust. Then he got down close and looked J.C. right in the eye.

'You suffer a little more J.C., then hell can burn you forever.'

As Aubrey slipped out the french doors J.C. yelled, 'Please kill me, please, kill me who ever you are, don't leave me...'

Aubrey came walking up to where Frank was still seated at the picnic table. Frank seemed lost in thought, then looking up.

'I see blood on your coat, I guess you killed him.'Aubrey sat down next to Frank then silence fell.

'You were right Frank, he wasn't worth killing, been dead for years.'

'A once persecuted white man and a once persecuted black man. Back to close the pain of it all. We were both banished from Eatonton. Me when I was 10 years old, and you when you were 37. We just didn't conform to the Eatonton standard. I'm glad we're not fake, Frank."

"We're real people not a made up Tar Baby set in the road to trick folks. Eatonton was made up so fake. Why didn't I see that, Aubrey?"

"It was your destiny to destroy the facade to help the real people that lived in Eatonton to live free. You remember what you told me, Frank, about what happened here?" Aubrey said.

"God, I have told you so much this day. Tell me."

"You once said because of what Doris and Bixby did to you, no longer could a person walk the sidewalks or pass a building or a house free anymore in Eatonton. Because of their actions, everyone lost their freedom on December 8, 1994. How do you know a camera is not set up in the trees to film you talking to a black man or a married woman? You have great courage, Frank, and I almost made the army my career. I saw my share on the battlefield of courage and valor in men. No, Frank, you didn't carry a gun or kill, although many times I don't see why you didn't, especially that bastard Bixby. You fought for what you believed in. Like that image you kept telling me about, the Confederate General on the horse. You have a great honor about yourself, Frank; you are a gentleman. I never will forget what you did for me and James." Aubrey pauses and looks down at the ground.

"I just don't know what to say, Aubrey.....I sure needed a speech like that two years ago. I never saw myself as courageous. Sure I hoped I could one day save a child from a burning building, or a person trapped in a car, but I guess God equips you to do what you can. "

"I guess the old saying of what comes around goes around one Monday night I was resting, thinking about the day, and the phone rang. It was Anastasia.

'Frank, I have got some good news for you. The F.B.I. met this morning while we were in court, at the Piggly Wiggly. About 40 of them swarmed down on Sheriff LaSurre's office like flies on honey. They arrested him and took out a truck load of papers. I think they got him on corruption charges, everything from gambling to laundering drug money. That's why LaSurre left court so early today. Remember that bastard Rick Mays rubbing his bald head like he was sick? That's LaSurre's number two man. You know, Frank, all of those faxes worked. The media didn't show up for you because they were covering the LaSurre raid. Isn't that great, Frank?' '

Chickens do come home to roost, Anastasia.' I couldn't believe what I was hearing.

"When I got to Arizona, Anastasia and Millie both sent me the front page clippings from the paper. 'F.B.I. Raids Sheriff LaSurre.' I was delighted at that victory, but I wanted them to get Bixby, and with a dose of patience on my part, they tied Chief of Police Ralph Riley and Bixby to LaSurre's corruption ring. Later, I heard they investigated Doris, but found nothing to link her. Just as well; she had created her own private hell to live in.

"Strange thing, Aubrey. Guess who LaSurre's Attorney was."

"Who?"

"Phil Fougerty, my first attorney, the spokesperson for the prosecution.

**iii**

"I headed for the drive out west to Arizona. I was flat broke except for the money Lynnette had lent me which was $500.00. Aunt Betty packed me a lunch and gave me her traditional talk of 'Now drive slow. We don't want any more police trouble and don't talk to strangers.' 'Yes, ma'am,' I said as I gave her a big hug. Lynn's aunts had fixed up a bag of travel supplies. In this bag were headache powders, a flash light, a piece of barbed wire and a female pad if I get cut.

"You headed out west with a female pad and barbed wire, Frank?'

"Only way to travel." Frank laughed. "My pickup was loaded with all my clothes and papers and, of course, my Samantha Gold watercolor of the boat. Almost at sunup, I reached the Alabama border, and I pulled off to the side of the road and took a picture of Alabama's Welcome Sign — Alabama, the Beautiful, and how beautiful it was to be in a free state.

"For lunch I dined on Aunt Betty's sandwiches and goodies in Vicksburg Park in Mississippi. Driving through the park, I saw a huge bronze statute of a Confederate General on a horse with sword drawn. Aubrey, it was what I saw in my dream. His face was full of valor and courage, determination. I looked up at the statute under the hot Mississippi sun for a long time. The inscription on the cast stone base read General—Confederate Army died in battle May 19, 1863. Aubrey, that's my birthday."

"Strange, Frank," Aubrey says.

"At a rest stop I encountered a woman with a small baby. She was a poor white woman with matted hair and was carrying a baby that equalled her unbathed appearance.

'Could you spare a few dollars?' she said.

'I have $6.00 to spare.'

'That would be great,' she replied. I felt bad, later, that I hadn't offered her some of my food. I reached Dallas, Texas, the first day and fell into bed in a local motel.

"The next morning at sunup, I hit the trail again. State after state clicked off. I was amazed at the abandoned buildings and houses as I drove through the Texas prairie. A lot of folks didn't make it. One unnamed town I stopped off at was near the Texas-New Mexico border. It was a strange ghost town, flat land with three huge two-story brick buildings rising up from the ground. Windows were broken and jagged panes of glass cut the remains of curtains. Most of the doors were boarded up, and graffiti was sprayed on the exterior walls. A huge department store with columns, and a large brick school house stood in town with monumental letters saying Founded 1912. Driving away, my imagination went wild, thinking of those who lived there and who walked the streets. What happened? Did a Doris Anthony destroy this place? I was drawn to this ghost town because of its old Georgia town square layout.

"Tuesday, August 29th, I reached Tucson at night and Peter, my long time friend and his wife and new baby Krista welcomed me with open arms, the refugee from Georgia. Peter and Lisa had given me the gift of not only a bed to sleep in and food to eat, but they had given me the gift of time. The time to heal.

"After settling in, I wrote letters to all of my family and friends. I wrote Leacy a letter. Somehow, Aubrey, she was always on my mind. It must have been three months after I reached Arizona when she called one night.

'Frank, this is Leacy.'

'God, I have missed you,' I said.

'Frank, you probably don't want anything to do with me.'

'No, that's not true.'

'I had so many problems to work out, one day at a time. Henry tried to get control of my money, but I took your advise and I am free of his ass. Frank, I felt like I never was there for you, through the Eatonton ordeal, but I always thought about you.'

'Leacy, I don't know what to say. I thought you were involved with someone else.'

'I was, Frank, a young guy, but that's over. He just used me for money like the others. I kept remembering what you told me of how my money is for my children, and no one else. You never used me, Frank. You loved me and treated me like a lady. I want to come and see you, Frank.'

'Let me know when and where and I will be there. Love you, Leacy.'

'I really truly love you, Frank.'

"That next morning I thanked God for a new life. The next weekend, I saw Leacy, and we talked and made love all weekend.

"We were married at Long Beach, California, at sunrise one June morning. The Queen Mary was in the background. With a single trumpet player playing, 'The Prince of Denmark March.' No one was present but Leacy and I and the Rev. James Weldon and the trumpet player. The waves broke slowly that morning and the sea foam raced back and forth on the shores as it had done for a thousand years. We said our vows and looked each other in the eye, and our souls met as if we had known each other a hundred years ago. In all of my searching I had finally found happiness, and Leacy and I were made one. James shook my hand and pressing tightly, he said, 'You both have found the flowers in the desert.' He hugged us and wished us well. As the sun started to rise, Leacy's long blond hair blew in the wind. The spray of flowers in her hair swayed back and forth. When we climbed the sand dune and stood on its top, I stopped and looked at her. That's the image of her I kept seeing all through my ordeal. She was always there for me, she was always in my mind helping me. Standing on that rugged cliff overlooking the sea.

**iv**

'Let's go and put an end to all this madness, and shake the dust from this crummy town off our shoes and not look back,' Aubrey said

We pulled into the Eatonton city cemetery. We parked the truck around the side entrance, so no one would see us. From a group of trees, we had a good vantage point.

"We're here, Aubrey."

"Yes, here we are, Frank," said Aubrey.

"Is your heart beating as fast as mine, Aubrey?"

"Sure is, Frank."

"I think we are early. I think they are just finishing the service. Forgive this young woman, Oh Lord," as the words of the unknown preacher drifted past the grave markers. "Let's get out of the truck, Aubrey."

"If you say so, Frank." Sitting on the front row was Doris' mother, Ms. Jeanette, and Ken, her daddy and her brother and sister, Kate and Jim. Other than that, I only saw a few others.

"To have claimed to have so many friends and family, where are they, Aubrey?" Frank whispered.

"Suicide is not a good way to go. Maybe Ms. Jeanette and Ken told everyone she died of natural causes."

"That would be a good cover." It wasn't but a few minutes later when the few people got up and walked away. I could see Ms. Jeanette and Ken. They weren't crying at all. They seemed somehow relieved that Doris was gone. Maybe I only knew half of Doris' demonic existence. Wonder if the ice cold Jeanette had anything to do with creating such a monster? Maybe Doris was raped by her daddy, who knows. "The sky is so grey, Aubrey. Everything is so quiet."

"Let's go, Frank." Aubrey grabbed Frank's arm.

"No, Aubrey, I have some unfinished business with Doris," Frank said. "Wait here, Aubrey."

"If anything goes wrong, I am coming after you, Frank Moss. That woman in Tucson loves you and so do those six kids."

"I'll be a little while, keep my back covered, Aubrey." Frank walked away from the tree toward the grave site. Aubrey took his wallet from his coat pocket and removed a newspaper clipping with a photo of J.C. LaSurre. Carefully, he tore it into a million pieces and threw it to the wind.

Everyone had gotten in their cars and left. Walking through the brown grass, a mixture of grass clippings and water stuck on Frank's polished black leather shoes. Looking at the ground reverently, Frank approached the grave site. He stood there under the green funeral tent, with a few simple flowers laying on the side. The marker next to Doris' grave read, Franklin Anthony. Just as I predicted, Doris was to lie next to her grandfather. Doris' casket had been lowered in the ground and a sweating black man started to fill the grave with the red soil of Georgia. Out of breath, the black man said, "Did ya know this one, sir?"

"Yes, I knew her quiet well. She changed my life."

Looking up from his shovel with a yellowish tint in his eyes, the man said, "Was she kin folk?"

"No, just a friend. I loved her very much."

"Ya know, sir, they say she killed herself. Put a gun in her mouth sitting in a rocking chair in her bedroom. They didn't find her for three days. All they found was a letter and a photo of that antique man she ran off a couple of years ago. Do you remember that, sir?"

"Yes, I remember." Tears ran down Frank's face as the red soil hit the metal casket. Frank reached in his coat pocket and took the August letter out along with his black diary.

*Enclosed is the material I received in the mail from you last week. With further reflection and upon counsel, I will not be preparing the lease for your use. I believe the idea you mentioned Friday about going to another lawyer is a good one.*

*I have had over 24 hours to think about your 'Visit' to my office this past Friday morning. I allowed myself this time so that everything I say to you will be well thought out and not said in the white hot anger I felt shortly after you left. I am writing and not confronting you in person because I do not want to enter into a shouting match with you, and I want to have my say without interruption. You have a way of commandeering a conversation.*

*Please listen to what I am saying; believe it and remember it. I do not want a relationship with you. The only relationship I ever envisioned, that of Business acquaintance and eventually friend, I no longer want. The possibility of that died when you came to my office last Friday.*

*When I first met you last winter, I looked upon you as a potential friend. At that time, as I told you at our first lunch, I was involved with someone and not looking for any type of relationship other than friend. We began to occasionally do things together. But early on, I sensed your feelings about me were different than mine for you. You started to try to express yourself physically in what I at first took to be completely innocent; hugging and later an attempted kiss or two. I asked you to stop hugging me as people would get the wrong idea about us; that is, would assume we were other than friends. I pulled away and didn't allow you to kiss me. I did not permit us to be in situations where this could be a problem. Even then I was not sure what you were thinking and hesitated to set you straight in the fear that perhaps I had misinterpreted your intentions and would embarrass you as well as myself. I should have followed my instincts and confronted you immediately as soon as I began to be uncomfortable. But, I tried to spare your feelings. This obsession of yours over my past relationships, especially your fabricated stories of my lesbian involvement, has destroyed any feelings I may have had for you. I thought if I continued to make it clear to you that I don't think of you that way, that you would get the point and back off, and we could still be friends. Obviously, I was wrong.*

*I thought you finally got the point when, after humiliating me in front of the entire community at the Riverwood Affair, I made it clear to you in my backyard that I didn't want you to touch me, and no, I didn't want to go to the beach with you. After that, I became even more withdrawn from you, avoided you more pointedly until the day you showed up at my house and told me all you had been thinking and feeling. When you told me how you loved me from the first, etc., I told you that I was sorry, that I did not now and would never return those feelings. We discussed it long enough that I considered you heard me and be-*

*lieved me. But that did not stop your unwanted attentions. You continued, intermittently, to call, wanting to take me somewhere so we could 'talk about us.' I continued to tell you there was no 'us', there was no reason for us to talk, and that I felt it was inappropriate and hurtful to you (and uncomfortable to me) to spend time together under the circumstances. (I remembered yesterday that it was during one of these conversations, the time you wanted to take me to dinner in Atlanta, that I tried to explain to you my feelings on the subject by analyzing our relationship to one I might have with a married man, and which you obviously also misinterpreted. What I said was not that going out with you was like going out with a married man, but that it was unwise in much the same way as it would be if I went out with a married man. Spending time alone with someone with whom I cannot, for whatever reason, have an intimate relationship is misleading and confusing to the man, and to others as well. My going out with you under the circumstances would have only misled you and confused you about my feelings for you. Also, it would have allowed others to continue to believe the untruth that we were 'dating.' That's all I meant when I compared going out with a married man with whom I was just friends). Every time we had one of these conversations, I hoped you would understand and respect my wishes to leave me alone, but after a brief period, you would try again. You had never been openly angry, demanding and abusive until you came into my office this past Friday morning and proceeded to berate me about a variety of things. I saw you the night you came to my house. And let me assure you, that I could press charges against you for trespassing on my property. - Again, the girl asleep in my bed was a girlfriend and not a lover.*

*How dare you come to my place of business and presume to close my doors and yell at me! I would not expect or tolerate that kind of behavior from a close friend, relative or husband, much less someone with whom I had a strained, tenuous 'relationship' at best. Whether or not I go to a function, business or otherwise, is none of your business. Whether or not I hire someone to work for me is my business. You are not my husband, business advisor or even close friend.*

*Never have I permitted or encouraged your advances. Never have I given you reason to think, or believe, that I thought of you as other than a potential friend. From the first moment you told me of your feelings for me and hopes for our relationship, I was completely honest about my feelings about you. I have never led you to believe, through word or action, act or omission, that I did, or would ever, think of you as other than a friend. You apparently have conjured up in your mind this imaginary relationship which has never existed. You know this is true.*

*With regard to your threat that you could 'shred' my business if you chose to, let me say this: I have more relatives in this town than you can count. I know you are openly on a shoestring with your antique business and I know about your notes to the bank. I have friends who work at the credit bureau in Atlanta. Believe me, I could make a few calls and make sure you could never borrow a dime again. I have made many friends here. I doubt that anything you could try to do to hurt my business could accomplish your threat. However, please listen and believe me when I tell you that I have confided in several close relatives and friends. They are on the lookout for anything derogatory to be said about me. If I hear one single whisper or suggestion of anything disparaging about me, or my business, which could possibly be attributed to you, I will take all appropriate legal steps to see that I am protected. Let me assure you that such sick, vindictive and unwarranted behavior on your part will only serve to hurt your business. And, oddly enough, personal feelings aside, I do not want to see you fail in Eatonton. You have had some good ideas and helped improve things — I would like to see you remain in business here, although only for that reason.*

*As for your assertion that you love me, I know that you do not. Love is not obsessive and possessive. If you truly did love me, you would have respected my wishes long ago and left me alone.*

*I have been astounded to learn that for months you have been telling people, leading them to believe, that you and I were 'dating.' You even told people that I dumped you! Since this is not true, your continuing to tell people that, or allow them to believe it, under the circumstances, is slanderous and damaging to my reputation. I hope that you will not continue to mislead people and will set things straight if the subject should arise.*

*Frank, I am not going to talk about this situation anymore with you or anyone else. The people in whom I have confided, including those who overheard your tirade last Friday, are not going to say anything.*

*Even if you believe something I have said in this letter is incorrect or unfair, it does not matter. We are not going to discuss it anymore. I am going to avoid being with you, but when I see you or am unavoidably thrown into a situation where we have to work together, I will be civil and polite. I would like to put this behind me. This is my plan and hope. It is contingent on your behavior, however. Please do not force me to show you my ruthless side. I do not want to get into a war with you or anyone else. Eatonton is my home, and I am not going anywhere. But I won't be a victim, and if you insist on forcing me into a corner, you will not like the result. Please forget about me, leave my family alone, and let's both get on with our lives and businesses.*

*I am enclosing a check in the amount of $200.00 in payment for the small cabinet you allowed me to take and use in my office last month. As I recall, this is the amount you quoted to me as the purchase price, if I decided after using it, that I wanted to buy it. If this amount is not acceptable, please do not cash the check, but return it to me by mail, and I will have the cabinet returned to you. Thank you.*

*In conclusion, please do not call me, write me, leave me notes or gifts, or come to my home or office. You ruined any chance I thought we might have of being friends, and I do not want any type of relationship with you.*
*Doris*

Frank dropped the letter and diary in Doris' grave. The grave digger looked up and paused; then he threw a scoop of soil on the letter. Frank walked away and heard voices from a distance past. "Hello, my name is Doris. You know, Doris Anthony, just like the movie Anthony and Cleopatra." Standing in the doorway of Frank's store, he saw Doris in her white linen dress with wind blowing through her hair. Frank put his hand on Doris' cheek and said, 'I forgive you, and all those you caused to hurt me.'

Approaching Aubrey, Frank wiped the tears from his eyes. Aubrey put his arm around Frank. "Frank, are you O.K.?"

"Yes, I'm fine."

"Let's go home, Frank," said Aubrey.

Driving back to Atlanta, I felt a great peace in my life, more than I experienced when I first went to Arizona.

"What happened to all the other bad guys?"

"Old Sheriff LaSurre, the bastard that raped your mother, the F.B.I. found so much dirt on him they sentenced him to 20 years, but the fat ass was killed in a car crash before they shipped him off. Remember that other fat ass Chief of Eatonton police, Ralph Riley?"

"Yes, I remember."

"Somebody told me he was putting up a T.V. antenna and was electrocuted. They said all that fat burned for a long time."

"Yeah, I heard that," said Aubrey. "Frank, how about that bastard Bixby?"

"I will tell you, Aubrey, I hated Bixby for so long. Just like you wanted to kill the LaSurre brothers, I wanted to put a bullet in that bastard's head so bad I could taste it. I remember calling my brother, Mike, one night when I was in Tucson, and I told him as bad as everyone wants to see me again, the first thing I would do when I got to Atlanta was to rent a car. I would drive to Eatonton and put a bullet in three bastards' heads. I think you know who would be on the hit list, Aubrey. From Arizona, I sent letters to everyone from the President of the United States, to the Attorney General, Senators in both states, Georgia and Arizona. I mailed letters to them all. I begged for legal counsel; even my own cousin turned me down. No one would lift a finger to help me. Politicians, what a crooked lot.

"Bixby and Doris Anthony even filed a $200,000 lawsuit against me and guess who their lawyer was? Duke Cody, my supposed attorney friend from the Kiwanis Club. Duke Cody, the two-faced bastard that stood up for me at the August 21st trial. A $200,000 judgment signed by none other than Judge Hines Carroll. The judgment didn't even have a court seal on it. It was plain extortion, Aubrey. Hell, you think the F.B.I. would do anything against another tin badge? After fighting for six months, I laid all of my weapons down and forgave my enemies.

"God, I starved to death in that God-forsaken Tucson, Arizona. I was so poor one time, a week before Christmas, I went to my church and asked for food. Oh, the years that Lynn and I gave, and now I was receiving. The exploited jobs that I had. I even worked as a maid like my maid Carrie. I did whatever it took to survive. You and I Aubrey, we are collector's items, and we both lived to tell our stories. We have experienced the three great motivators in life. Fear, hate, and love, and in the end, we have come to the realization that love for our enemies is the greatest motivator.

We flew back to Tucson from Atlanta and carried on our conversation in the plane.

"I devised in my mind every torture known to man as a fate for that sack of shit. Bixby deserved to die more than any man alive. But I figured I never could as a human come up with a death plan that would be suitable for such a bastard, so I turned the entire matter over to God. Like I told you today about J.C. LaSurre, I figured He had a plan far worse for Bixby than I could ever come up with, and, boy, did he. The F.B.I. tied Bixby to LaSurre's corruption ring, and they sentenced Bixby to five years. He wasn't in prison a month till some drug dealer that Bixby had screwed got him. They say they tied Bixby to a cot, bound his hands and feet with wire and poured lighter fluid over him and set him on fire."

"My God, Frank, did that really happen?"

"What I heard, Aubrey. Remember April Preston, the bitch I helped out and who later sided with Doris? No one ever knew what happened to her. I know for a fact I saw her lying in Doris's bed. No one ever saw her again. Figure that one out. Aubrey, did you read a couple of weeks ago about another bastard, Judge Hines Carroll?"

"No, what was that, Frank?" said Aubrey.

"I read in the paper someone sent Carroll a Merry Christmas package in the mail. Damn thing blew up, and they said they had to scrape Carroll off the wall like dog shit. Said his hand and arm were still on the package. Same hand that signed all those legal papers on me. They all got what was coming to them, and so time will tell. God worked fast on some of my enemies. I told him to put a rush on it," laughed Frank.

**V**

"Back in Tucson. Let's get off this plane, so we can roll down the window and breathe free air. Maybe the two of us sent Eatonton to B'rer Rabbit's laughing tree." Frank pulled up in front of Aubrey's house, and James ran out the front door.

"Daddy, you're home!" Aubrey hugs his son and turns and shakes Frank's hand. With a strong determined look, Aubrey looks Frank in the eye.

"Thanks for your story Frank. I am glad you chose me to go with you. I will tell my grandchildren about you, Frank Moss," and with one last squeeze of a handshake, Aubrey, arm and arm with his son, went into the house.

"Our pain is over, Aubrey," Frank said. "Yes, the scars will always be there, but the pain is over." Rounding the corner to Porter Street, I saw home. As soon as I pulled in the driveway, the front door swung open, and Leacy and all six kids came and surrounded me.

Willie grabbed my pants leg and hugged me and said, "Mr. Frank, you're home."

"Yes, Willie, I'm home." Leacy's eyes met Franks. Frank hugged little Willie, this blond headed little man that he loved so much. "Did you see B'rer Rabbit?"

"Yes, I did." Leacy put her arm around Frank's waist and hugged and kissed him.

"You have got red mud on your Sunday shoes, Mr. Frank."

"So, I do Willie." The red mud from Doris' grave, I thought, but after all, Chickens Do Come Home to Roost.

*The End*
DAVID MORELAND